JAMESON'S SALVATION

RILEY EDWARDS

Jameson's Salvation
Gemini Group Book 2

Riley Edwards

Cover design: Lori Jackson Designa

Written by: Riley Edwards

Published by: Riley Edwards/Rebels Romance

Edited by: Rebecca Hodgkins

Proofreader: Julie Deaton and Rebecca Kendall

Jameson's Salvation

Ebook ISBN: 978-1-7339667-8-8

First edition: September 24, 2019

To my family - my team – my tribe.
This is for you.

CONTENTS

1.	Jameson	1
2.	Kennedy	11
3.	Jameson	23
4.	Kennedy	34
5.	Jameson	44
6.	Kennedy	60
7.	Jameson	72
8.	Kennedy	79
9.	Jameson	91
10.	Kennedy	98
11.	Jameson	107
12.	Kennedy	120
13.	Jameson	132
14.	Kennedy	148
15.	Jameson	162
16.	Kennedy	171
17.	Jameson	178
18.	Kennedy	187
19.	Jameson	196
20.	Kennedy	208
21.	Jameson	217
22.	Kennedy	227
23.	Jameson	237
24.	Kennedy	247
25.	Jameson	260
26.	Kennedy	276
27.	Jameson	290
28.	Kennedy	300
29.	Jameson	308

30. Kennedy	316
31. Jameson	322
32. Kennedy	334
33. Jameson	341
34. Kennedy	347
35. Jameson	356
36. Silver	362
Riley's Rebels	365
Also by Riley Edwards	367
About the Author	369
Acknowledgments	371

1

JAMESON

Jameson Grant was sitting on an old stump drinking a beer, looking at his buddy and former teammate's old yellow barn. He was hot, tired, and his body ached from old-fashioned manual labor. He was doing that while thinking life was good—and since Jameson hadn't had all that many really good days in the last fifteen years, he was thinking life wasn't just good—it was fucking fantastic.

Cold beer, no neighbors for miles other than his best friends who lived with him on the old Swagger Farm, and of course Nix and McKenna who lived on the other side of the woods that surrounded the property. But other than that, no one. Nothing but the summer corn crop to his right, and a soybean field to his left.

He was living a goddamn country song and he couldn't have been happier.

Business was good, money was rolling in, not that he needed much, but it was always nice to have.

So, life was perfect for Jameson Grant and it was about damn time.

His head tipped back, he took a few more swallows of the icy brew, and his attention went to the rumble of an F150 driving up the lane. The truck passed the house and continued the last quarter mile up to the barn, and suddenly Jameson's life wasn't so great.

He hated visitors. The only thing he hated more was when someone came calling unannounced. He watched as the pickup slowed, and he was happy to see it was filthy, that the seventy-five-thousand-dollar truck was used for working and not just for showboating. Said a lot about the truck's owner.

Jameson hated when people showed off their money. Like anyone gave two shits you could afford a luxury vehicle. Or more appropriately, the bank owned it, and they were really living paycheck to paycheck like the rest of the population, yet pretending they were highfalutin'. He'd seen enough of that shit to last a lifetime.

It was safe to say, Jameson didn't like much. People accounted for the majority of his gripes. That was because he'd learned the hard way that people sucked. They robbed, they lied, they cheated, and they killed. It was the last part he struggled with the most. Some could say he, too, was a killer and they wouldn't be wrong.

He had indeed taken a life, many, as a matter of fact. One did not serve as a Navy SEAL for nearly fifteen years and not earn the black hashmarks he now had. One didn't carry the burden of death and wonder if everything he'd done would be forgiven when he knocked on the

Pearly Gates. Perhaps Jameson Grant would be an unwelcomed, unannounced visitor, the kind he detested so much.

Whatever was in store for him on the other side, was something he spent a good amount of time trying not to think about. And right then, as the driver of the pickup was opening their door, wasn't the ideal time to be thinking about his morality.

The sun was setting and the last rays of the day were glaring off the windshield, making it impossible to see the occupant. Jameson stood and squinted as he waited for the driver to make an appearance. And when she did, the glimmers of light highlighted her shiny golden hair and Jameson was extra-pissed.

Kennedy Lane.

He'd seen her arguing with a man in her front yard, not two weeks ago. She'd been relieved when Jameson had appeared on the street, and with nothing more than a glare from Jameson, the man who had been yelling at Kennedy took off. She'd tried to show her gratitude by inviting him in for an iced tea.

Christ, an iced tea. For a moment, Jameson had thought he was living in Mayberry and not a small town on the Eastern Shore of Maryland. Though by the look of the town, and the feel of it, too, he might as well be on the lookout for Sheriff Andy Taylor and Barney Fife.

Though, the last man that had served as sheriff of Kent County was a dirty piece of shit who'd tried to kill McKenna, Nixon's woman. Thankfully, that scumbag was six feet under where he deserved to be. He'd been terrorizing the county for two decades. Just thinking about Sheriff Dickhead Dillinger made Jameson furious, and yet again reminded him why he disliked most everyone.

"You following me?" Jameson barked.

Kennedy jerked back in surprise before she smiled.

Good God, the woman was lethal. Her smile alone was enough for Jameson to break all his rules and ask her to sit and stay awhile.

"Hey. Jameson, right? How ya been? I'm actually lookin' for Nixon. He around?"

Her musical voice floated across the barnyard and just as it had done the first time he'd heard it, it slammed into his chest, making him feel funny.

"Nixon?"

"Yeah. I need to talk to him."

"'Bout what?"

Jameson had no clue why he was being nosey. It was out of character for him and he knew he should just tell Kennedy, Nix wasn't there and be done. But he couldn't stop himself from wondering why she wanted to see his friend.

He told himself it wasn't jealousy and he was just looking out for a buddy who didn't need a very beautiful woman causing trouble for him. And Kennedy Lane had trouble with a capitol T written all over her.

"Heard he set up shop," she answered. "I know most of the gossip you hear around town you can't believe but I thought I'd take a chance and see if it's true."

"And what'd you hear?"

"That he's some sort of PI."

That wasn't entirely true, but it wasn't false either. Gemini Group did more than private investigations.

"Why do you need a PI?"

Kennedy's smile faded and she unnecessarily looked around the yard. They were alone. Holden was at the office where he spent most of his time. Weston and Chasin were taking their Saturday to go kayaking on the Chester River. Nixon was at his house with his woman and her siblings. So that left Jameson alone on the farm to finish painting the roof of the old milking parlor.

It had taken a shit-ton of man hours and elbow grease, but the old farm had been restored to its former glory. No more peeling paint, rusted tin, falling down barns, and the forest of weeds and grass had been mowed down. The place looked great, and he was happy to help. Nixon had been seriously depressed when he'd come home and found his father's farm in disarray after he'd passed away.

Nixon Swagger loved his old man and the land he'd grown up on. After Nix had separated from the Navy his plan was simple; come back to Kent County, fix up the house and barns, and rent out the land. Then he was supposed to go back to Virginia Beach and they were going to start their business there. But he'd met McKenna. Everything had changed for him and he decided to stay. And if Nixon was there, the rest of them would be, too. They were a team.

"You remember the guy who was in my face at the Tea Party?" she asked.

Jameson remembered. He'd been walking around the

street fair and when he couldn't take another minute of the crowd and people bumping into him, he'd split and taken a walk down a residential street. He was enjoying the solitude until he saw Kennedy and the man. He was indeed in Kennedy's face yelling at her, and the beauty was yelling right back.

The first thing Jameson had thought was, he was impressed the woman was standing her ground and not taking shit from a man who towered over her and outweighed her by at least a hundred pounds. It wasn't muscle that accounted for the size difference, the man had looked like he'd never met a cheeseburger he didn't like and had never seen in the inside of a gym. Or knew that such a facility existed.

His next thought was, she was crazy. She should've gone back into her house and called the police. People did fucked-up things, especially in anger, and the man had looked furious. But so had Kennedy.

"Yeah, I remember him."

"Well, he's a pain in my ass. I guess I don't need a PI to find him, since I know who he is, I just need something on him to make him stop. I was thinking that maybe Nixon could find that something."

"You wanna blackmail him?"

"Blackmail's an ugly way to put it. I don't want anything from him other than for him to stop harassing me. And men like Reggie Coleman don't stop just because you ask them to. And most especially if you're a woman."

Jameson's eyes narrowed and his body went tight. "What do you mean, especially if you're a woman?"

All sorts of crazy thoughts were floating through Jameson's head. Ones that made him want to mete out violence. Was the man sexually harassing Kennedy? Had he physically hurt her?

"Reggie's a good ol' boy. You know the kind."

"No, I don't know the kind," Jameson lied.

He did know plenty of men who behaved like assholes because they thought just because they were male they could treat women like they were inferior. It was bullshit, it went against everything Jameson believed in. Even though he hated most things, one thing he never wavered from was women were precious and should be protected and treated as such. And just because he felt the need to protect them didn't mean they weren't equal. As a matter of fact, in Jameson's eyes women would always be superior to men.

"He's a land developer and he lives by the notion, you don't pitch the bitch."

"What does that mean?" Jameson had never heard the phrase.

"When he's working his contracts trying to pay pennies on the dollar for land he's trying to strong-arm the owner into selling, he never speaks to the woman. Even if she's the landowner. He'll try to circumvent her and go to her father, brother, male cousin, hell, even a friend if it means he can speak to a man."

"He was talking to you," Jameson noted.

"Only because my dad's dead, I'm an only child, I

have no cousins local, he tried approaching my friends' husbands and they all told him to take a hike. So that leaves me. As you saw, he's not happy about it, and even less so since I've told him to fuck off more than once."

"You told him to fuck off?"

Jameson was impressed, Reggie Coleman sounded like a dick.

"Well, yeah. I didn't start out being so crass. I tried to politely decline his absurd offer but he likes being told 'no' by a woman only slightly less than having his balls twisted. So after the twentieth time of him coming around I finally told him to fuck off."

Jameson couldn't help it, his lips tipped into a smile.

"You had first-hand knowledge on his thoughts about his balls being twisted?"

"I see your point, I don't. Perhaps Reggie Coleman enjoys that sorta kink. You never know what floats someone's boat. Now that you mention it, I could see him getting off on it."

Jameson couldn't help it, he was enjoying the woman's banter, so he continued to engage even though he knew he should just tell her Nixon wasn't there and send her on her way.

"I didn't mention anything. You're the one that seems fascinated with the man's balls."

"Ew. That's gross." Kennedy's face scrunched in disgust and Jameson chuckled.

Needing to steer the conversation back to something more appropriate—and to a topic that didn't make

Kennedy's sharp wit come out along with cute gestures that made Jameson want to laugh—he moved along.

"What's he want?"

"My land," she answered.

"Your land?"

"Yep. He bought the farm behind me when Mr. Nickels passed away. His widow didn't want to sell, but after a year of not being able to find someone to rent the property to who could till it, she had to. Her only son lives in New Jersey and he never had any interest in farming. The land taxes were coming up and she couldn't afford to pay them from her social security. Not to mention, you can't leave nearly four-hundred and fifty acres unattended. She was growing a weed crop and the farmer next to her was pissed."

None of that meant anything to Jameson. He had no clue why a neighboring farmer wouldn't be pleased the fields next to him were growing weeds and didn't understand what any of it had to do with Kennedy's land.

Luckily, she continued. "Now that he owns the land behind me, he wants mine, too. I only have fifty acres but I have the most street access."

"I take it you don't want to sell. Even at fair market value."

"Over my dead body. That land is mine. I've worked hard for it. And I'm not selling to anybody, but most especially not to that snake so he can turn it into a development."

Jameson was taken aback at the vehemence in Kennedy's voice. Gone was the sweet lyrical tone. And in its place was steely determination. He was impressed and more than a little curious about the feisty woman who'd fight to keep her patch of land.

It was out of inquisitiveness he asked his next question, an offer he hoped didn't bite him in the ass. But he'd decided the moment she'd stepped out of her truck and smiled at him he was going to ask it. Even before she'd told her tale of woe.

Now he had an excuse for his odd behavior, and the truth was, Reggie Coleman sounded like a man who needed to be taught a few lessons. Luckily for Kennedy, Jameson was a good teacher.

"Wanna go on up to the house?"

"The house?"

"The house, Kennedy. The place you passed on your way up here."

"Smartass," she said with a smile. "You think Nixon can help me?"

There was that jealousy again. Jameson tamped it down and answered.

"Yeah, I think *we* can help you."

Jameson wasn't entirely sure why he put so much emphasis on the *we*, but for some crazy reason it was important to him. Almost as important as her accepting his invitation.

2

KENNEDY

I seriously hoped Jameson couldn't tell how nervous I was. My hands may've been shaking, though since I'd shoved them in my pockets, I couldn't be sure.

Had I known I was going to run into the man, I wouldn't have come, or at least I would've gone home and changed out of my dirty clothes, maybe washed some of the dirt and dust off me, and run a brush through my hair. But I hadn't done any of those things because I'd been red hot mad and I'd thought I was coming over to talk to Nixon.

While Nixon was one good-looking man, he wasn't as hot as Jameson. And, well, he was just Nixon. I'd grown up with him. He was a cute kid when we were in elementary school, but I could still remember him picking his nose. And when we got to middle school and he'd shot up two feet over the summer—okay that was an exaggeration, but he'd had a growth spurt and started to fill out—he'd become even cuter. However, I couldn't forget the way his voice had cracked, making him sound like a frog for a full six months. In high school, he'd come into his own and there was a presence about him that everyone wanted to be around. But by then, he was just Nixon.

My buddy.

So, I'd appreciated the boy-man he'd become but I'd never looked at him as more than a friend, even on the night I'd almost screwed everything up. A boy I could pal around with and know I was safe to do silly teenage stuff, because Nixon Swagger was a champion for girls. Sure, he'd nailed quite a few of my classmates, but he'd never broken hearts. And when Rich Dillinger had hurt some of my friends, it was Nixon who'd stepped in and helped.

Bottom line was, I had no issue with Nixon seeing me looking like a ragamuffin as my mom would say. I had no interest in Nix and if the rumors were to be believed, and considering I'd seen him in town with McKenna Wilson, he was very much taken and officially off the market.

But Jameson was a whole different story. He was the kind of man who made you do a double-take. I didn't want him to see me looking like a farm hand with filthy clothes and messy hair. But it was too late for that. There I was, standing in front of the sexiest man I'd ever seen, looking like shit.

I'd been so pissed that Reggie had cornered me—again—and had again threatened me, I'd marched my happy ass straight to the Swagger Farm to ask for help. I wasn't sure what Nixon could do, but I needed someone to do something. And while I could fend for myself, the situation was spiraling out of control and I couldn't go at it alone. Not anymore.

I'd had enough.

It had been annoying six months ago. It became tiresome three months ago. And in the last month it was infuriating.

"Kennedy?" Jameson called.

"You work with Nixon?"

"Maybe you shoulda asked that before you told a stranger about your problems."

I couldn't help but smile. He was a little gruff and a whole lot short, but there was something about his grumpy attitude that made me want to make him smile, like I had a moment ago. I'd bet he didn't smile that much.

"You're not from around here," I stated.

Having grown up in Kent County, I would've known him if he had. First, because there was only one county high school, and second, a man like Jameson couldn't be forgotten. He was a giant, almost a foot taller than me. Big, broad shoulders, and hair so black it could be described as inky, or maybe midnight.

"Yeah."

"But you obviously know Nixon."

"And?"

"If you're a friend of Nixon's that means you're good people. And if you're at his barn and he's not here, that means he trusts you."

"You're correct on all accounts, but I don't see how

that explains why you told a stranger about Reggie Coleman."

Perhaps it was a KC thing. But the company you kept and who extended their trust to you went a long way around here. And your word and your reputation still meant something. Deals were made with a handshake and a nod. Jameson wouldn't be standing on Nixon's land if he didn't like and trust the man.

"Well, if Nixon trusts you, I know I can, too."

Something flashed in his eyes and he didn't look happy.

"That's not smart. You shouldn't trust someone you don't know. People are assholes."

"That's cynical."

"That's real. You need to be careful to whom you extend your trust. You don't know me and just because Nix does doesn't mean shit."

"Are you telling me I can't trust you?"

"No, I'm telling you, you need to be smart or you'll get hurt."

"Right. I can only be who I am, Jameson. I extend my respect and trust until someone proves they don't deserve it and if I get hurt in the process that says more about them than me. If I allowed every asshole who I've run into over the years to change me, I wouldn't like myself very much. If you guys can help me with this Reggie Coleman situation, I'd appreciate it. Of course, I'd pay y'all. I'm not asking for a freebie."

Jameson was still studying me and I fought not to wilt under his scrutiny. He probably thought I was some naïve hick who didn't understand there were dishonest, shitty people in the world. But his assumption would be incorrect. I understood to my bones how unfair people could be. How they made judgments about you before they knew you. How they lied to get what they wanted. How they'd step on your back and crush you to get ahead. That was precisely why I tried my best not to behave that way toward others, and often times it was at my own expense. But I'd rather be hurt than turn into someone I wasn't proud of. Someone my father wouldn't be proud to know.

"Let's go up to the house and talk," he suggested.

"You wanna ride up?" I offered and started back toward my truck.

Jameson looked at my dirty truck, down the lane to the house that was less than a quarter-mile walk, then back to my pickup. His own two feet would probably get him there quicker than it would take me to start up my truck, turn around, and drive up—but still, the polite thing to do was offer, even if I was hoping he'd decline. I wasn't a slob, my house was always clean, but my truck was another story. And I'd spent the day working so the interior cab looked worse than the mud slung all over the outside.

"Sure. Thanks."

Well, damn. Looks like Jameson was going to be treated to my mess.

He was still looking at me funny when he broke eye contact to walk to the passenger side. At least he was no longer looking at me like I was some hodunk who needed her head examined for talking to strangers, but he was still trying to figure me out. And that was okay. I had nothing to hide from him. I was who I was and I was alright with that. I was honest and hard-working and I didn't give a shit what people thought about me beyond them being able to confirm I was both.

"Sorry about the mess," I mumbled as Jameson swung up into the cab. "It's been a crazy week. I was gonna clean all this out today but I ended up needing to work on a project."

"What do you do? For work?" he asked, and was gracious enough not to comment on the empty water bottles at his feet and mound of shit in the back seat.

"A little bit of everything," I told him and pulled farther into the yard so I could turn around.

I was pushing up in my seat with my ass off the bottom cushion as I backed my beast up, careful not to hit the five-gallon paint buckets that had been left in front of the old milking parlor.

"You know you have a backup camera, right?"

"Yeah, sure, but I never use it."

"Why's that?"

"My daddy taught me to drive. Old habits, I guess. When he was teachin' me he'd read me the riot act if I didn't look fully behind me. Admittedly, he taught me to drive when I was about seven and it was on an old Oliver tractor, but still, he'd yell if I didn't look."

"Never seen anyone have to stand up in their seat to back up before."

"I'm not standing." I smiled. "I'm just lifting my ass so I can see."

"Right."

I could hear the smile in Jameson's voice and I really wanted to look over at him but I refrained. Barely. And only because I didn't want him to think I was some sort of weirdo.

After I'd straightened and sat back in my seat, Jameson asked, "Tell me about a bit of everything."

"Huh?"

"You said you did a little bit of everything. What does that mean?"

"Oh. Um." I wasn't sure why I was hesitant to explain what I did for a living. I was proud of myself. I worked seven days a week. I wasn't rolling in it, but I made enough money to support myself and help my mom. But I certainly wasn't what someone would call successful. Hustler was more like it. Or at least what my dad had always said, *my, Kennedy, she's always hustling.* And he'd always said it with a proud smile. "I work odd jobs here and there. But in the summer, I sell my crops at the farmers market along with the honey I make. I also make candles from my beeswax and sell those in some local shops. I also make some pottery and necklaces. I sell those local, too, and at the market. During the winter, I do other stuff since the farmers market is closed, and, well, you can't grow tomatoes and sugar corn in the winter. So, a little bit of everything. Whatever will pay the bills."

"And the lumber and tools in the bed of your truck? Is that part of a bit of everything, too?"

"No. That's what's left over after I built a ramp for my mom today."

I pulled to a stop in front of Nixon's farmhouse and cut the engine. Jameson was staring at me. He obviously had no such hang-ups about *me* thinking *he* was weird, because he wasn't trying to hide that he was looking.

"You built your mother a ramp?"

"Yeah," I sighed.

Another point of irritation. Not only had I been battling it out with my mom's insurance company about paying for a handicap ramp, and I use the word *handicap* with great objection considering I hated that word, but there was no denying my mom needed it. So after all of the back and forth and them delaying, I decided to build it myself. Which was not the complaint—hard work didn't scare me and building a ramp was not rocket science. But the lumber had cost a mint, and with summer turning into fall, which obviously led to winter, I needed to bank all the money I could. Winter months could get tight. And if that wasn't bad enough, that was when Reggie had ambushed me. I hadn't even had a chance to clean up my tools when the pompous prick pulled up and started in.

"My mom had a stroke about nine months ago. She's doing better but she still has some paralysis on her left side. She can't walk down the stairs to leave the house, which means I have to go over there and carry her down. She has a friend who's a retired nurse who comes and looks after her, but Miss Janice isn't steady enough on her own feet anymore to help mom. So she needed a ramp.

Miss Janice can either push her down in her wheelchair or my mom can use her walker."

Jameson's eyes narrowed and something that looked like anger flashed before he covered it up. "And why wouldn't the insurance company pay a contractor to build it?"

"That's a great question. One I've been trying to get answered for six months. My mom couldn't wait any longer and I can't afford to hire someone, so I did it."

"Right."

"It wasn't like it was all that hard. It was like building a front porch, only it slopes at one end. I framed it up yesterday and finished it today."

"By yourself?"

"Yeah. It wasn't—"

"I know, it wasn't hard," he said through gritted teeth, and I was starting to wonder what his problem was. He didn't strike me as the type of man who thought a woman should sit in the house barefoot, but like he'd said, he was a stranger. Though I couldn't see Nixon tolerating any friend of his having that line of thinking.

Before I could ask him what his issue was, he opened his door. "Come on, let's go inside."

I wordlessly followed him around the back of the house and through the sliding glass door into the dining room.

"Wow. This place looks great," I noted.

"You've been in here before?"

"Yeah. I used to help Mr. Swagger bale hay in the summers. And before that, when I was a kid."

"You know Nix well?"

There was something in his tone again I couldn't place. I really hoped he didn't think I was after Nixon.

"You know that I know Nixon is with McKenna, right?"

His body jerked and he leveled me with a pissed-off glare. "Why would you say that?"

"I don't know, the way you asked me if I knew Nix gave me the impression you were trying to figure out if I was gonna cause trouble for him or something. Nixon and I have been friends since we were five. Or I should say, we were friends until he left for the Navy. And since high school graduation I've talked to him a total of two times. Both when he was home visiting. I don't want to cause any issues. I just need some help."

"And you asking for help, is that gonna cause an issue, whether you mean for it or not?"

"Maybe this was a bad idea." I turned to go back toward the door and immediately started thinking of other ways I could deal with Reggie. Now that Sheriff Dillinger was gone, the police would be more help. Not that I had any evidence Reggie was harassing me, but it wouldn't hurt to file another complaint.

"Why's that?" Jameson's question stopped me.

"Sorry to say, you're kinda a jerk and after the day I've had, I don't need the hassle."

Jameson's full lips tipped up into a smile, before he roared with laughter.

Sweet baby Jesus, he was something else when he

laughed. Gone was the thorn-in-his-ass bear and hello Mr. Sexy.

"Sorry to interrupt," a male voice startled me and I let out a squeak of surprise.

Both men's attention came to me as my hand went over my beating heart.

"Holy fracking monkey balls, you scared me."

"Did she just say monkey balls?" the man asked Jameson.

"I think she has a fascination with balls. That's twice she's mentioned them in thirty minutes," Jameson answered.

"I'm not fascinated by balls," I defended.

"You're not?" Jameson asked. "You seemed fairly concerned about Reggie Coleman's balls being twisted."

"I was not. I said he didn't *like* his balls being twisted, not that I was concerned about them."

"Right." Jameson chuckled.

"Why are we talking about balls?"

"I don't know. You're the one that keeps bringin' them up."

"Well, can we please stop talking about balls?"

"Who's Reggie Coleman and why are we concerned about his balls?" the stranger asked.

"Sheesh, I don't care about his balls," I huffed.

"Reggie Coleman's an asshole who's been harassing Kennedy here, trying to get her to sell him her land. Land she doesn't feel like parting with. She came here to talk to Nixon about diggin' some shit up so she can use it to make the dickweed stop."

"You go to the police?"

What just happened? How did we go from quite possibly the most embarrassing conversation of my life, one that under normal circumstances would've had me praying for a black pit to swallow me whole, to talking about the police?

"Yes. Several times," I answered and Jameson's brow went up in censure. "What? He's in Nixon's house. You're talking to him and you told him about Reggie. So, you seem to trust him but you're gonna scowl at me for talking to him because he's a stranger?"

"You don't know him," Jameson unnecessarily noted.

"Jeez, Jameson, should I ask to see his ID? A background check, maybe? I answered his question, I didn't tell him where the bodies are buried."

"You have bodies buried?" Jameson countered.

"Can't tell you that, I haven't completed your background check yet." I smirked and Jameson nodded his approval.

"Now you're catching on."

Why did joking around with Jameson feel so good? He was kind of a jerk, albeit a good-looking one, and he frowned at me more than he smiled. But still, the banter between us was comfortable, entertaining. It made me want to bicker with him some more to see if I could get the grump to laugh again.

Don't go there, Kennedy. Your life is already complicated enough.

3
___

JAMESON

Kennedy Lane was something else. Jameson hadn't enjoyed spending time with a woman as much as he'd enjoyed being in Kennedy's company in a long time.

He'd been called a lot worse than a jerk through the years but no one had ever apologized and meant it before slinging an insult at him. The woman intrigued him, and she shouldn't have. Jameson had to admit, she was beautiful. But she was too bubbly, too cute, too sweet for his liking. She was the type of woman who would normally drive him to insanity with the look-on-the-bright-side attitude she had.

Jameson wasn't a bright-side-of-anything type of guy.

"Yo! Where's everyone at?" Nixon asked, walking in. He stopped, scanned the room, and when his gaze landed on Kennedy, his back shot straight and his eyes widened before he schooled his features. "Kennedy Lane. Long time."

What the fuck was that about?

"Hey, Nix." Kennedy shuffled from foot to foot. She looked nervous as all hell. "Sorry to come by unannounced, I need to talk to you."

"You came by to see me?" Nixon glanced at Jameson, then Holden, who'd only come home from work right before Nixon had stopped by, and finally back to Kennedy. "Everything all right?"

"Wish I could say yes, but you remember Reggie Coleman?"

"Yeah. He's a contractor, right?"

"More of a developer now. Or at least that's what he likes to call himself. He's been acquiring land. You know that big development on the river?" Nixon nodded and she continued. "That's his project."

"How'd he get the permits to build there? It's a tidal marsh."

"When you're drinkin' buddies with the county commissioners, and you play golf with the head of planning and zoning, you can get whatever you want. You haven't been gone long enough to forget the good ol boy mentality."

Nixon and Kennedy shared a knowing look and Jameson felt a pang of jealousy. A feeling that was not only new, but very much unwanted.

"What's Reggie got to do with you?" Nixon continued.

"Reggie wants my land and he's not takin' no for an answer. Hate to say it because I know how much you hate gossip, but I heard you do PI work. I was hopin' you could find something on Reggie to make him back down."

Nixon was quiet for a moment and Holden's movement caught Jameson's attention. He'd opened his laptop and his fingers were flying over the keys.

When he found something, Holden said, "According to tax records, he owns quite a bit of land. He also has permit applications in on several lots and an application to subdivide a farm that was in agricultural preservation."

"He does?" Kennedy asked. "He'd have to buy that farm out of ag preservation or the permit will never be approved. That would take a lot of money."

"He have that kind of cash?" Jameson asked.

A few keystrokes later, Holden answered, "Not liquid, but he has a hefty line of credit."

"How do you know that?" Kennedy asked.

"Can't tell my secrets to a stranger." Holden winked and Jameson had an overwhelming urge to punch his friend. "I'm Holden, by the way."

What the hell was going on? Was Holden flirting with Kennedy? It sure looked that way to Jameson and he couldn't for the life of him figure out why that bothered him so much. It shouldn't have even hit his radar. He'd seen Holden pick up hundreds of women—they loved him and flocked to his fun-loving disposition and quick smile. Why would Kennedy be any different? And why in the hell would the sight of it make Jameson so irate?

"What made you decide today to ask for help?" Jameson interrupted the Holden lovefest. He couldn't stand to watch her beaming smile aimed at his friend any longer.

"After I was done at my mom's house, I was putting

away my tools and Reggie stopped for a chat. I'd had enough of his badgering months ago, but his visits are happening more frequently and today he told me if I thought things were tight now, they were about to get worse—"

"He threatened you?" Nixon cut her off.

"He's *been* threatening me, Nixon. That's how he gets people who don't want to sell to sell. That's why I'm here. I need to find a way to make him leave me alone, before things get any worse. I know he's fuckin' with me, but I can't figure out how. I can't prove anything, and I don't know what he's planning next."

Nixon's jaw was clenching and Jameson knew his friend hated to bring up the sheriff's department but it needed to be asked. "Have you reported him to the authorities?"

Kennedy gave him a sad smile. Obviously having heard what Sheriff Dillinger had done to McKenna and her family softened her features and she nodded before she answered, "I have. Each time I went in, I was told there was nothing they could do. That Reggie wasn't doing anything criminal by offering me money to purchase property. Rich Dillinger practically laughed at me and said he didn't see an issue with Reggie's offer no how, and I should sell before I lost my land to the bank."

"Fuckin' dick," Nix sneered and Jameson had to agree. "You in danger of losing your property?"

"I wasn't."

Jameson could feel his muscles tighten as his body went taut with anger. The thought of sweet Kennedy

Lane, who busted her ass to help her mama and worked hard to get what she had...she shouldn't be in any kind of danger. She shouldn't be feeling the stress of losing something she clearly loved.

"But you are now?" Jameson practically growled his question.

"It's not that bad, but a few more shitty months and I'll be seriously scrambling. And with my mom needing the extra help, and her insurance not kickin' in to pay for Miss Janice, and paying out-of-pocket to build that new ramp, let's just say it was a hit. But I do have money saved for a rainy day so I can pay you. I figure it's raining now and I'd better patch the hole and put a stop to it before it's pouring and I flood. So please, don't let my financial situation stop you from helping. I can—"

"You're not paying us."

Three sets of eyes swung in Jameson's direction and he'd have to admit he was as shocked at his declaration as they were.

"No, really—"

"As you said, you've known Nixon since you were five. You've helped his dad on this farm. We're not taking your money."

"I'm not a charity case, Jameson. I have money. Not a lot, but I've been saving my whole life for an emergency."

"Didn't say it and didn't think it, Kennedy, so I know you're not a charity. It's the right thing to do. Neighborly, even." Jameson knew his excuse was lame but it was the only one he had for his out-of-character behavior.

He'd known when she first told him about her situation they wouldn't be charging her. But finding out about her mom, and more about Reggie Coleman, cemented Jameson's resolve.

"I don't take handouts. No way, no how. Either I pay or I find someone else," she proclaimed and Jameson couldn't help but notice how cute she was when she was trying to be stern.

"It's not a handout, it's a public service. You said it yourself, he strong-armed the widow who lives next to you into selling when she didn't want to. And I know I haven't lived here long, but I pay attention and I find it difficult to believe she couldn't find a farmer to rent her land to. Which means Reggie Coleman made it so she couldn't. So if he pulled that shit with an old woman, God knows who else he's done it to."

"What's this about? What widow?" Nixon interjected.

"Mrs. Nickels," Kennedy sighed. "She couldn't find anyone who wanted to rent the land after Mr. Nickels died, so she had to sell. Of course, Reggie Coleman was there to scoop it up, and at a ridiculously low price."

"All of it? Or did you buy your land back?"

"All of it. Even if I could've afforded to buy it back from her, I couldn't go it alone. I tried for a year, but even being only two-hundred and fifty acres, with the old equipment and everything that goes into the daily operations, I had to admit it was too much for me. It sucked when Mom had to sell it off, it sucked more when Reggie got it."

Nixon's face was stone and Jameson knew his friend

was feeling Kennedy's loss. Nixon loved his dad's farm and had given up a lot to come home and take care of it. Jameson hadn't had much of anything growing up. His mom had done the best she could after his dad bailed, but they'd had to move a lot, so he'd never grown attached to places or things because he'd known he wouldn't have either for long. He couldn't begin to comprehend the connection either of them felt.

"Jameson's right, we're not takin' your money." Nix lifted a hand and stopped Kennedy's protest. "Hate to have to pull this card, especially because I knew your dad and he was a proud man, never took nothing from nobody without payment. But you're in the position to let pride get in the way. You need our help, we're gonna give it, and there'll be no repayment. I don't want to get into your personal business but unfortunately, we're gonna have to do that, too. Jameson's gonna take you to the sheriff's station and you're gonna talk to Jonny Spenser. But before you do that, Holden's gonna check and see if Dillinger or anyone else in that office actually filed a report—"

"There are no reports filed involving Reggie Coleman harassing anyone. No reports on him for anything, actually. Not even a speeding ticket in the last twenty years," Holden cut in.

"Didn't think so," Nix continued. "When you're done at the station, head over to Kennedy's. Her house is situated back from the road and surrounded by trees—I want cameras up ASAP." Nixon's directive was aimed at Jameson so he nodded his understanding.

Kennedy frowned. "Wait. Cameras? Is that necessary? All I wanted was some sort of dirt I could use to make him stop," she protested.

"We'll find that. But in the meantime, you need to be safe. I'm assuming you live alone."

"Well, yeah."

"Right. You gotta man that stays over regular?"

Jameson once again stiffened. The thought hadn't crossed his mind that she might've had a man. But now that Nixon had brought it up, Jameson's gut soured and he held his breath waiting for her answer.

"I don't have time to clean out my damn truck, you think I have time for a man?" she joked, but there was something behind her flippant comment that made Jameson believe Nix had hit a sore spot.

"Then yes, the cameras are necessary. It's better to have them up and not needed than need them and not have them."

"But—"

"How far back do you want me to dig?" Holden asked Nixon, cutting off Kennedy's protest.

"As far back as you need to go to find something," Nix answered.

It was time to leave. Holden was going to start asking questions that Jameson didn't want her to hear. But more than that, he didn't want her freaked out, and there was no doubt, Nix and Holden's conversation would do just that. A man like Reggie Coleman didn't just wake up one morning and decide to be a prick—he'd been perfecting his tactics for a good long while. And Jameson would bet

Mrs. Nickels the widow wasn't the first woman Reggie'd fucked over, he'd bet she wasn't even the fifth. So if sweet, pretty Kennedy Lane didn't already know, Jameson wanted to keep it that way.

"Come on, Kennedy, let's head to the station."

"But—"

"I want to get to your place before it gets dark."

"Can I talk?" she snapped.

"Sure, when your ass is planted in my truck and we're on the road."

"But we need to talk about me paying."

"We did, and it was decided you're not paying."

Kennedy's whole body transformed as she looked like she was getting ready to lose her shit. Her face was tinged pink, steel infused her spine, and she stood taller. And finally, her sexy bedroom eyes flashed with anger.

"No one decides anything for me, Jameson. You two may *think* you've decided, but that doesn't mean it's a done deal."

"Think about—"

"I am thinking, Nixon, and I'm thinking that you doing this for free feels like shit. I pay my bills. I make my own way. And it has nothing to do with pride and everything to do with what's right. I don't take advantage of other people's kindness. You're already doing me a favor by looking into this on short notice. I won't have you doin' it for free and I certainly won't have you come outta pocket on it. I pay or I'll find someone else."

"How many summers did you come over here and help my pop?" Nix asked.

31

"He paid me."

"How many?"

"I don't know, Nix. Every summer since I was thirteen until the year he passed."

"Right. And when he got sick, you come over here and help out around the house? You mow his grass, even though he bitched he didn't want you to? You bring him food? You come over and check in on him, keep him company?"

Kennedy didn't say anything and Jameson knew Nix had made his point.

"Not the same thing, Nixon, and you know it. I loved your dad—he was there for me and my mom when my dad died. And I should've done more for your dad."

"It is the same thing. There's a debt to be paid, and it's mine. I owe you. And you know if my pop was around, he'd have my ass in a sling if I didn't take care of you. You and I may not have spoken in many years, but my dad told me everything you'd done for him. How much he appreciated your help, especially in the end. And if you don't think me knowing that you were here taking care of my old man when I couldn't didn't go a long way to help my guilt, you'd be wrong. Don't fight me on this, Kennedy. We're taking care of this for you."

Kennedy's body slumped as she realized Nix wasn't backing down. Jameson hadn't known all that the woman had done for Nixon's dad, but hearing it, he wasn't the least bit surprised. Kennedy Lane was a good person, through and through. And as much as Jameson liked hating everything and everyone, he just might like Kennedy.

And now that he knew he liked her as a person, it was going to make the attraction he felt toward her even harder to tamp down.

Someone as bright and cheery as Kennedy didn't need Jameson's bad attitude and black soul to darken her world. No, she belonged in the bright, brilliant light, and Jameson knew he was best left to his cold solitude.

The fuck of it was, for once Jameson wanted to know what it felt like to be wrapped in warmth.

4

KENNEDY

I was annoyed Nixon had pulled his father into the money conversation. It'd been a low blow. But once he'd started ticking off the things I'd done for Mr. Swagger, like I was some goody-two-shoes, I knew I'd lost.

I hadn't helped Mr. Swagger because I wanted gratitude, I hadn't even done it to return the kindness he'd showed my mom and me after my dad died. I did it because all I could think about was my own mom. If I'd been off serving my country like Nixon had been and my mom was all alone, I'd want someone to help her.

I truly believed you reaped what you gave. I knew that some people thought I was a pushover because I never said no when someone needed help, and I offered my time more than I received back. But the truth was, even though I had very little, I had more than some. I would never allow others' inability to do the right thing make me a pessimistic bitch. That didn't make me a pushover, it made me a good person.

"I'm sorry," I told Jameson as we pulled out of Nixon's lane.

"For what?"

"I'm sure a trip to the sheriff's office wasn't how you'd envisioned your afternoon going. Or should I say evening."

The sun had sunk farther into the western sky, streaking the horizon with yellow and orange. Even though Jameson had said he wanted to look at my place while he still had daylight, I didn't think that was going to happen.

"Had nothing else planned," he said, not taking his eyes off the road.

"Well, at least you shoulda let me drive my own car. That way you didn't have to go back to Nixon's to drop me off and waste more of your time."

"Need to go back there anyway, considering that's where I live."

"You do? I didn't know that."

"Yep. Nixon moved out a while ago and moved in with McKenna, Zack, and Mandy. All of us live there."

I didn't know who all Jameson was talking about, but I assumed he meant Holden and the other guys I'd heard he'd worked with.

"I love that for Nix. I'd heard he moved in with McKenna, but I also know you can't believe half the shit you hear."

"Only half?"

"No, you're right. It's more like you can't believe ninety percent of what's floatin' around."

"Now that I believe." Jameson smiled and once again the small gesture changed his whole appearance.

I wasn't nosey by nature but I was curious as to why he always looked like he was pissed about something. To say he'd perfected the resting bitch face would be an understatement. Only on him it was more like a, 'I'm a total badass and could snap you in two so don't even think of talking to me', face.

At some point in Jameson's life he'd been burned, that much was obvious. But what I didn't know, and it'd never be my place to ask, was why he'd kept picking at the scab. Maybe whatever happened was so bad, he used the fresh pain as a reminder so he didn't fall prey again.

It was none of my business but I felt a little sad for him. Likely a man like Jameson wouldn't appreciate me feeling any sort of way about his private life, but it didn't make the sadness any less true.

"You said, all of us live at Nixon's old place. Who's all of you?"

"Me, Holden, Chasin, and Weston. Though I don't know if you saw it, but Holden lives in his Airstream. He has it parked up at the barn."

"Why does he live in a trailer?" I asked before I thought better of it.

"Don't let him hear you call his fully restored, prized possession a trailer. He can get snippy about the Silver Bullet." Jameson was joking, I could hear it in his voice and it made him sound way more likeable.

"Noted." I smiled back even though I doubted I'd be in the man's presence again.

"And he lives in it because he likes his privacy maybe only a tad bit more than I like my own. There's three bedrooms in the farmhouse, none of us were real keen on having to double-up, but even if it was a ten-bedroom mini mansion, he'd still prefer his Airstream."

That was a little strange—opting to live in a trailer by a barn—but hey, to each their own. And I'd never had an issue with privacy, considering I was an only child and it'd been me and my mom since I was seventeen. Hell, some days I wished there was someone else's voice or mess in my house. But then I remembered why it was that I still, at thirty-one, lived alone, and immediately redirected my depressing thoughts. No one wanted a tomboy who had barely enough time to shower every day, forget about making time to actually date or buy a dress.

Plus I was that tomboy and I had no interest in finding the time to buy a dress. If a man couldn't like me in my work jeans with my hair pulled up, then he wasn't worth the effort. So, why did I care that Jameson had seen me in my daily grubbies, and not freshly-showered at least?

"Where'd you go?" Jameson asked, pulling me from my thoughts of growing old alone with only the buzzing of my bees to keep me company.

"Huh?" I looked at him, and since he was stopped at one of the few red lights in town, he was staring at me.

"You looked like you were a hundred miles away."

"Oh, I was just thinking about all the chores I have left to do tonight," I lied.

Jameson nodded and went back to looking at the

road. I had a feeling he knew I wasn't telling the truth, but he'd said he liked his privacy so I suspected he was giving me mine.

It was a damn shame, too, because I figured it wouldn't have taken much coaxing from him and I would've spilled my life story and how tired I was of always carrying the weight of the world on my shoulders. That just for once I wished I had someone to talk to. Sure I had friends, and they'd take the time, but most of them were now married and had their own concerns. And my friends that were still single were only that way for short periods of time, then they'd find themselves a man and get lost in the newness of passion until they realized they'd picked another Mr. Wrong and go back on the prowl.

I wasn't prone to feeling sorry for myself, I didn't have the energy or time for it. But all this Reggie business, and being afraid that one more misstep or financial hit and I'd lose the rest of the farm my dad had worked so hard to give us, was wearing me down.

I just needed to sleep on it and tomorrow I'd be back to my old self. Strong. Independent. Resilient. That's what my dad used to always say about me. He'd believed in me when his friends had chuckled at his daughter out working the fields with him. He'd always say, 'My girl's just as strong as any boy and she works harder.' And I did work harder, I had to. In this small town, being a girl didn't work in your favor, not if you wanted to do anything that resembled *man's work*.

Thirty minutes later, we were walking out of the sheriff's office after talking to Jonny Spenser. Of course, I knew him and he knew me. We'd gone to school together and with both of us never leaving Kent County, we'd had plenty of occasion to run into each other since graduation.

He was a good guy in high school and he'd grown up to be a good man. I couldn't understand how he was still single other than to say, he seemed to enjoy his throne as KC's hottest bachelor. He'd probably nailed every good-looking woman in the county and he was still well-liked and you rarely heard a cross word spoken about him. Said a lot about a man, when he could still be friendly with his exes. Or maybe it said he was great in bed and they were all hoping for another go-around so they were still nice to him in the interim.

"You hungry?" Jameson asked, and at the very mention of food my stomach growled.

"A little."

"You want to stop for pizza?"

Pizza sounded great, but I had food at home and I hated wasting it. I guess it could keep for one more day—

"What's wrong?" he asked, interrupting my internal struggle.

"Nothing."

"Stop doing that."

"Doing what?"

"Lying to me. I can't stand liars."

I jerked in my seat at the accusation.

"I'm not a liar."

"I didn't think you were, but twice you've lied to me. Both of them while we've been in my truck. You didn't lie to me when we were at the barn. I asked you what was wrong and you laid it out for me, bold as brass, not caring you were talking to a stranger. Now? Now you're lying."

I thought about what he said and I had lied to him, once. And the second time he was making reference to, wouldn't have been the lie he'd thought it was if he'd allowed me to finish.

"You cut me off before I could finish my last statement. Nothing's wrong. But I was going to add I have a roast in my crockpot at home and I don't like eating out when I have food at home because it's a waste. But since you mentioned pizza that sounds better. But then I was thinking it's a big roast and maybe you'd like to come to my house and have some. But then I remembered that the last time I invited you into my mom's house as a thank you for running off Reggie, you turned me down. So I didn't think my ego could take another hit like that, so I was going to tell you pizza sounded great."

"Your house for roast it is."

"Come again?"

"We're going to your house to eat the roast you're cooking."

"Um."

"You're right, no sense wasting good food. You a good cook?"

"I've never had any complaints."

Jameson's brows pulled together before he rested his features and said, "Great. I haven't had a real meal since McKenna took pity on me and invited me over for supper."

He drove past the shopping center that the pizza place was in and I wondered if he knew where he was going.

"You're gonna have to give me directions."

Well, that answered that. I told him where to go and when I was done, he asked, "Why'd you lie to me? The first time when I was stopped at the light and you were staring off into space looking like someone kicked your cat."

I didn't own any cats—yet. Though I was starting to get worried I would be buying a menagerie of pets in the not-so-distant future.

"Because I was embarrassed to tell you what I was thinking, so instead I told you I had chores."

Jameson nodded. "I understand that. But in the future, if there's something you don't want to talk about, tell me to mind my own business, don't bullshit me."

I was looking at Jameson, really looking at him, and for some reason this meant something to him. Something big. Even though his demand was abrasive and frankly kind of rude—not to mention, I had no plans for any sort of future where I got to know him better—I still wanted to give him this, so I did.

"All right," I agreed.

"The second part to that is, I understand not wanting to share, but if you find yourself wanting to, you never have anything to be embarrassed about. I'm the last person to judge. I may be an asshole and I do my best to avoid human interaction, but I don't judge the people I like."

"And I fall into the category of people you like?" I stupidly asked.

Jameson was quiet for a while and I was starting to panic a little when he finally spoke, "Yes, strangely, you do."

I realized two things. The first was, Jameson didn't just say things. He took the time to measure his answer and make sure what he was saying was what he meant to say. And I had a feeling, if his answer would've been the opposite, he still would've told me, even if it was impolite to do so. Jameson Grant did not do social grace.

The second was, he was oddly confused about liking me. He sounded genuinely surprised.

"Thanks for your help," I told him.

He shifted in his seat. "You already said that."

"No, I didn't. I said I was sorry to put you out."

"Same thing. Your appreciation was implied."

"You don't take others' gratefulness well, do you?"

The slightest smile. "No, I do. I just haven't done anything to earn yours, yet."

I'd never met anyone like Jameson. He was forward to the point of being abrupt. One could even call him bad-mannered. But I felt oddly comfortable around him. I'd spent very little time with him, yet I knew exactly where I stood and I liked that. I knew he liked me enough to offer me his time. I knew he didn't like to be lied to—

which no one did—but he didn't even like the smallest of omissions, he preferred straight out honesty. I knew he didn't like most people. I knew he was loyal, probably to a fault, just like me. But mostly I knew he was a good man.

To sum it up, Jameson was a strange bird. One I wanted to get to know. And that scared me to death. A man like him had the power to squish me like a bug under his boot. Not that I thought he'd do it intentionally. But I knew myself—no matter how many times I'd been hurt, I still wore my heart on my sleeve.

I just hoped I was as resilient as my dad always said I was. I had a feeling I was going to need to be.

5

JAMESON

"No complaints, huh?" Jameson looked down at his now-empty plate and wondered if he had room for thirds.

"What was that?" Kennedy asked.

Her head tipped to the side and her hair fell over her shoulder. It was pulled up in a ponytail but the ends brushed her left breast, drawing Jameson's attention to her chest, and once there he couldn't help but take his fill. She had perfect-sized breasts for her small frame. Not too big, not too small.

Jameson knew it was rude how he was checking her out, so he forced his gaze to her face and took a moment longer to enjoy how pretty she was. No makeup, no subterfuge, no charade. Kennedy was who she was, she didn't try to hide the fact she worked hard and that work included manual labor. There was no girly polish on her short nails, and he'd bet she didn't even own a bottle. Her hands were work-roughed, her clothes were worn for comfort, and her hair was messy.

Jameson liked that, all of it.

"You're a damn good cook," he finally answered.

"Kinda hard to screw up a roast. I just threw it in the crockpot this morning."

"Right. And the stewed tomatoes? Did you make those?"

"Of course I did." Jameson smiled at her disgruntled response. "I picked them fresh from the garden this morning. The bell peppers and zucchini, too."

By the time they'd gotten to Kennedy's house, the sun had set and Jameson couldn't see much. Nixon had been right though; her house was secluded. She'd mentioned her property line ended at the county road but her house was not street side. Much like where Jameson lived, you had to drive down a dirt lane lined with trees to get back to the old farmhouse.

His headlights had provided enough illumination to see the barn behind the house, and beyond that her neatly planted garden. But he hadn't been able to appreciate the extent of her crops.

"Hard work taking care of all of this by yourself," Jameson noted.

Kennedy sat up straight and held herself tight. "Nothing I can't handle."

"Didn't say you couldn't. Just stating the obvious."

She nodded but didn't say anything and Jameson knew he'd struck a nerve. And for some inexplicable reason he wanted to know more.

"Someone tell you you couldn't handle it?"

Kennedy sighed and slumped back in her seat, and

for a moment he thought she was going to lie to him. His jaw clenched in preparation. He hated liars. If he asked a question he expected honesty, even if that honesty was as simple as telling him it was none of his business.

"Lots of people have told me I was stupid for wanting to keep my dad's farm. After he died, some people pitched in to help me, but there's only so long they can help before they have to get back to their lives. When my mom ended up having to sell off some land, I felt like a failure. Like I was what everyone was saying, a silly girl trying to do a man's job farming.

"It took me a long time to realize even though we couldn't keep it, I didn't fail. I tried my best with the tools I had. Unfortunately, there's not a lot of money farming, and tractors and other equipment are expensive. My dad didn't believe in carrying debt, so everything we had was old. He knew how to fix just about anything. But when stuff started breaking down on me, I didn't have the knowledge he had. We had no choice but to sell. It was that or go into debt, and that wasn't right to put my mom into financial hardship just because I had a point to prove."

Jameson was damn impressed and more than a little pissed-off on her behalf. He'd never bought into the notion there was a distinction between a man's job and a woman's. Of course there were things that men were more prone to excel at than women, but that didn't mean a woman couldn't do it. It simply meant that the woman who took on the task would have to be determined.

And by all accounts, Kennedy was determined.

"Glad to hear you know you didn't fail. Too many people think that when something doesn't work it's a failure, instead of realizing the experience was a lesson. The only failure is when you don't do anything. When you sit on your ass and expect the world to hand you what you want. And I have a feeling you've never sat around a day in your life. You impress me."

Kennedy's head tipped down and her cheeks pinked. Jameson's fingers itched to reach out and touch her. Lift her chin and make her look at him. But he refrained. It was not his place to touch her anywhere, no matter how badly he wanted to.

"Yeah, well, I don't have time to sit and do nothing. There's always something to do. I might not have all two hundred and fifty acres we once had but I still have fifty, my bees to tend to, and not to mention, this old house would fall down around me if I didn't keep on top of it."

Jameson looked around the dining room and wondered if she'd restored the woodwork all by herself. There was crown molding at the ceiling, a bullnose chair rail that went around the room on three sides, and by the look of it someone had removed a wall, opening the dining room up to the kitchen.

"Did you do the restoration in here?" Jameson asked.

"Yeah. I wanted to open it up. The house was built in 1909. It was just the kitchen and this room downstairs and the two bedrooms upstairs. The original outhouse is still out back. Back then every room had a door so you could close it off to keep the heat where you needed it." Jameson thought about the kitchen and had noticed there was a fireplace in there, as well as one in the dining room. "In the thirties, they put in a bathroom upstairs. It was crazy small. And in the forties, they built an addition that almost doubled the size of the house. But anyway, with everything closed off it was stuffy and dark. Thankfully the wall I wanted to remove wasn't load-bearing, so it was a cinch to demo."

Just as Jameson had thought, Kennedy was remarkable.

"You did a great job."

"Thanks." Her gaze slid away again and Jameson couldn't help but smile.

"Seems you're the one that has issues with praise," he noted.

"Maybe I'm just not used to it."

How in the hell was that possible? The woman was astonishingly capable and obviously talented.

"What's that mean?"

There was another sigh and she looked over at him and shook her head. "That's for another conversation."

"Is that your nice way of saying it's none of my business?"

"Pretty much."

Jameson chuckled and a strange feeling hit his chest. One he'd never felt, therefore couldn't place, but it felt so damn good he didn't try and stop it.

"Would you like dessert, a tour of the house, or neither and you can take me back to get my truck from your house?"

"Are your keys in your truck?"

That was something Jameson had learned in the last few months he'd lived in Kent County. Everyone left their keys in their car and most didn't lock their doors. It was beyond weird and something Jameson didn't think he'd ever get used to.

"Yeah."

"I'll have the guys bring your truck over."

"Why would you bother them when you have to go home and I can drive myself back?"

"It's not a bother, and even if it was, you're dead on your feet from workin' all day. You don't need to be going out again, not even to drive your truck home."

"I don't like favors, Jameson." She pinned him with a stare and it was cute how she'd narrowed her eyes and thought she could get him to back down.

Jameson was contemplating how to explain himself without Kennedy thinking he was more of an asshole than he was sure he'd already made himself out to be. Which was something else new. He couldn't remember a time he cared what someone else thought. He didn't guard his words or his reactions, but he found he cared what she thought.

And Jameson thought that just because a woman *could* do anything didn't mean she *should* have to, or that while he was around, he'd allow her to.

"It's not a favor when it's offered."

"Feels the same."

"It might, but it's vastly different. You didn't ask me to do anything. I offered. And I did so because I don't want you out driving this late after you've worked your ass off all day."

"It's barely nine o'clock."

"What time did you get up this mornin'?" he asked.

"Five, same as always."

"That means it's late and it will be later if you go pick up your truck after you give me a tour of your house. Holden and Weston can bring your car over. Their lazy asses didn't get up until seven."

Kennedy's lips twitched and Jameson reached in his pocket for his cell.

"Seven's hardly lazy." She smiled.

"It is when you're up at five."

Jameson sent his text, and before he could put his phone back in his pocket, Holden had replied they'd bring her truck over now.

"I still think it's unnecessary, but I'm gonna pick my battles and just say thank you."

"Pick your battles?"

"Yeah, I have a feeling there will come a time with you when I'll need to fight for my corner. So I'm saving up all my ammunition for that battle. No sense in using it all up on something I really don't care about, even if I think it's silly to bother your friends. But in the grand scheme of life, it's no skin off my nose if someone drives my truck."

Jameson liked that a helluva lot. He wasn't exactly sure why, but he couldn't deny the feeling.

Kennedy took Jameson upstairs to show him the work she'd done ripping out an old bathroom, and how she'd converted the old one and a small bedroom into a master closet and new en suite. The workmanship was pristine— she'd spent a lot of time remodeling her home. It was updated but somehow she'd kept the house authentic.

She was showing him her latest project in one of the bedrooms when two sets of headlights swung into her drive, signaling Holden and Weston were there.

"Are you going to go down and talk to them?" she inquired.

"Nope. They said they'd leave your keys in your truck. I'll grab them and bring them in before I go."

"You can leave 'em in the truck. I never bring them in."

Jameson clenched his teeth and badly wanted to school her on personal safety, especially with the asshole Reggie circling. But he didn't. He, too, would pick his battles, and getting Kennedy to change a habit she'd had since she began to drive was unlikely.

"If you need any help in here, let me know," he said instead. "Hanging the molding will be easier with two people."

"Thanks, but it's not that hard. I just have to cut it into manageable sections and butt the joints. By the time I putty them and paint them, you can't see my breaks."

Jameson found it ridiculously attractive she not only knew what the term 'butt the joints' meant, but she'd been correct, Jameson couldn't find where she'd scabbed the two pieces of wood together.

"Offer stands, four hands make for easy work."

Kennedy muttered her thanks and Jameson hoped

she understood he hadn't offered his help because he'd thought she was incapable. He'd offered because, well, he didn't know why he'd offered. The fuck of it was, he just wanted to be around her.

She turned off the lights and they wandered back downstairs. She stopped in the living room and with much trepidation she asked, "Would you like a beer?"

He hated that she was uneasy, and he knew it was because the first time she'd asked him in for iced tea, he declined. Not only that, but he'd tucked tail and bolted.

Time to set shit right.

"Got anything stronger?"

"Sure. Jim Beam, Johnnie Walker, and Jose Cuervo."

A woman after his own heart.

"Will you join me?"

"Sure, I'll have a few fingers of Johnnie." Kennedy's face flamed and she quickly added, "I mean, I'll take a pour."

"I'll have the same."

"'Kay. Have a seat and I'll be right back."

Jameson watched as Kennedy scampered out of the room, and the moment he was alone he wondered what he was doing and why'd he'd been so intent on staying. If he was honest with himself, which he always was, he hadn't accepted her invitation for a drink so she wouldn't suffer another blow to her ego as she'd earlier explained his first rejection had done. It was because he was intrigued.

And his fascination with her went beyond how impressed he was by her. He was simply enthralled.

Jameson was definitely interested in her. He just wasn't sure if he should act upon it. Jameson wasn't relationship material. He never had been. He had major hang-ups about commitment and he was smart enough to understand where those issues stemmed from.

So while he'd like nothing more than another tour of the upstairs, this time one that included the master bedroom—complete with testing the thread count of Kennedy's sheets—he wasn't going to make a play.

He had no doubt she'd catch his play. There'd been a few times Jameson had caught her staring at him with blatant interest, but it was unclear what that curiosity entailed. He had no idea if she was a serious relationship type of girl on the lookout for a husband, or if she just wanted a roll in the sack and a good time. The former was a no-go, the latter he could provide in spades.

However, there was the small problem she was Nixon's friend, and however loose that connection, he wouldn't exploit it. Not even for dynamite sex and a taste of the pretty Kennedy Lane. And Jameson was sure the woman would be a great lay.

"Here ya go," Kennedy said, handing him his whiskey.

"Thanks." He waited for her to take her seat, then sat himself, trying to keep a respectable distance. "You don't have a TV," he observed.

"I probably sit in this room once a month if I'm lucky. I do have one in my bedroom but I couldn't tell you the last time I turned it on. By the time I come in, eat, and shower, I'm normally too tired for much of anything else."

Damn, did he understand that. Jameson wasn't a big TV watcher either.

"When I say that out loud, it reminds me how boring I am."

"Boring because you don't numb your mind with TV?"

"No, because I don't have a life. I do go out on occasion. I mean, I do have some friends, but most are married with kids, so luckily they can't get out much either. I don't know why it's important to me that you know this, but I'm happy with my life."

Jameson was more pleased than he should've been that Kennedy had opened up and given him that small truth, but he couldn't deny the feeling.

"Why would you think that I'd think you weren't happy?"

She sighed and he was beginning to see a pattern. When she was getting ready to say something that she thought would be embarrassing, she'd exhale and brace for ridicule. The gesture pissed him off. Not the act itself but the reason behind why she did it. Someone in her past had not been kind to her, and he didn't think it was her dad. She was too fond of her home and the land for it to be him. She wouldn't've tried so hard to save it if he'd been a dick to her. And it wasn't her mother. Every time she spoke about her, love crept into her voice.

"Because my life revolves around work. But I'm fortunate enough to love what I do. I like working my garden and taking care of my bees. I love making honey and candles, and canning my vegetables. It may sound boring, or like I'm not ambitious, or I settled for this life because I didn't have big dreams. But honestly, this is the life I always wanted. I enjoy a hard day's work. I like to be a good steward to the land. I like selling what I make at the market. Everything I sell, I make or grow. I can look at everything around me and know each day I accomplished something."

"I'm not sure who in your past made you feel like you weren't ambitious, but I'd bet you get more accomplished by eight a.m. than most people do in a week. There's nothing wrong with an honest day's work accompanied by a shit-ton of elbow grease. I'm glad you're happy, I don't think there are many people who can say they love their job. But you can. I don't think you're boring. I find you interesting and I want to know more. I wanna watch you finish the demo work on your bedroom upstairs. I have a feeling you could teach me a thing or two about finish carpentry. As a matter of fact, Kennedy, I can't remember a woman I've ever found more fascinating than you."

Kennedy's shy smile made his admission almost worth it, though he was mentally berating himself for revealing too much. He never should've told her he wanted to know more about her. He knew he was giving her the wrong impression and almost shot back his whiskey so he could once again hightail it away from her.

Good God, he'd turned into a pussy.

He watched as she took a healthy swallow of her drink and chuckled when her face didn't scrunch up like most women's did when they sipped whiskey.

"What's amusing?"

"You obviously like your Johnnie Walker, you didn't grimace."

"I do," she confirmed. "Now, when I shoot tequila that's a different story. I was happy you didn't choose Jose or I'd be making all sorts of funny faces and you'd think I was some kinda pansy-assed girl."

"Babe, you're a girl all right, but I wouldn't say there's a single thing about you that makes me think you're a pansy."

"You haven't seen me drink tequila yet so you can't say that."

Jameson took his own sip and savored the warmth as it hit his chest.

"So what made you move to Kent County? It isn't exactly a beacon for excitement," Kennedy inquired.

Jameson was happy to see some of the shyness gone, but he didn't particularly enjoy sharing.

"The short answer is, I moved here because of Nix."

"And the long one?"

"How 'bout we save that for a night filled with tequila?"

"Gotcha."

Kennedy smiled and relaxed back, sinking farther into the couch cushions, taking no offense to him tabling the conversation.

They both sat there in companionable silence and he liked that about her, too. She didn't need to fill the void with needless chitchat. She could simply be and enjoy her whiskey.

Yeah, Jameson liked that too much.

With both of their drinks drained and Kennedy stifling a yawn, Jameson reluctantly ended their evening.

"I'm gonna head out," he told her and stood.

She followed him to her feet, her gaze lingering on his chest a moment before she brought her eyes up and smiled.

"You're really big," she blurted out, then quickly tried to cover her blunder. "I mean, you're really tall. Obviously, I knew this. I mean, you're tall-tall so it's easy to see, but standing this close to you and really seeing the height difference...well, it...never mind, I don't know what I'm trying to say. My brain is malfunctioning."

Jameson chuckled at her stuttered explanation and let her off the hook. "I get what you're saying," he started. "But maybe our height difference has more to do with you being a tiny little thing."

"I'm not tiny," she huffed. "I'm five-seven. You're just a giant."

"I'm six-three, not eight feet. And compared to me, you're a little thing. I could toss you over my shoulder and run five miles and still not notice you."

"I have no doubt," she mumbled.

He really needed to leave. Now that he was picturing Kennedy's lean, sexy body thrown over his shoulder, he was not thinking of PT-ing—he was fantasizing about carrying her up to her bedroom and showing her just how big he was.

His body was so much bigger it would easily cover hers, but her long legs would still wrap around his waist.

He had no doubt they'd be a perfect fit. The mere thought of Kennedy withering under him while moaning her pleasure made Jameson's dick twitch in excitement.

It was really time to leave.

"I'll walk you to the door."

That was a brilliant idea, he needed to be shown the door. As much as it was his suggestion it was time for him to head home, he was having serious trouble with his feet taking him where he needed to go.

Kennedy opened her front door, leaving the glass storm door closed, and looked up at Jameson with tired eyes and licked her lips. He fought back the groan that was threatening, seeing the moisture her tongue had left behind. He'd bet those full, pink lips would feel great wrapped around his cock.

Goddamn. He was kicking his own ass for thinking dirty thoughts about a woman when he had no business going there with her. But if they did...

"Thanks again for today," she broke his train of thought.

"No need. I'll be in touch tomorrow. Will you be around?"

"Yeah, I have a full day in my garden."

He didn't even want to think about her bent over, ass in the air, tempting all his strength as she harvested her crop.

"I'll be over around noon."

"Okay." Her answer was timid and she went as far as to look away.

"If that's not—"

"No. Noon's fine."

"Then why are you being shy again?"

She didn't reply for a moment and Jameson was wondering if he should've kept his mouth shut, when she straightened and with a smirk she answered, "I'd rather not say."

He should've known she'd politely tell him to mind his business.

"All right, babe, I'll see you tomorrow."

Jameson pulled open the storm door and made his way in the dark to his truck. First thing on his agenda tomorrow was to get her motion-activated lights.

He was almost home when a thought occurred to him —was Kennedy acting shy because she thought he was going to kiss her? She was staring up at him expectantly, she had licked her lips. But neither of those things supported his notion. Maybe it was his imagination running wild. Maybe she was nervous because she *didn't* want him to try something.

Maybe Jameson just needed to cool his jets and stop thinking about all the ways he'd like to fuck Kennedy, and treat her with a little more respect.

But Jameson suspected his fantasies were the tip of the iceberg.

6

KENNEDY

For the first time in a long time, I didn't want to get out of bed when my alarm sounded. I wanted to roll over and enjoy the rest of my dream. But I knew if I'd hit snooze, I'd continue to do it five more times and I had work to do.

Besides, what was the chance I'd fall back into the same dream? Luckily, in my dream, Jameson had already done all the good stuff. When the buzzing started, my Dream Jameson was cuddling me close after he'd given me multiple, really great orgasms.

Unfortunately, it was a dream in every way. In my limited experience there was no such thing as multiple orgasms. Actually, there was no such thing as an orgasm being the result of sex, period. But in my dream, Jameson had indeed made me quiver and shake and scream his name. That was another myth about sex, the screaming. No one actually shouted during sex. Nothing felt that good. But holy hell, in my dream Jameson had been taking me so hard from behind, hitting all the right spots, I was crying out and doing it loudly.

Too bad that particular fantasy would never come true.

There was no way the man had any interest in me other than helping me with Reggie Coleman.

He was crystal clear about that last night when he was leaving. He couldn't have avoided making any sort of contact with me if he'd tried. Well, he could've if he'd left through the back door while I was holding open the front.

When he'd asked me why I was acting shy, I was shocked he'd called me out. Most people wouldn't notice, and if they had, they certainly wouldn't have asked about it. But not Jameson, no, he asked about everything. I'd rather poke my eyeballs out with toothpicks than tell him I was thinking what it would be like if he'd leaned down and kissed me goodnight.

Today I had to face him again, and after seeing Dream Jameson naked, I wasn't sure how I was going to do that and not turn a shade of red.

I looked down at my watch and decided it was time to go in and wash up. Jameson would be here any minute and I'd been out in my yard for the last five hours and I was a sweaty mess. I had enough vegetables to take to the market this week and cover the orders I already had for the local restaurants who purchased from me. I'd spend the rest of the day washing and boxing everything up so tomorrow I could jar the honey I'd collected yesterday.

I was carrying the last crate to my back porch when a shiny, red Ram pickup pulled up my lane and my temper spiked. Jameson did not drive a Ram, he drove a Tundra. And his wasn't flashy red, waxed to a high-gloss shine. No, Jameson's was a man's truck. It was metallic gray, with a blacked-out grill and rims. It looked tough, like the man who drove it. The interior was much cleaner than mine, but his was still a workhorse, not as a way to compensate for a potbelly and low testosterone.

Reggie hefted himself out of his truck and started toward my house. I cut him off before he could reach my newly laid brick walkway.

"Get off my property," I snapped.

"You should take my deal," Reggie returned.

"I told you no."

"Now, listen here, Kennedy, a smart girl like you—"

"Get. Off. My. Land," I cut off his condescending speech.

I'd heard it before and I wasn't in the mood to hear it again.

The sound of tires eating up the gravel driveway caught my attention and I wasn't sure if I was ecstatic Jameson was there, or if I was twice as pissed at Reggie that I hadn't had time to wash up and Jameson was going to be treated to me looking like I worked in a field all day. Which I had, but I still didn't want Jameson to see the dirt on my hands and I was sure I stunk to the heavens.

"This is the last time I'm gonna make you an offer," he stated.

"Great."

"I don't think you're understanding me. I won't be offering—"

"What won't you be offering?" Jameson asked, entering the conversation.

Reggie took a step back, probably thinking he had more time to threaten me before Jameson was in earshot.

"Private business matter. None of your concern, son."

Jameson's eyes narrowed on Reggie and I had a feeling that was the wrong thing to say. Jameson towered over Reggie by a lot—he was not a tall man. And the size difference was tremendous. Where Jameson was a big wall of muscle, Reggie was a short stack of hotcakes with puddling in between the layers.

"I'm thinking any business that relates to Kennedy is my concern."

"I don't—"

"What'd he say to you this time?" Jameson asked me, interrupting Reggie's rebuttal.

"Oh, the usual. If I was a smart girl, I'd take his offer. Then he told me this would be the last time he makes an offer. You interrupted him before he could get to the good part."

Jameson's lips twitched, not missing my mocking tone.

"Yeah? What's the good part?"

"Well, he normally spouts off about how when times get hard, I'll have no choice but to sell. Then he tells me his offer won't be as high. Then sometimes he explains that the cost of taking care of my mother is going to wear me down and when it does he'll only offer me half of his current offer, so I should give it to him now. And I would be giving it to him at the price he wants to buy at. He likes to come at me with all sorts of shit. But this is the first time I'm going to explain to him that if he comes onto my land one more time, he'll be met in the driveway with my shotgun."

I turned from Jameson to look at a red-faced Reggie and announced, "I've asked you to leave. You're trespassing. So I'm gonna tell you one more time, I'm not selling. Not today, not ever. Now, I'm going in this house, I'm going to my safe, and I'm getting my gun. If you're still out here when I get back, I'm shooting."

"You wouldn't dare shoot me," Reggie told me with a broad smile.

Smug bastard.

"You willing to take that chance? Because I'm telling you right now, your pretty red truck's gonna get the first taste of my buckshot. After that, we'll see."

I turned and walked around to the back of my house. I didn't wait to see what Jameson was doing. I didn't wait to hear if either man had something to say about my promise of brandishing a weapon. I marched into my house, went straight into my mudroom where my safe was at, spun the dial, opened the heavy metal door, and pulled out my favorite Remington Model 870. It was my dad's and had been passed down to me.

I remembered as a kid Dad teaching me how to shoot this gun. I also remembered him teaching me never to aim it at something I didn't intend to shoot. He also told me never to kill an animal I didn't intend to eat unless it was threatening something I loved or trying to kill our livestock.

I wondered what my daddy would think about me shooting Reggie Coleman's truck. Knowing my dad, he'd be proud. Reggie was a nasty pig and he was threatening something I loved—what was left of my dad's farm.

He wouldn't get it. Not ever. I'd told Reggie once and I'd meant it, over my dead body, he'd take this land.

"Whoa there, Annie Oakley." Jameson appeared.

"He gone?"

"Yep. I think you promisin' to shoot that fancy-assed truck 'a his did it."

"It would. He loves that damn thing. Never seen a speck of mud on it. Bet he carries one of those shammy towels with him, in case he gets caught in the rain."

Jameson studied me for a moment and his eyes flicked to the shotgun in my hand before he looked back at me and smiled.

"You all right?"

I thought about lying and saying I was fine, but Jameson would sniff that out in a second so instead I told him the truth.

"No. I'm sick of him bothering me. I'm scared he's gonna make my life hell and somehow force me to sell like he did Mrs. Nickels. I know he put the word out for no one to rent her land. I'm not sure what he can do to me, but I do know I don't want to find out." I stopped and took a shaky breath. "Thank you for coming when you did. You stopped me from committing a felony. Or at least a visit from the police and Reggie suing me to fix his truck."

"Right place, right time. Or should I say, Reggie

picked the wrong time for his visit when I was on my way over. Were you really gonna shoot his truck?"

"Yep. I was gonna shoot out his windows and enjoy the sound of glass shattering. Probably not the smartest plan, but he will not leave me alone. This is my land, he has no business coming here. I've tried being nice, but it doesn't work. I lost my temper."

Jameson continued to look at me for a long time. He looked like he was wrestling with his thoughts, and finally with a nod he asked, "Babe, do me a favor, yeah?"

Babe?

Why did hearing him say that give me a warm, tingling feeling?

"Okay."

"Go put your gun away."

Was he nervous I had a gun?

"I know how to shoot. I'm not gonna accidentally shoot a hole in my ceiling."

"No doubt. But Weston's on his way over and I want to—"

"Weston?"

"Yeah, remember, he works with me."

"I remember who he is, but he's comin' here?"

"That a problem?"

I glanced down at myself and seeing as I was in filthy clothes and looked like a sweat-drenched pig, it was a big problem.

"I'm not fit for company." I shoved the shotgun at Jameson. "Here. The safe's still open. Will you put that away and lock it up for me?"

He took the gun from me and shook his head. "What does that mean? Not fit for company."

"Look at me. I'm a wreck. I need to go rinse off."

"Um." Jameson chuckled. "I'm standing here. Do I not count as company?"

"No. Friends don't count. I'll be right back."

I didn't wait to see if Jameson was locking up my shotgun—I was sure he knew his way around guns and would understand how to lock my safe.

I jogged up the stairs and rushed to undress, tossing my dirty clothes on my bedroom floor, and made my way to the bathroom. I turned on the taps and my mind was going a mile a minute while I waited for the water to warm up.

I was halfway through my very fast shower, rinsing the shampoo out of my hair, when the water went ice cold. I screeched at the shock and jumped out of the spray.

"Goddammit!"

Suds still covered my body and soapy water was sluicing down my face. I blindly felt for the taps to turn off the now unbearable cold water, then opened the shower curtain to reach for a towel to wipe my face.

"Dammit, *dammit,* dammit," I angrily muttered.

"You okay?" Jameson asked. His voice was close and I was naked with the curtain open.

With my eyes still closed, I scrambled to yank the towel off the bar and in my haste, I pulled too hard. I heard metal clank on the tile floor and started to stumble back.

Why had I insisted on tiling the shower floor? Why hadn't I gone with a plastic insert? The shower bottom was slippery as hell, especially when it was covered in shampoo. I was going to fall and break my neck in my own shower. Jameson would find my naked dead body and Reggie would surely scoop up my property.

"Son of a bitch," Jameson bit out.

Two strong arms grabbed my biceps and I was hauled forward, slamming into a hard wall of muscle. My hands and the towel were trapped between us, and if my eyes weren't already screwed shut to prevent soap from blinding me, I would've closed them in humiliation.

"Can you stand?" he asked.

"Sure," I mumbled.

"Don't move."

He stepped away and I heard the vanity cabinet open and close and the faucet turn on then off. I adjusted the towel and prayed it was covering my lady parts. I tried to remember when the last time I shaved and trimmed was. If my parts were on display, a big hairy bush would only add to my mortification.

Get a grip, Kennedy. Who cares if your pubes are out of control? Me. I care, dammit.

I jerked in surprise when a wet washcloth was pressed against my forehead. Then Jameson carefully commenced washing the soap off my face. He went back and rinsed the washcloth and repeated his efforts, paying close attention to my eyes.

"That should do it. Open your eyes."

I slowly opened them and blinked. When I didn't

feel the burn of shampoo in my eyes, I stopped blinking. That was when I came face-to-face with Jameson, a look of concern on his handsome face.

"Are you okay?" he asked.

"Nope."

"Care to explain."

"I'm standing in my bathroom naked, not sure what the towel I'm holding is covering or what you saw—"

"I wasn't looking, Kennedy. I was more concerned about what had you screaming."

Well, that was somewhat of a disappointment and further hammered home his disinterest. I mean, I was grateful he didn't get an eyeful, but at least he could've lied and said he was too gentlemanly to gawk.

"The water went cold," I explained.

"The water went cold? It's damn near ninety degrees outside, you were taking a hot shower?"

"No, not hot. But it was warm, then it was suddenly ice cold and it shocked the shit out of me. I didn't mean to scream, it was just...well...shocking."

His eyes flitted down to my chest before they came back to my face and gone was the concern. His gaze heated and I became acutely aware of how close he was standing. His hand came up and picked up a soapy hank of my hair and rubbed it between his fingers. When he set it back down the back of his knuckles brushed just below my collarbone. Slowly they skimmed down my bare skin, over the swell of my breast until I lost his touch because the damn towel was in the way. My nipples started to tingle and I doubted the terrycloth material would do much to prevent Jameson from feeling the hard nub as his knuckles grazed over it.

I stood motionless, our eyes locked, and in deep contemplation wondering if I should drop the towel. It would be easy, my hand was the only thing holding the bunched material to my front. Before I could summon up the bravery, Jameson dropped his hand and stepped back.

"I'll let you figure out how you're gonna rinse your hair and let Weston in." His voice was deeper than I'd ever heard it—almost hoarse.

The gravelly sound made other parts of me tingle and my body shook. His hazel eyes flashed and I knew he saw it. *How embarrassing.*

"Kennedy?" he called.

"Yeah?"

"Rinse your hair and get dressed."

"Right."

But he made no effort to move and neither did I. I couldn't tear my eyes away from his. There was something sparking between us and I didn't want it to end. It may've only been one-sided, that side being mine, but it felt damn good.

"Now, babe."

"You're the one that needs to move," I reminded him. "I'm the one standing here practically naked."

"Son of a bitch," he repeated his earlier remark and stepped away.

He turned and left and I remained rooted in place.

What the hell just happened?

I shook myself out of my stupor, shut the bathroom

door, and looked at my sink. With no other choice but to rinse my hair in the small basin, I turned on the water and caught sight of myself in the mirror.

Hoping the towel had slipped some since I walked out of the shower, because if it hadn't, Jameson had gotten quite a look. The material stopped just above my nipples and barely had covered my crotch.

Why did that knowledge excite me more than it embarrassed me? Why couldn't I get his husky voice out of my head? Maybe because, that was what my Dream Jameson had sounded like, when he was ordering me to ride him harder. Maybe because I hadn't been so attracted to a man ever.

Maybe because I was a silly girl and my mind was filled with nonsense.

7

JAMESON

Jameson walked down the stairs as slowly as humanly possible and adjusted his hard dick in his pants. He'd done his best not to look at all of Kennedy's exposed skin, but good God, he couldn't stop his eyes from roaming. His body's reaction to her was instant and visceral. He couldn't stop his dick from responding and he'd tried his best. Never had he not had control of every part of his body before.

He'd seen plenty of women in more of a state of undress and had never had to fight from getting hard. He was not one of those men who was led around by his dick. His mind was always in full command of his actions. But Kennedy tested all of his strength and he'd failed.

By the time he'd reached her front door to greet Weston, his dick was no less hard and he had to stop and take a second. Maybe he should've been ashamed of his reaction but he wasn't. He also wasn't ashamed he'd woken up with a raging hard-on this morning after a hot dream starring the two of them having wild sex. And the only thing that had stopped him from ripping the towel away and carrying her to her bed to see if she sounded like she had in his dream when his head was between her legs and his mouth latched onto her pussy, was because he'd heard Weston pull into the drive.

He wasn't sure if he was pissed at his friend for his punctuality, or grateful.

The knock on the door pulled Jameson from his thoughts and thankfully the pulsing in his dick started to subside.

He opened the door as his friend's hand was up and ready to rap on the wood again.

"Took you long enough." Weston smirked.

"You knocked once, jackass."

"Yeah, but I know you heard me drive up."

"Whatever. Come in."

Weston stepped inside Kennedy's remodeled farmhouse and he looked around. "Nice place."

"It is. She did the reno herself." Jameson hoped Weston didn't hear the pride in his voice.

"Seriously? Herself?"

"Yep. Tore down walls, re-plastered, did all the trim and molding herself."

Weston glanced around the open space again and nodded. "Good work."

When Weston's gaze came back to him, he knew by the smile of his friend's face he was about to catch shit.

"Heard she was smokin' hot."

Jameson's eyes narrowed and his body went taut.

That wasn't what he was expecting.

"Did you?"

"Sure did. Holden said she's a—"

"Careful," Jameson snapped.

"Careful?"

Jameson had walked right into Weston's trap and gave away more than he should've.

"Was gonna say, Holden told me she's a nice, sweet woman."

"Right."

Weston smiled at his feet, shook his head, and muttered, "People in hell must be drinking ice water."

"Come again?"

"Nothing. Where's she at?"

"Shower."

Weston's brows hit his hairline and he chuckled. "That was fast."

"Don't be a dick. She was working outside all morning and wanted to clean up before you came over. Before she comes down, I need to fill you in..."

Jameson quickly retold the story of Reggie Coleman being at the house when he'd pulled up. Through the brief, Weston's irritation rose to the surface.

"She got her shotgun?" he asked.

"Yep. She was gonna let loose on his truck."

"I think I like her already."

Jameson wasn't sure why his friend's innocent, off the cuff comment pissed him off but it did.

"Yeah, well, as amusing as it would've been to see, it would've bought her a metric shit-ton of problems."

"It would've, but the asshole would think twice about coming back," Weston noted.

"Or it would've made the asshole double-down in his fight to take her property."

"Hey. Sorry," Kennedy said, bounding down the stairs.

Jameson wanted to groan at the sight. Short cutoff shorts that showcased her long, tanned, toned legs. Tight tank top that not only clung to her midriff but to her perky tits, too. And bare feet that padded down the stairs. Clean and fresh, with her hair still wet hanging long around her shoulders, she looked younger than he knew her to be.

Weston cleared his throat and under his breath Jameson heard him mumble a *good God*. He knew why that comment pissed him off. Jealousy reared its ugly head.

The day before, Jameson had caught Holden staring at her, but he knew Holden had less interest in more than a one-night stand than Jameson did. Holden was a shameless flirt but would not touch a woman who had a hint of sweet. He preferred women who'd been around the block a couple hundred times and wouldn't attempt to call him the next day. He'd been hung up on a woman named Charleigh since before she'd married their buddy, Paul.

Charleigh made her decision and chose Paul over Holden and he'd never recovered. After Paul died in combat, Holden had stayed away from Charleigh and her daughter, Faith, at all costs.

But Weston? He was looking for something permanent. Had been even when they were all still in the Navy. He wanted a wife and kids and had no problem admitting it.

By all accounts if someone was going to try to hook up with Kennedy, it should be Weston. She was exactly his type. Hell, she was every man's *type*. Beautiful, smart, capable, strong, and extremely sexy.

"Did I miss anything important?" Kennedy was looking between the two men but her eyes landed on Jameson and suddenly he felt like he was ten feet tall and made of steel.

The small gesture meant nothing, Kennedy was simply looking to him because Weston was a stranger to her. But it felt great all the same.

"Nope. Kennedy, this is Weston," he introduced.

"Nice to meet you," she replied, but made no move to shake his hand.

"You, too," Weston returned, openly staring at her.

The overwhelming urge to punch his friend was becoming harder and harder to tamp down.

"Jameson told me about today's run-in," Weston informed her.

"Yeah. I don't often lose my temper but that man pushes my buttons like no one else."

"Have you scouted the perimeter?" Weston tore his gaze from Kennedy and faced Jameson.

"Not yet."

"I'll go start. Nice to meet you, Kennedy."

Weston tipped his head and started for the front door.

"I'll be right out," Jameson called to his friend.

Jameson waited for the door to shut and moved to Kennedy, closing the space between them.

"You okay?"

"Yeah?"

Her answer was posed as a question so Jameson went on.

"It wasn't cool of me to barge in on you while you were in the shower."

Kennedy smiled and her face flamed red. "Told you I could act like a pansy girl. I'm a little embarrassed I screamed from a little cold water."

He was happy to hear that was all she was embarrassed about and not that Jameson had practically seen her naked. And if he was honest, he had caught sight of her tits before she covered them. The vision was something he wouldn't soon forget.

Needing to get one last thing out of the way, he held her eyes and apologized. "I shouldn't've touched you the way I did." A flash of disappointment shone in her green eyes and Jameson wished he was a different sort of man. "I shouldn't—"

"I get it," she cut him off.

Her wounded gaze was his undoing. She'd thought he was rejecting her—again.

"Babe, you don't get it. You don't have the first clue why I couldn't stop myself from touching you and why it can't happen again. I am insanely attracted to you, seeing you wet, barely dressed...well, let's just say it took all of my control not to test that attraction. This is me protecting you from me."

"Why do you think I need protecting?"

"Because I know myself. I know the kind of asshole I am. And I know you deserve better than what I can give you."

"What is it you think I deserve?"

"A man who will give you more than a great fuck and a couple of orgasms. A man who will call you the next day. A man who's ready for commitment and one who doesn't hate the world."

Kennedy stood straight and pushed her shoulders back, which only drew Jameson's eyes to her chest. Pretty, rose-colored nipples were hidden behind the navy blue tank she wore and he couldn't help but wonder if they tasted as sweet as they'd looked.

"That's mighty presumptuous of you."

"Say what?"

"You presuming I have the time or energy for a commitment—or that I'd want one."

"Right," he muttered disbelievingly.

"You're awfully full of yourself. Not to mention, you're making some pretty big assumptions about what I want. But your message is received loud and clear."

She took a step back and Jameson immediately hated the distance. But this was what he needed. Her to be the strong one and push him away. Kennedy thinking he was an asshole now was better than acting on the attraction and hurting her later.

8

KENNEDY

It had been seven days since I'd seen Jameson.

He and Weston had looked around my house, declared they were installing six cameras and a motion sensor flood light, and left to get what they needed.

Only Weston had come back.

He didn't make excuses for his friend's absence. He simply got to work and only stopped when I went outside to offer him a bottle of water.

I'd found Weston was easy to be around. Mainly because he was funny and friendly. He joked and jabbed at me and called me Farmer Jill until I went out in my garden, picked us a cantaloupe and cut it up. The second the juicy square passed his lips, he announced he would be my farm hand if I paid him in cantaloupe and watermelon.

Before he'd left for the day, I packed him up two of each to take home with him.

Then with a wave and a smile, which was more than I got from Jameson, he packed up his tools and left.

Since then, I heard from Nixon. He'd called to tell me they were working their way through Reggie Coleman's life and they'd hopefully have something soon. I'd also received a call from Holden to tell me the cameras that were installed were working and not to walk around outside naked because the house was being watched. I knew he was kidding but it was a little disconcerting to know I was under surveillance, even if it was for what Nix had called 'my own protection.'

And the final call I received was from Jonny Spenser from the sheriff's department to tell me that Reggie Coleman had filed a complaint that I'd threatened to shoot him. I explained the situation and referred him to Jameson as my witness. Jonny's only advice was to not shoot Reggie and avoid him. I figured both options were good, however I knew only one would happen. It didn't matter if I tried to avoid Reggie, he always found a way to harass me.

The person I had not heard from was Jameson, which made my cellphone ringing and the display announcing he was calling a shock. I was just leaving the organic grocery store and I was somewhat stunned because after five years of stocking my honey, they'd just informed me they were no longer going to carry it. The owner had apologized but wouldn't budge, even when I'd offered to drop the cost of a case.

Not in the mood to talk to anyone, I swiped left and declined the call.

I hadn't even made it two steps and my phone started ringing again.

This time with a scowl on my face, ready to tell Jameson I wasn't in any sort of mood to be lectured or told what I wanted or needed from a man so he could keep his stupid thoughts to himself, I answered.

Before I could say hello, he was speaking. "Where are you?"

"Why?"

"Kennedy, where the hell are you?"

"You—"

"Where?" he barked.

What had crawled up his ass? It was none of his concern where I was and I certainly didn't appreciate him barking at me.

"None of your business."

"Don't fuck with me right now. Where?"

The anger in his voice gave me pause, but then I remembered he was Nix's friend. He may've been mad but he'd never hurt me.

"In town."

"Where in town?"

"In front of Nature's Choice. Not that it's—"

"Go back into the store and stay there. Do not leave the store until I get there."

"What's wrong with you?"

"Promise me, Kennedy. Go into the store now."

"What's—"

"Please trust me."

Maybe it was the way he'd asked, his tone of voice

pleading. No longer mad but more worried.

"Okay. I'll wait for you."

"Inside?"

"Yes, Jameson, I'll go back inside. Though I'm not all fired up about hanging around here since the owner just told me he was no longer buying my honey. I'll feel more than a little stupid."

"Fuck. I wouldn't ask if it wasn't important."

"All right. I'm going in."

"See you in a few minutes."

I tossed my phone in my purse and wandered around the store, staying as far away from the front counter as I could. I was more than a little upset that Jonas Brown had terminated our agreement, and a little hurt, too. I'd thought we were friends, but I guess not when the man wouldn't even explain why. I was browsing the essential oil selection, pissed because I needed to stock up on a few bottles but I'd be damned if I purchased them from Jonas.

Suddenly Jameson was at my side, his eyes angry and head going from side to side scanning the small grocery store.

"What's wrong?"

"Come on."

He grabbed my hand, laced our fingers together and tugged me out the door, and didn't stop until we were at his truck, which was illegally double-parked. He opened the passenger door, hoisted me in, jogged around the front, and got in behind the wheel.

He was pulling away when he told me. "Someone broke into your house."

"What?"

"As soon as Weston saw someone was on your porch, he went straight over..."

I could no longer hear what Jameson was saying because all that I could concentrate on was that someone was in my house. The word echoed in my head and I couldn't believe it. No one would break into my house. I didn't live in a community where people stole from each other.

"Babe? Are you listening to me?"

"No."

"Hopefully they're still in there when Weston gets there."

"Hopefully? That's dangerous. He could get hurt."

I was looking at Jameson in profile but I saw his jaw clench, obviously displeased.

"Don't worry about him, he's a big boy, he can handle himself."

"I'm sure he can. But I don't want anyone getting hurt on my account."

"Anyone, or just him?"

"What?"

"Never mind. We're headed to the office to wait for his call. When we have the all-clear I'll take you over there. Or if you prefer, Weston can come and get you and take you himself."

"What does that mean?"

"Exactly what I said."

"Why are we talking about Weston when you just told me my house is being robbed?"

"We're not talking about Weston, we're talking about how you want to handle the situation."

"And why would you think I'd want Weston to take me home? Or better question is, why would you care?"

He didn't answer. Instead, he parked in front of Fountain Park and cut the engine. He remained silent when he got out and made his way to my side of the truck. And further he didn't say a word when he helped me down and grabbed my hand again and yanked me to follow.

I would've protested all of this if I wasn't shocked someone broke into my house, and confused by his odd behavior. He unlocked a door between the distillery that had recently opened and a clothing store that had opened before I was born. We were halfway up the steep staircase when I pulled him to a stop.

"Am I in danger?"

"No."

"Then what's with the urgency to get to me?"

"Didn't say you *weren't* in danger. But you sure as fuck aren't now."

"I have to go to my mom's."

If Jameson thought there'd been the tiniest chance I was in danger, I had to check on my mom. I couldn't leave her vulnerable.

"Holden went over there."

"What? She can't know this is happening."

"Didn't say he was gonna waltz up to her front door. He's just sitting on her house. But I think you need to talk to her so we can put cameras up around her house, too."

Holy shit.

"Do you think it was Reggie who broke in? I mean, the guy's a prick, but home invasion isn't his style."

"I don't *think* anything. Facts are all I care about. The person in your house isn't Reggie, that's a fact. The man was slimmer and much younger. But what I can't rule out is Reggie isn't behind it. And until we know that, I'm not taking chances. You said your mom can't get around well, which means if someone breaks into her house, she's a sitting duck."

I felt my body shiver at the thought of someone in my mom's house.

"Babe, that's not gonna happen. Holden is over there now, and if we need to we can place a man outside twenty-four seven. Cameras would also be good."

"I can move in with her."

"You just got done telling me you didn't want her to know what was going on."

"I won't tell her."

"So you suddenly moving in wouldn't make her ask questions?"

"No. I'll...um...my water heater. I'll tell her I'm moving in because my water heater's still broken."

"Jesus."

Once again, Jameson started pulling me and I waited for him to unlock another door before he ushered me into an open room with the coolest dinged-up hardwood floors I'd ever seen. The far wall was brick and five arched windows allowed light to spill into the room. There were two wingback chairs sitting in the corner with a table set between. There were also two big bookcases shoved full of books. They looked out of place in what would be considered the reception of an office, but what did I know about what the inside of a private investigation firm looked like.

It was clean and masculine.

He pulled me down a hall and I noted a large conference room to my left and another set of stairs at the end of the hall. After we ascended those stairs, he finally spoke.

"Nixon and McKenna's office." He pointed to the first door. "Holden's. Weston's. Chasin's." He tapped each closed door as we passed and he opened the last door, stepping aside so I could enter, then he shut the door behind us.

"I take it this is yours."

"Don't be cute."

I hated when people called me cute. There was nothing cute about me. And I certainly wasn't trying be cute now. I was trying to be a smartass because I was annoyed at the way he was dragging me around, but more worried about someone being in my house and Weston rushing over there to try to catch them.

If he got hurt because of me, I would never forgive myself for pulling them into this mess.

"Your water heater's broken?"

"Yeah." Why was he looking at me like I had a third eyeball in the center of my forehead? "You were there when it broke, remember?"

Under normal circumstances I probably would've

blushed talking about that day, but right then I was too aggravated to care I'd just reminded him he'd seen me near-naked before he'd given me the brush-off.

"No, Kennedy, I do not remember." He was stalking toward me and I felt it imperative to step back. Only I couldn't take more than a few paces before my back was to the wall. Well, fuck me running, I was trapped and Jameson was still advancing.

He didn't stop a respectable distance; he invaded my space and rested his hand on the wall next to my head, caging me in. My heart rate spiked and I fought the urge to either punch him or kiss him. I wasn't sure which one I wanted to do more, but both emotions were swirling around battling for supremacy.

"What I remember is hearing you scream, taking your stairs two at a time, rushing into your bathroom, being treated to the sexiest fucking view I'd ever seen before you ripped the towel loose and I lost sight of your tits. Then I remember washing the soap out of your eyes and getting to openly study your pretty face without you knowing. Then I remember insanity taking over and the need to see if your skin was as soft as I'd dreamt it would be. So I touched you to find it was softer. Then I distinctly remember feeling how hard your nipple was under that towel and I desperately wanted to take you to your bed and do a variety of filthy things to you. Nowhere in my memory of that day—and, babe, it is seared into my brain—do I remember you telling me your water heater was broken. And my head may've been full of images of you taking my dick, but I would've remembered that."

Did he? Did he seriously just say that? I'd never heard anyone talk like that.

"Kennedy?"

I didn't know how to respond. I knew how my body was responding—the wetness between my legs couldn't be ignored—but I wasn't sure what I was supposed to say.

"You never came back," I accused.

"I told you I wouldn't."

"No, you didn't."

I remembered everything he said to me and he never informed me I wouldn't see or hear from him again.

"I told you I was protecting you."

Now I was super-pissed. I didn't need protecting, nor did I want it.

"Protecting me, or protecting yourself?"

"You don't know me to say that."

"Oh, but you know me well enough to say I need to be protected from you? I'm not the one that says I hate everyone and everything. That's you."

"Someone like you, whose head is full of sunshine and rainbows, couldn't handle a man like me. So yes, I'm protecting you from me."

"You're a tad arrogant, don't you think? Who said I wanted to handle you?"

Jameson's face lowered and a cruel smile pulled at his lips. "Don't try and lie to me, Kennedy. We both know I could have your ass up on my desk, your legs spread wide, and you screaming in the next five seconds."

The nerve of this asshole.

"And that makes me what? Easy? A slut? Because I'm a woman, it's different for me? So what I think you're hot and I haven't had sex in a long time and I think you'd be good at it. So how about we say, you're scared because you know *I* could sit my ass on your desk, and without much effort get you to fuck *me*. And maybe you'd like it enough to want to call the next day. Then what? Your 'I hate everyone' façade would crack? So again, how about all I want from you is a few good orgasms and for you *not* to call? Did you think of that, Big Guy, or were you too busy thinking I was some stupid naïve girl who doesn't know that sex and relationships aren't the same thing?"

"I don't think you're stupid."

"Right. My head is just full of sunshine and rainbows. Which may be the most insulting thing anyone has ever said to me. I do not need anyone to protect me."

"You have no idea the type of man I am, what I've done, or what I've seen. There's a good reason I am the way I am."

"And you don't know the type of woman I am or what I've seen. And there may be a reason but I doubt it's a good one."

"You can't imagine."

"I can't?" I spit out and lost all control on my mouth. We were nose to nose and I was red-hot pissed at his audacity. "I think I can. I'm the woman who witnessed my father being murdered when I was seventeen." Jameson's body jerked back and his hand fell from the wall. "I'm the woman who picked my mother up when she had a nervous breakdown. I'm the woman that worked and supported my mother until she could get back on her feet. I'm the woman who tried to keep my dad's land so we wouldn't lose what we had left of him. I'm—"

"Kennedy, stop."

"No. You think you know me. You don't. You don't have the first goddamn clue. I've worked my ass off for what little I have. I've been fucked over. I've been cheated on. I've lost more than I should've before I hit twenty. And even with all of that, I walk around with a smile on my face and still give those around me the benefit of the doubt. Because the alternative is I turn into a cynical, hateful bitch. And I don't want to be that woman. So I don't walk around thinking the world is sunshine and roses. I walk around knowing that someone killed my dad in front of me but I am strong enough to pull my shit together and be a good person."

"Babe."

"I don't wanna hear it, Jameson. Yes, I thought you were hot. Yes, I would've made it easy for you to get me into bed. No, I wouldn't've expected anything after. And if you had been as good as you said you were, I would've welcomed you back for seconds and still not expected anything. But you're a presumptuous asshole. And that's something I can't look past."

"Can I please explain?"

"Nope." I popped my P and headed for the door. "I'll walk back to my truck and wait for Weston to call me."

I threw open the door and calmly left with a lump in my throat and a suspicious hurt in my heart.

9

JAMESON

It took a moment for Jameson to come out of his stupor. Kennedy had rightfully laid him out and he was in shock. He would've never guessed she'd gone through what she had.

Not the way she smiled.

Not the way everything about her was light and airy and projected so much beauty.

No, he would've never guessed she'd seen such a horrific event.

By the time his feet came unglued, Kennedy was already down the stairs and quickly making her way across the reception area. He had to double-time it to beat her to the door.

"Wait," Jameson said, placing his hand on the knob so she couldn't open it.

"Please move."

"Not until you hear me out."

"I think we've both said enough."

He was smart enough to know he needed to choose his next words carefully or she'd be gone and he'd never have the chance to make things right.

"I'm sorry I was an asshole."

"Thanks."

"Don't do that, Kennedy."

"Do what? Thank you for your apology? Saying you're sorry doesn't change anything."

"You're right, it doesn't. I'd like to explain."

"Why? It doesn't matter. Nothing changes. It's not like we were even friends."

"You're my friend."

The admission felt strange. Jameson didn't have many friends and that was by design. Kennedy was right, his hateful attitude prevented most people from wanting to get to close to him. She'd been right about a lot of things.

"Right. So we have one drink together, and you don't call me for a week. And when you do, it's only because my house is getting broken into."

If there was ever a time to practice what he preached about honesty, this was it. But, damn it was hard.

"I didn't call you because your house was getting broken into. I called you because even though I didn't see your car there, I didn't know if you were inside. And when you didn't pick up your phone my heart felt like it was going to explode. I was an asshole when I finally got you on the phone, because all I could imagine was you in your house alone and some man breaking in. I didn't handle it well, because I'd never felt panic like that before. And considering I spent years in the desert killing bad guys, that's saying something.

"And you were right. I am scared that I'll be the one who will want to call the next day. As a matter of fact, I know I will. I can't stop myself from thinking about you. I can't stop wondering what you're doing. And that scares the ever-living shit out of me because I know you're too good for me and I know it won't take you long to figure it out. Then where will that leave me? Fucking crushed."

Jameson let go of the door handle, stunned at what he'd admitted. He didn't think there'd ever been a time when he'd confessed he was scared of something.

"Why do you think I'm too good for you?" she asked.

"Because I know you are. And what you just told me upstairs confirmed it. You're stronger than I am. I've allowed the things I've seen to blacken my soul. You're too good to have someone like me darken your doorstep."

Jameson's phone buzzed in his pocket. He pulled it out to see Weston had texted that he'd cleared Kennedy's house and she could go home to check if anything had been taken.

"What have you seen?"

Jameson hated that she'd asked.

"Enough to fill me with hate."

"Right," she mumbled. "Full disclosure and honesty from those around you but you get to keep your secrets bottled up."

"What I've done and seen isn't dinner conversation, Kennedy."

"Good thing we aren't eating dinner then."

She had a smartass comeback for everything and it was annoying as hell.

"I didn't ask you to come down here and talk to me. You followed me. You apologized, and I'm sorry I lost my temper. We can simply be done now and walk away. If we see each other walking down the street, no hard feelings, we can wave and say hello. And while I'm the type of person who gives second chances, I don't give thirds, so please don't ever try to feed me your bullshit again."

Why did the thought of them going their separate ways make Jameson's gut tighten? He'd gone a full week without speaking to her and it'd been torture. He'd actually gotten into his truck twice to drive over to see her and had to force himself to go back into the house.

What was it about Kennedy Lane that drove him to the brink? He'd never met a woman who'd called him on his shit, and there'd certainly never been one who'd accused him of being scared.

"Come on, I'll take you back to your house."

"Sure," Kennedy whispered her sad response.

He knew it wasn't what she wanted to hear, but he wasn't sure he could tell her about his life, or if he even should. She'd been right yet again, nothing would change. He still couldn't have her. Not for the long haul. And sex with Kennedy was out of the question, he knew that would be the biggest mistake he could ever make. He wouldn't call for seconds, he's simply keep calling until she stopped answering.

JAMESON HAD SPENT two hours with Kennedy at her house as she walked through it, checking to see if anything had been taken. Weston continued to comb the outside for anything that the suspect had left behind. Even though they had the guy on video, Weston had wanted more.

When Kennedy declared nothing had been taken, she called Jonny Spenser to report the break-in and Weston had left to go back to the office to email a copy of the recording to the sheriff's office.

Jonny had come out to take a report and was frustrated when he found out the guy had worn gloves. He'd taken Kennedy's statement, told her to keep her doors locked, and left.

Holden had called and said there was nothing going on at Kennedy's mom's house, but he was staying for a while longer just to be safe.

After Jameson had ascertained that Kennedy would be all right by herself for a bit, he left.

Now he was on his way back to her house and he knew by the way she'd said goodbye to him, she didn't think he was coming back.

The second his truck pulled to a stop, he saw the curtain in her living room pull back and he knew she was freaked out and probably standing guard.

He grabbed the bag on the seat next to him, made his way to her front door. She opened immediately, a wary look on her face.

"Is everything okay?"

"Yeah, babe, sorry I scared you." Jameson held out the bottle.

"What's that?"

"That's for after I'm done."

After she took his offering, he went back to his truck and opened the tailgate. The water heater was going to be a bitch to carry by himself but he didn't think she had a dolly and he hadn't stopped by the farm to pick one up. He could've called Weston for help, but he didn't want the intrusion.

"What are you doing?" Kennedy asked, standing behind him.

"Replacing your water heater."

"Why?"

"Because there's no way in hell you're taking a cold shower after the day you've had. Pissed as shit you've been doing it for a week and I didn't know."

"I was planning on replacing it tomorrow."

"Well, it looks like your day just freed up."

"You can't buy me a water heater, Jameson."

"Do you ever not argue?"

She stared up at him, stunned and clearly thinking about her answer.

"No."

"Right. As long as you're standing here, help me carry it in. It's not heavy, but it's awkward."

"I can't accept this. It's too expensive."

"Fine, write me a check for two hundred dollars."

Kennedy smiled wide, thinking she'd won.

The check would be ripped up and tossed in the trash before he left her house.

But in an effort to get the new water heater installed so they could move to the second part of their evening, he'd agree to anything if it meant she didn't argue.

10

KENNEDY

I was taking a nice warm shower and I hated to admit it, but I felt better knowing that Jameson was downstairs. Earlier, when he and Weston had been in the house with me as I looked for something missing, I hadn't been scared. I was pissed someone had been in my house. When Jameson told me he was leaving I didn't think anything about it, until I was alone.

Then irrational fear had crept in. Irrational because I knew Weston and Jameson both had searched my house from top to bottom and no one was hiding under a bed waiting to jump out and kill me, but damn if it hadn't felt that way.

I'd never paid attention to the creaks and groans my old house made. I'd lived in it my whole life, I was used to the sounds it made. But as I stood in my kitchen looking for something to make for dinner, debating what I was going to eat, every noise made me jump. Then I starting thinking about the fact my truck was still in town, which meant if someone did break in, all I could do was run.

So I opened my safe and grabbed my shotgun. Once the double barrel twelve gauge was within reach, I felt a little better. But not much.

Someone had been in my house. And what freaked me out more was they hadn't stolen anything. At least nothing I could find. So what the hell had the guy been doing? I'd watched enough movies to know there was plenty of sick shit he could've been doing in the fifteen minutes he was alone in my house.

I finished my shower, grateful it wasn't ice cold and quickly dried myself off and dressed. I took a look around my room. Nothing was out of place but I still yanked the sheets off my bed knowing there was no way I'd be able to sleep in them tonight.

I walked down the stairs and stopped when I found Jameson sitting on my couch. His ass was on the edge, his legs bent and spread wide, elbows on his knees, and his head was bowed. He looked deep in thought and when his gaze came up to meet mine, I knew I was right. He wasn't masking the stark pain.

He lifted his chin in a silent question and I explained. "I know it's silly but I don't want to sleep on sheets that a stranger could've...done stuff on."

He nodded his understanding but said nothing. I spotted the unopened new bottle of whiskey sitting on the coffee table in front of him and wondered why he'd brought his own when I had plenty.

I didn't inquire as I walked past him, through the

kitchen and into the laundry room. I dumped my sheets into the wash, started the machine, and stopped to grab two glasses out of the cabinet. Then I made my way back into the living room.

I placed the glasses on the table and sat next to Jameson.

"Unless you wanna drink straight from the bottle." I gestured to the glasses. "Which is cool with me, too."

He uncapped the bottle, took a healthy swig, and passed it to me. I followed suit, my swallow not quite as healthy as his but enough for the liquid to burn down my throat and warm my belly.

"There's a lot I can't tell you," he started. "The missions I went on are top secret. And just because I'm no longer in the Navy doesn't mean I can talk about them."

"Okay." I wasn't sure where he was going with the conversation but it didn't look pleasant.

"I'm struggling," he admitted, and clenched his jaw like it was the worst feeling in the world. "I don't know what to do with you. Straight up honesty here, I've never met a woman I've wanted to talk to about my past. And not because I want to unload my burdens, but because I wanted her to understand why I am the way I am." He stopped and took another drink before he looked me dead in the eye and continued. "I'll never be like you. I'll never be the type of person that rolls with the punches, takes one on the chin, and still looks on the bright side of life. That will never be me. I'm not wired that way. It's ingrained in me to protect, to watch for danger, to predict it, to stop it before it happens. And when I can't, I react to the threat in a manner that eliminates it permanently."

Jameson handed me the bottle and waited for me to take a drink before he took a deep breath and went on.

"I was a total dick earlier. I made assumptions about the type of woman you are, because I've never met anyone like you. You confuse me and surprise me. Neither of which I'm used to. The physical attraction between us is undeniable. We both feel it. You were right about all of it. Everything you said was spot-on. And that's another thing, it bothers me that you barely know me, yet you can see right through me. I've never been in love. I've never had a relationship. Hell, I've never dated or had a girlfriend. I've gone to great lengths to keep my emotions in check and you make me want to test the waters. You scare the ever-loving hell outta me."

"Not even in high school, you didn't have dates or a girlfriend?"

I found that hard to believe, Jameson was a good-looking man. I was sure as a teenager he was just as good-looking. Teenage girls would've gone crazy trying to get with him.

"Didn't say I didn't hook up in high school, but there weren't movies and ice cream involved."

"Oh."

That made more sense. Of course he would've gotten some action, but the thought of him never opening himself up to anyone made me kind of sad.

"My dad walked out on my mom. And I saw what it did to her. She fell apart in her grief. I remember her telling me how much she loved him—that was years after he'd left and she still loved the asshole. She waited for him to come home, prayed about it, begged God to answer her one wish. When I left home to join the Navy, she was still prayin'. I wanted no part of that. If that was what love did to you, I never wanted to find it."

That I could understand. I'd watched my own mother break down after my dad died. But he didn't leave us intentionally, he was taken from us. And even though it was painful to watch my mother have a nervous break-down there was beauty in it. She loved my dad so much she couldn't cope with his death. She couldn't imagine a life without him. But I wouldn't tell Jameson that—the situations were vastly different, and his father didn't deserve the kind of love and devotion his mother had offered.

"What if I'm like my dad? What if that's in me?"

"What if what's in you?"

"Whatever is so fucked-up in him that he could walk away from a good woman and his kid. My whole life I've been told by everyone in my family I'm just like my dad. I look like him, I'm built like him, I was a good athlete like him. So what if he gave me that, too; that fucked-up gene that makes me destroy my family?"

"He didn't."

"You can't say that. I know I'm an ass—"

"He didn't, Jameson, and you already told me why you could never be him. You're not wired that way. It's ingrained into you to protect."

"I'm a product of my environment. If he hadn't left, I

wouldn't've had to step up and be the man of the house, care for my mom, support us. I would've been a normal kid going through life. I would've been like everyone else, looking for love and wanting a family. Instead I'm this man, the one who won't touch emotion with a ten-foot pole because his father taught him love hurts."

Damn, I kind of hated Jameson's dad. What kind of dick leaves his family? And by the sound of it, severs contact with his own flesh and blood.

"Maybe you wouldn't have had a skewed view of love and relationships. Maybe you would've found a sweet woman and married her and had a couple of kids by now. But that didn't happen. What happened was, your dad's a jackass and left, his decision sparked a chain reaction, and that made you into a man that has a burning desire to protect those around him. And because of that, because of him, and what he taught you, you'd never inflict that type of pain. He taught you a great lesson."

"Oh, yeah, what's that?" Jameson huffed. "How to be a cynical, distrusting prick?"

"No. He taught you everything you didn't want to be. And sometimes that lesson is more important. You're the man you are today, because you knew the man you never wanted to be."

Jameson picked the bottle back up and I watched the muscles on his neck constrict and his Adam's apple bob as he swallowed. Every inch of his body seemed to have muscle piled on top of muscle. I'd never in my life found a man's neck sexy, but all I could think about as Jameson drank was how much I'd like to run my tongue over the corded lines and trace a path.

It was crazy that six hours ago I was standing in Jameson's office pissed off as all hell, yet there I was once again thinking about how much I'd like to touch him. It's funny what a little honesty does by way of forgiveness and understanding.

Trying to find the good in people and the reasons behind their actions didn't make me a doormat. I was telling Jameson the truth—I gave most people a second chance, because everyone screws up and says hurtful things. But the chance is only given if there's sincerity behind their apology. And I believed Jameson was a good man. Twice now, he'd admitted he was scared, and for someone like him, I imagined it was a difficult confession. One I would not squander and throw in his face.

"How drunk are you?" Jameson's odd question took me by surprise.

"I'm not."

"Tipsy?"

"No, it takes more than a few sips of whiskey to get me buzzed. Why?"

"Because, I'm going to kiss you, and I need to know if you're sober."

Butterflies took flight in my belly and nerves set in. Somewhere in the back of my mind I wondered if I'd ever get used to Jameson being so forward. Jameson didn't give me time to process my thoughts because his hand went to the side of my face and slid into my hair, and simultaneously he pulled me toward him and he leaned in.

Our mouths met and his tongue brushed my bottom lip. Without thought or hesitation I opened for him. Not that I was doing much thinking as his tongue swept in and tentatively slid against mine. I'm not sure which one of us moaned, but the sound echoed in the silent room. Jameson deepened the kiss and lifted me up off the cushion and pulled me astride him.

Gone were the butterflies dancing in my stomach. The excitement of the kiss pushed everything aside. I could feel the hard length of him pressed tight against my wet center and I rocked my hips. His grip in my hair tightened and he slanted his head, taking a seriously hot kiss and making it hotter.

I'd never been kissed like this before. Never felt the raw need and passion. Jameson wasn't kissing me, he was devouring me. All I could do was follow his lead, let him take me where he wanted us to go. I was more than okay with that, I didn't want to do anything but feel the antici-pation he was building.

Without warning, he broke the kiss and shoved his face in my neck. I would've been seriously disappointed but his tongue lashed out and he was doing exactly what I'd fantasized about doing to him, blazing a trail down my throat to the swell of my breasts. His hands went to my hips and he easily lifted me higher so he could continue to lick and suck on the skin there.

"Sweet Christ, I knew it'd be good," he said without lifting his head. "But I had no idea."

Needing the friction back, I adjusted myself back over his hard-on and ground down.

"Fuck, Kennedy," he groaned.

One of his hands left my hip and went to the collar of my tank top. I heard it tear as he yanked it down, settling it under my breast.

His mouth latched on to my nipple through the lace of my bra and my back instinctively arched.

"More," I begged.

He sucked harder and I moaned.

"More."

He tore the lace down and his tongue flicked against my bare breast.

My hips were moving on their own accord. I wasn't thinking about anything other than how good he felt under me and the sensation his mouth was creating.

All I knew was I needed more. All of him. I wanted the layers of clothes between us to be gone so I could really feel him.

11

JAMESON

Jameson was fighting for control.

He'd had no clue that the reality of Kennedy would be so much better than anything he could've dreamed up, or he would never have kissed her.

He wasn't sure if either of them was ready to go any further. But damn if he didn't want to fuck the hell out of her. There was nothing timid or shy about Kennedy, he'd been stupid to think there was. The moment their mouths had touched, he knew he was in trouble. And when she'd swung her leg over him and started rubbing herself on his dick, he knew he had a bigger dilemma than he'd been prepared for.

The woman was incendiary.

And his plan to take things slow had gone up in smoke.

Kennedy's hands went to the hem of his tee and he had no choice but to sit forward so she could pull it over his head. Unfortunately, this meant he'd lost the pleasure of her nipple in his mouth. And damn if she didn't taste sweet.

Before he could stop her, she had his pants unbuttoned and the zipper pulled down. With her gaze downcast watching what she was doing between his legs, he couldn't see her face but he could see her forehead wrinkle—probably in shock finding he went commando. Without the barrier of boxers, the head of his dick was in full view. And he didn't need to look to know it was dripping.

Her finger smeared the liquid around the tip and a shock of excitement flooded his body. He had to shut this down. They were already edging on the wrong side of his good intentions. Another touch and he may give into what they both wanted.

"Baby." His hand went to hers and grabbed her wrist, bringing her hand up and settling it on his chest. Though he quickly found, that was no better. It didn't matter if she was touching his dick or any other part of his body, it sent waves of need through him.

"Please, Jameson. More." Her tiny hand was rough from working and scraped his skin as she roamed his chest and abs, ratcheting up his desire.

She was going to be the death of him.

"Slow, Kennedy."

"I don't want slow." Her eyes snapped to his and the passion swirling there took his breath. "I want you, now."

Jameson had known he'd reached his breaking point, but he hadn't known all it would take was a declaration for him to shatter.

If she wanted more, he'd give it to her. He was finding he'd give her anything she wanted if she asked. When she pleaded with those big green eyes of hers, he worshipped at her feet.

Jameson flipped her to her back, tugged her shorts and panties down her legs and tossed them aside. He placed one of her legs over the back of the couch and the other one went over the side, her foot on the floor as he spread her wide.

"Is this what you want?" he asked.

"Yes." Kennedy lifted her hips in invitation and Jameson lowered his mouth to her pussy. And with a long, hard swipe he took his first taste.

His tongue traveled over her trimmed curls, over her belly, finally stopping as he circled one nipple. Needing to get his fill, he pulled the other cup of her bra down and drew her puckered nipple into his mouth before he nipped the hard nub, loving the way she moaned and pressed closer.

After he spent a good amount of time teasing and licking her breasts, he lifted his head and looked down. The sight was beyond sexy, bra and tank top askew, her nipples were tight and raw from his attention. His gaze went to her face and she stared at him. So damn beautiful, she wasn't hiding her hunger from him and goddamn if that wasn't hot as fuck.

"You're sure you're ready for this?"

"Yes." She wiggled under him.

"I can get you off with my mouth, I don't need to fuck you to make you feel good."

"I want *you*." She tilted her hips, and with his pants undone and his dick exposed, her movement scraped the head of his cock against her pussy and Jameson went dead-still. One more move and the tip would notch in. "Oh, God," she moaned.

The head of his cock was dangerously close and before he could do anything about it, Kennedy surged up and the first few inches of his bare cock was inside of her.

"Fuck!" he shouted. "Do not move, Kennedy."

"More, Jameson," she whined and his eyes closed and he tried to block out the feel of her pussy hugging his throbbing cock. It was too much.

"I'm not wearing a condom. Give me a minute."

Jameson didn't need a minute to fish a condom out of his wallet, he needed it to gather some sense before he took her bare and blew his load like an untried virgin.

"I'm on birth control." Jameson's insides clenched and his mind spun out of control. He'd never had sex without a condom. "Please hurry. I need you."

"Kennedy." His voice sounded tortured even to his own ears. "I've never..." His words died in his throat when she pulled off his dick, leaving just the tip in, before she lifted back up, taking more of him. The heat of her excitement coating his cock was too good. It was too hot. It felt better than anything he'd ever felt and he knew he was going to give in.

"You need to be sure, baby."

"I'm sure."

"Really goddamned sure. We can stop right now and I'll eat your pussy until you're screamin' down the house.

But if you keep movin' on my cock I am gonna fuck you, and there will be no coming back from that. I won't do the right thing and walk away. I'll keep coming back. I'll keep taking anything you're willing to give. The choice is yours, but you better make it quick."

"I'm sure." She tightened the walls of her pussy and he slipped in a little farther. "Fuck me, Jameson. Now."

He surged forward and Kennedy's head flew back, pushing into the cushion behind her as she took his full length, the open zipper of his pants pressing into her ass.

"Ohmygod!" she shouted.

Jameson eased out and slowly pushed back in. "You want more?"

"Yes," she hissed.

He gave her a few more slow strokes and was enjoying the look of wonder that had sparked in her eyes.

"More, baby?"

"Oh, god, yes."

"Keep your legs wide for me."

Jameson adjusted himself on the small couch. Coming up on a knee with both of his hands balancing on the armrest, he gave her more. He took great pains to keep his thrust slow and steady, giving her time to accommodate his size.

He waited until she was lifting her hips, meeting him stroke for stroke with her back arching, before he asked her again.

"You ready for more?"

"More?" The sound of wonder was hard to miss but so was the desperation.

He lowered himself to his elbow and used one hand to lift her ass higher, the angle allowing him to go deeper, and his head swam with overwhelming lust. His balls started to tingle and his cock swelled. He used every ounce of willpower he had to tamp down the urge to come.

With his mouth close to her ear he whispered, "Yeah, more, baby. I'm gonna fuck you until you see stars and scream my name."

"Thought that's what you were doing."

Jameson gave her a hard thrust and he felt the puff of her exhale on his neck.

"Not even close."

"Oh, God."

"You think you can take it? I can get us there just like this if you can't."

He'd been holding himself back and would continue to if Kennedy wasn't ready, but damn if he didn't want to see her lose her control. She was giving as good as she was getting and it was hot as sin. She was so goddamn hot between the sexy sounds she made, the way she moved with him, her tight, wet pussy that had threatened to unman him before more than two inches of his dick was inside of her. But he knew she had more to give, he just had to get her there.

"I can take it."

He grabbed the leg that was draped over the couch and bent it toward her body, resting the back of her thigh against his bicep, hitched her ass up higher, and used the hand near her head to hold on to the armrest for leverage and pounded in.

It took less time than he'd expected for both of her hands to go to his back and her nails to dig in.

"Jameson," she panted.

His mouth slammed down on hers and in a dual assault, he drove his cock deeper and stoked the already out-of-control blaze higher.

He knew it was going to burn. He knew he'd never recover. He knew that there would be no floating back down to earth. When Kennedy figured out he was no good for her he was going to plummet down thirty-thousand feet and it would end him.

But he didn't care. He was too lost in the feel of her. Lost in her goodness and light and he'd chase that feeling until she refused to allow him to take anymore.

Kennedy wrenched her mouth free and sucked in much-needed air before she wheezed out his name.

Not good enough.

"You seeing stars yet, baby?"

"Jam-e-son," she stuttered. "Oh, God."

"Not good enough, Kennedy. I want you screamin'."

He pumped harder, and her nails clawed at his back, the bite of pain brought him closer and he prayed he could keep up his pace. He was dangling over the edge and ready to tip over.

"Holy shit!" she shouted and her pussy convulsed.

He adjusted his angle again and slammed into her harder. "My name, Kennedy."

Her eyes closed, her head thrashed, her mouth opened in a silent scream and finally she shouted his name as her orgasm hit. The force of it made Jameson explode.

Come shot up from his balls and scorched as it shot out of the head of his cock. The roaring in his ears prevented him from hearing Kennedy's cries of pleasure. Emotion slammed into his chest and took his breath. Her nails dug in harder, their bodies still violently crashing together, and Jameson's orgasm seemed to last forever. Once the last of his come spilled into her, he slowed, enjoying the way his dick glided in and out—their combined excitement eased the path.

He waited for the normal need to extradite himself from the act of sex before it became personal to come, but it never did.

Kennedy leisurely came back to herself and recovered long before Jameson did. Their eyes were locked, her arms were still around him, and his dick was still buried inside of her, but all Jameson could feel was her shine. The warmth her smile provided as she laid under him, staring at him, like he'd given her something more than an orgasm. Like he'd given her something special.

"I never knew," she whispered.

"Knew what, baby?"

"That sex was that good."

"It's not."

"Huh?"

"It's not that good, Kennedy. Sex is mediocre at best. It's simply the tool for a release."

"I don't get it. That was good, really good. I used to

think that screaming during sex was a myth perpetuated by the porn industry." Kennedy paused and her forehead pinched together. "Was that not good for you?"

Her question cut Jameson deep. She'd misunderstood.

He leaned forward to kiss the wrinkles on her forehead, and while he was so close, he moved to her lips for a quick, wet kiss before he pulled back and looked down at her. She'd never looked prettier, face flushed, hair mussed up, tits still out of her bra and shirt. His dick twitched and went from softening to recovering.

"Sex has never been that good for me," Jameson told her. "I've never experienced what we just shared, not once. I've never been so lost I was prayin' I was never found. I've never had a woman lose control and tear my back bloody and want more. I've never felt anything better. I've never wanted to come so badly but then not want to come because I didn't want the feeling to end. I've never been so fucking hard I could feel myself throbbing. I've never been so confused about a woman but simultaneously sure." Jameson pulled his now fully hard dick out a few inches before he pushed back in. "I've certainly never been so turned on I was ready to go again minutes after I've come. So, no, sex is not that good. Sex with you is better than good. It's a religious experience."

"I've never had an orgasm during sex," she blurted out.

"No?" Jameson smiled, happy to know he'd been the one to give her the first.

"No. I've never lost control and tore up someone's back. Sorry about that, by the way."

"Don't be sorry. It was hot as fuck. And I would've been seriously disappointed in myself if you didn't let go and give me wild."

"I've never begged for sex," she admitted. Jameson's smile grew. "Don't be smug."

"Hard not to be, when you're telling me you've never had an orgasm during sex and you went off like a rocket for me. And before I gave you your first ever sex-induced orgasm, not only were you beggin' but you were fucking yourself on my dick."

Kennedy's eyes narrowed. "I'm not being smug that you said you'd never been so hard you could feel your dick throb."

"You should be. You're sexy as hell. You make me lose my mind. And straight up, I think I shot off harder than I ever have in my life and I want to fuck you again so bad, my dick is twitching. Your pussy is so tight and hot, I might come again from just being inside of you. So, baby, you should be lying there satisfied in the knowledge I've never had better. And I'm not ashamed to tell you, you had me on the ledge and I was hoping I didn't go before you. That's never happened. I've never not had to work for it, to find it for myself."

"What's that mean?"

Jameson paused, not sure this was the right time to have this conversation.

"You sure you wanna hear this with my cock buried inside of you?"

"What does it matter to me? I'm the one lying under you after you came so hard, *you* saw stars. I can't be jealous of women who weren't better than me."

Kennedy smiled and Jameson tipped his head and roared with laughter.

"Can't dispute that logic," he said through his hilarity.

"So? Tell me."

"First you have to promise that after I tell you, you're gonna let me take you upstairs and fuck you again."

"There are no sheets on my bed."

"You don't need sheets on your bed to ride me." Kennedy's eyes flared and Jameson smiled. "You wanna ride me, baby?" She nodded and Jameson's dick jumped. "Good, because I want your tits in my mouth while you bounce on my dick. And now that you've taken the edge off, we'll see if we can't get two more orgasms out of you."

"Oh, God," Kennedy moaned and her pussy convulsed. "Hurry and tell me."

Jameson thought about how to explain what he'd meant. He figured she probably wouldn't like his answer, but she was right, she was the one lying under him, and she didn't have a damn thing to be jealous about because no one could hold a candle to her.

"It means in the past, I had to get creative to make myself orgasm. I hold myself back from everyone—that included during sex."

"What's creative mean?"

Goddamn, he did not want to have this conversation.

Jameson sighed and held her eyes. "It means I had to

think about something else to get myself off. And most of the time the orgasm wasn't worth the effort involved to have it."

"Oh."

He could see the flicker of thought starting to work behind her eyes and he needed to shut that quick.

"Don't go there, Kennedy. I told you the truth and if you don't believe my words the fact that my dick is hard and has stayed rock hard even though we've been talking for the last five minutes should tell you I'm being honest. I wouldn't know what my recovery time is because I've never fucked the same woman two times in one night. But I can tell you, never has my dick gotten hard before it fully went soft. Not when I was a randy teenager and was discovering sex, not ever.

"I was with you every second of the way. From the time our lips touched until I came. The only time I wasn't thinking about your sleek warm pussy and the way it was strangling my cock was when I was counting backward from one hundred in an effort to make you come before I did. No other thought crossed my mind. I let myself go and held nothing back from you. And I swear on my life, that has never happened before."

"I believe you," she whispered.

"Good." His eyes drifted closed in relief.

"Take me upstairs, Jameson. I want more."

Jameson pulled out and severed their connection, and just as he'd suspected when he stood and lifted her off the couch, he'd give Kennedy anything she asked for.

They were walking into her room when she asked,

"You think maybe this time you could take off your pants and shoes?"

And for the second time that night Jameson threw his head back and laughed.

"Yeah, baby. I think we can arrange that."

Kennedy smiled and Jameson knew he wasn't in trouble. He didn't have a dilemma, he was exactly where he was supposed to be.

12

KENNEDY

It had been two days since I'd learned there was such a thing as multiple orgasms and I still ached in all the right places. And it had been three nights in a row that Jameson had spent the night in my bed but hadn't done more than kiss me since the first night.

Frustration was mounting. He was a great kisser, I thoroughly enjoyed making out with him. What I didn't enjoy was him not allowing it to go any further. And if I tried, he'd pin my hands to the bed, kiss me hard and wet, then roll me to my side and tuck me close.

The cuddling part was nice, too. And a complete shock. Never in a million years would I think Jameson Grant was a cuddler. He looked more like a wham-bam-rollover-and-don't-touch-me type of man. But, nope, he'd pull me close and wrap his big arms around me. I'd fallen asleep like that, and woken up the same way.

The guy who'd broken into my house had been identified as Peyton Marshall. I'd known Peyton a long time.

His family had moved to Kent County when he was in third grade and I was in sixth. We'd gone to school together off and on since then. He was a brat at eight, he was a menace at twelve, and by the time I'd graduated high school he was a complete douche.

It didn't surprise me he'd turned into a criminal. But the thing was, his record was clean. He'd never been charged with a crime, but considering the old sheriff was as dirty as mud, that didn't surprise me either. Peyton was a day laborer and worked construction, though he wasn't employed by any one company. He floated around and took whatever jobs he could get when a crew was short. That meant he wasn't very good at showing up for work so no one would hire him permanently. Again, I was not surprised.

But Peyton seemed to have vanished, and in a county as small as ours, that was a feat. No one had seen him, and he hadn't shown up on the job site he was working. He'd taken nothing of value from me to pawn, and even if I couldn't find evidence he'd taken anything from my house, I didn't have anything valuable enough for him to hock and go on the lamb.

Until Peyton was found, Jameson was insisting he stay at my place. I didn't fight this, because I liked him being there. And a small part of me felt better knowing he was there.

I'd just finished labeling a hundred mason jars of honey and was wondering what I was going to do with my bounty when my phone rang. Now that Nature's Choice was no longer stocking my stuff and sales had been down at the farmers market, I was going to have to start branching out. But I didn't know how to begin.

I picked up my phone off the work bench and saw it was Weston.

"Hey," I greeted.

"Is Jameson there?"

I glanced at the clock on the wall and realized I'd lost track of time, something I often did when I was working in my shed. Last time I'd talked to Jameson he'd said he was stopping by his house before he came over, but it was later than I'd thought he'd be here.

"Don't think so, but I'm in my shed. Let me go look."

I walked around the side of my house and Jameson was sitting in his truck in my driveway. His head was pressed back against the seat rest and his eyes were closed.

"Um. Yeah, he's here. You need to talk to him?"

"Yeah."

I didn't like the tone of Weston's voice. Something was wrong. "Everything okay?"

"Just put him on, yeah?" His sharp biting answer was all the confirmation I needed.

Jameson's eyes opened as if he sensed my approach and he got out of his truck, pinning me with narrowed, accusing eyes. Something was wrong with him, too.

"What's wrong?" he inquired.

"You tell me." Jameson's answer was to clench his jaw. "Here, it's Weston."

That earned me another weird look and I handed him my phone.

"Yo," Jameson said when he took my offering.

The conversation was mostly one-sided. There were a few "whens" and "wheres" and finally a "see you in a minute" then he disconnected and handed me my phone.

"Gotta go," he told me.

"What's wrong?"

"Not now, Kennedy. I have to go."

He started to swing up into his truck and I made a split-second decision and jogged to the passenger side and hopped in.

"Kennedy. I have—"

"So go."

"Need you to get out, babe."

"Nope. There's something wrong. So drive and tell me what's going on."

"Kennedy—"

"I'm not getting out, Jameson. So if you have someplace to be you should start driving."

His eyes did a full body scan and I wasn't sure what he was looking for, but when he was done, he fired up his truck and backed out. He was silent until we hit the main road.

"This isn't cool," he finally spoke.

"What's not cool, is your friend calling my phone wondering where you are, and then me finding you in your truck looking like something is very wrong."

"Got a lot of shit on my mind. I was taking a minute."

"Taking a minute? From me?"

"Yes."

Well, that fucking hurt.

Perhaps I'd made the wrong choice insisting on going with him. Jameson didn't mince words and sometimes honesty stung. Maybe I should tell him to let me out at the next stop sign and I could walk home.

"I told you I'd call the next day." That was a weird statement and I wasn't sure why he was bringing it up. "Told you I wouldn't walk away."

He looked pissed and he sounded it, too. Normally my first thought would've been he was going to break up with me, but there was nothing to break. We'd had sex, we kissed, we had a few meals together, we talked about our days while sitting on my couch, and we had slept in my bed. But we weren't together in the traditional sense. He could leave at any time and owed me no explanation.

But I'd be lying if I said it wouldn't have hurt.

"I don't understand why you're mad about that."

"I'm not mad. I'm confused. I needed a minute and I was taking it."

Now I was confused.

"You don't have to stay at my house, you know. I'll be fine by myself."

"I *want* to stay at your house. I *want* to sleep next to you. I can't stop thinking about the next time I get to see you. Hell, I just plain can't stop thinking about you."

My belly started feeling funny at his admission. I liked hearing he felt the same way about me as I felt about him. I couldn't wait until Jameson came home from work. I loved hearing him walk in my front door. Maybe I should've been more cautious. Maybe I should've kept my feelings in check, but that wasn't my style. I didn't want to deny I liked him and I wanted to spend time with him. I wore my heart on my sleeve and it'd gotten me into trouble on more than one occasion but I wouldn't change who I was. And if this ended badly and Jameson left me brokenhearted, I'd pick myself up, and move on. Nothing ventured, nothing gained, right?

"But if you need some time alone—"

"That's the thing. I don't want to be alone. That's the fuck of it. I don't think you understand, I'm always alone. I prefer it, I crave it, I need it. My whole life I've held myself away from everyone—even my closest friends. But, now, with you..." He trailed off, his statement hanging thick in the cab of his truck and I held my breath. "You've changed everything and I don't understand why. I've known you just over a week. A fucking week, Kennedy, and I can't stand being alone anymore."

I didn't say anything mainly because I couldn't breathe and my heart was pounding in my chest.

"You don't have to be alone if you don't wanna be," I whispered.

"Are you sure about that? You don't know me, Kennedy, not really. The things I've done, the things I can't tell you, they've marked me. Tainted me. Are you really willing to take the chance that a man like me won't ruin you? I'm fucked-up, babe. I like the silence because I can get lost in my head and not think about what I've seen. Silence means no one is around to see how screwed-up I am. I thought I was confused about how I felt about you. But I'm not. I'm struggling with what to do with those feelings because I'm afraid I'm going to snuff out your goodness, and I'd rather die than see you lose the shine in your pretty eyes. I don't want my bad attitude and judgment to rub off on you. After all you've been through, it's a fucking miracle you're still so giving and bright. I can't live with the thought of crushing that spirit."

I needed to get a few things straight with Jameson. He seemed to have the wrong impression about me.

"If you keep putting me up on a pedestal, you're gonna be disappointed," I told him. "You seem to have painted this perfect picture of me that's not real. I like that you think those things about me, but you have it all wrong. I am the way I am, because the alternative isn't acceptable. I watched my dad die, Jameson." I watched as he flinched, but as unpleasant and heartbreaking as the topic was, it had to be talked about.

I'd long ago dealt with the tragedy of losing my dad. The horror of watching him gunned down in front of me.

"The anger bottled up so tight in my chest I wanted to explode. I lashed out at everyone. I hated the man that killed my dad. I hated God for taking him. I hated my mom for falling to pieces instead of taking care of me. I hated the town, the police, the court system who would allow a mentally unstable man on the streets and that man shot my dad. In. Front. Of. Me. I was seventeen, out of control, and using alcohol to numb the pain. For six months I failed myself and I failed my father. I hated that I froze when I saw the gun. I hated that I didn't die that day instead of my dad.

"I went off the rails. Completely. My grades went in

the toilet. My attitude sucked. And again, I was going out and drinking whenever I could. I lost my virginity at a party drunk out of my head. I don't remember anything about it other than it hurt. And not a physical pain. My soul hurt and I found I liked that feeling. So I got drunk again and did it some more.

"I hit rock bottom when I came on to Nixon. I was tore up, I think I'd had a bottle of vodka to myself and I tried to talk him around to having sex with me." I knew this was going to piss Jameson off and it made me look like a total whore, but he had to know so he could understand.

The only sign of anger coming from Jameson was his white knuckles on the steering wheel. Other than that he stayed quiet and I appreciated it. I wouldn't have been able to get this all out if he spoke.

"I can't remember much of what I said or did, I just know I was pressin' him hard to take me home. After a bit he put me in his truck and off to the Swagger Farm we went. He parked next to the pond and walked me into the woods. Everyone knew about the famous Swagger Shack. No disrespect to McKenna, but he'd nailed a lot of girls in there. He was young and good-looking and playing the field. So we went into the shack and I quickly sobered up.

"He did not take me there to have sex with me, he took me there to lay into me. We had a huge fight. Rip roaring, yelling match. That night he told me I was someone he didn't want to know. I was embarrassing myself and if my dad could see me, he'd be disappointed in me. Coming from Nixon, someone who was a close friend, it hurt."

Even now, all these years later my heart twisted thinking about how mad Nix was at me. How he'd looked at me with disgust. If I'd been sober at the time, I would've known Nix would've never taken advantage of a girl while she was drunk. Hell, he never would've touched me in the first place. We were friends—only friends.

"That night, Nixon told me exactly what I needed to hear at the exact right time. When I'd hit the bottom of a very dark pit. I wasn't only hurting myself, I was hurting everyone around me, too. When we first met and you scowled at me for telling you about my personal problems because you were a stranger and I explained it was only because you were a friend of Nixon's, can you understand now? Nixon changed my life that night. He saved me from myself. He could've done whatever he wanted to me that night, I was so drunk I wouldn't've stopped him. But instead he proved to be the friend I knew he was. A friend I could trust with my life."

"Sounds like Nix," Jameson mumbled.

"I had a choice in that moment. Continue to be hateful and self-destruct or find the person I was before my dad was taken. I chose peace. I chose to live my life the best way I could and that was by not being angry at everyone. I didn't like myself, Jameson. I wanted to die and I didn't care how long it took. I was selfish and mean and half the time I couldn't breathe because all I wanted to do was feel pain.

"There's nothing perfect about me. I screwed up. I own what I did and sometimes it's still embarrassing living in this small town where I know everyone else remembers, too. I avoided Nixon for a long time, because I was so ashamed of how I'd behaved. I don't belong on a pedestal.

"And I'm sure I want to take my chances and get to know you better. I'm sure that the things you've seen and things you've done have left a hole in your heart. But you, too, have a choice. And whatever decision you make is yours, and I will never change who I am. I won't ever go back to a place where I'm ashamed to look in the mirror."

Jameson was quiet as he processed all that I'd told him and I appreciated that, too. It was hard for me to tell him how I'd felt and how I'd behaved. It had taken me a long time to forgive myself, many years of living my life the best way I could to finally cut myself some slack.

He pulled his truck in front of Fountain Park and cut the engine. I unbuckled to get out and without warning, I was hauled into Jameson's lap and his mouth crashed onto mine.

The kiss was deep, wet, and quick. When he pulled back, his face was still hard but his eyes had gone soft. I guessed Jameson didn't think less of me after hearing how I'd behaved. Either that or he'd just given me the best goodbye kiss known to man.

"You belong on that pedestal, baby, high above the rest of us. Your strength is one of the many things I'm attracted to. And everything you just told me proves you're as strong as I knew you already were." He kissed my forehead and smiled. "And I'm happy that story ended without me having to kick my friend's ass."

"Did you really doubt Nixon's integrity?"

"No, not his integrity, but I have first-hand experience how hard it is to say 'no' to you."

"What's that supposed to mean?"

"Seriously?"

"Yes, seriously. You have no problem saying 'no' to me."

Not that he verbalized his refusal to do what I wanted, he simply redirected me, but the end result was the same.

"Babe, I fucked you on your couch, with my shoes and pants still on, and I did it bare. Twice."

"Yeah, and it was hot," I told him, then added. "And the second time you weren't dressed."

"It was hot. And I did manage to get you undressed the second time. Which in case I forgot to tell you, might've been better than the first, but only because I got to watch you ride my dick. However, the point is, I wanted to take it slow, I had no intention of having sex with you. I wanted to kiss you, then things got a little heavy and I couldn't say no to you."

I liked that he couldn't say no to me. I liked that he was in the moment with me. What I didn't like was he hadn't lost control since then.

"But you've said no the last two nights."

"Because I needed to make sure you understood what you were getting into without sex muddying the waters."

"Now you're insulting me again."

"No, I'm not. But how 'bout this, I needed to understand where I was without sex fucking with my head."

That was a little better.

"And now? Do you need more time to understand where you are?"

"No." I couldn't help my smile and Jameson groaned. "She's gonna be the death of me."

"Maybe. But at least you'll be seeing stars and moanin' my name when you go."

I watched Jameson's face transform as humor took over. I continued to stare as the smile hit. And further, I sat on his lap and not only heard but felt him shaking with laughter.

All of it I liked—a whole lot.

13

JAMESON

Jameson couldn't remember the last time he'd felt this relaxed with anyone. And considering when he'd pulled into Kennedy's driveway he'd been in knots, it was doubly shocking. But Kennedy had a way about her that calmed his racing thoughts.

He'd been alone in the office all day and was crawling out of his skin. That's when he'd started thinking about how much he'd changed. The timespan wasn't lost on him. In a little over a week, he'd gone from wanting seclusion to needing to be near Kennedy.

It didn't help that as he was pulling into Kennedy's drive, one of his favorite songs came on the radio. He'd parked his truck and let the lyrics soak in. The Cody Jinks song summed up his life. Right down to the part about life never being the same. Every time he'd heard the song in the past, he'd zeroed in on the part about bad news always finding him.

That's what his life had felt like, bad news seemed to follow him.

But then there was Kennedy, and he understood why the Cody Jinks' lyrics had called to him. His life would never be the same, and the thin line between joy and pain was forefront in his mind. And for the first time in his life he wasn't scared of falling in love and hurting the other person. He was afraid he'd be the one to get hurt.

Or had that been his fear all along?

"Why are we here?" Kennedy's question pulled him from his thoughts.

"Weston was over in Baltimore serving a subpoena and caught a blade to the arm and needs me to stitch him up."

"What?" she screeched and scrambled off his lap.

"Then why are we sittin' in the car makin' out?"

"We weren't makin' out, babe. We were talking."

"Why are we still sitting here now? Wait! Why isn't he at the hospital?"

Jameson tried not to laugh at the expressions she was making. She was flustered for sure, but she looked damn cute trying to shift through her thoughts.

"He doesn't need a hospital; he just needs stitches. He would've done them himself but he can't reach."

She opened her car door and Jameson followed suit. He met her at the hood and grabbed her hand. She was nearly dragging him across the street in her haste to get to Weston.

Jameson unlocked the front door and Kennedy bolted up the stairs and stopped on the landing. As soon as he'd made it to the top, her eyes widened and her mouth dropped open. When she recovered, she asked, "You're going to give Weston stitches?"

"Yep."

He opened the door and waited for her to precede him.

"Took you long enough," Weston growled as soon as Jameson closed the door.

"You said it was just a flesh wound. I would've driven faster if you'd nicked something important."

"Yeah, a flesh wound that's bleeding like a motherfucker."

"Did you clean it and try glue?" Jameson asked.

Weston shot Jameson a look that couldn't have been mistaken for anything other than what it was and Jameson smiled. His friend wanted to tell him to eat a bag of dicks, but he wouldn't say it. Not in front of Kennedy.

"Sit down," Kennedy commanded, coming out of the bathroom with a towel and a wet washcloth.

Weston did as he was told and she pulled the bloody shirt he'd used as a tourniquet from his bicep and winced. The wound was on his bicep but went far enough back out of sight Weston wouldn't be able to tie off the sutures.

Jameson studied the three-inch laceration and luckily it was a clean, straight slice. It would be easy to close up.

"Yep, that needs stitches all right. I'd guess twelve, maybe fifteen," Jameson announced and Weston flipped him off.

Kennedy pressed the washcloth against Weston's arm

and her other hand went to his back to steady herself as she applied pressure.

Suddenly and with shocking clarity, Jameson understood Nixon. The man was positively insane when it came to McKenna. None of them could get near her without him looking harassed. Therefore, his friends did it more, just to get under his skin. They'd hug her hello, hug her goodbye, pat her on the back when she worked her magic and found them the intel they needed. Anytime they could, they'd touch her in a brotherly way. Nixon hated it.

Seeing Weston sitting with his shirt off and Kennedy's hands on his bare skin sent him ballistic.

"Did the big asshole just growl?" Weston asked. "Possessive asshole. Maybe if you weren't sucking face outside in your truck and you'd come up here sooner, your woman wouldn't be worried about me bleeding out."

"You're not gonna bleed out, idiot."

Not wanting Kennedy's hands on Weston for any longer than necessary, Jameson told them to go into the conference room and he went to the bathroom to wash his hands. The med kit was in the other room and the chairs were leather. It would be easier to clean up blood should any drip when Jameson was sewing Weston up.

Once again, Weston was seated and Kennedy was tending to his arm when Jameson entered the room. Jameson pulled out the med kit and rooted around for what he needed. Once he had everything laid out, he put on a pair of surgical gloves and turned to Kennedy.

"I take it you're okay with blood."

"Not fond of seeing someone I know bleed, but otherwise yes."

"Go wash up and put on a pair of gloves." Kennedy didn't move but her brow did raise and her lips flattened. "If you wouldn't mind, I could use your help," he added and she still hadn't budged. "Please."

Kennedy waited for Weston to take over holding the washcloth on his arm and she left the room.

"Knew you had it bad, but goddamn."

"You sure you wanna do this right before I'm gonna stitch you up?"

"Might have to start calling you a house kitten. You and Nix both seem to have traded your balls for—"

"Unless you want me to make you cry like a bitch in front of Kennedy, I wouldn't finish that statement."

Weston tried but failed to hold back his shit-eating grin. "Right. Happy for you."

"Happy about what?" Kennedy asked, walking into the room with her hands in front of her, bent up at the elbows like a doctor on one of those TV dramas does when they walked into a surgical suite.

"Nothing, babe. You're gonna need some gloves, too."

Kennedy easily put on the two-sizes-too-big latex gloves and waited for Jameson's next instruction.

He explained what he needed her to do and got to work. Twenty minutes later, Weston had thirteen stitches and Jameson was cleaning up the mess when Kennedy asked, "What happened anyway?"

"Asshole wasn't too happy when I handed him the subpoena. Didn't think much about it, the guy's being disposed in a civil case. Apparently, he's not willing to give testimony and was pissed we'd tracked him down. It was sloppy on my part; I should've been ready for anything. But goddamn, the man was quick on the draw and caught me on the arm before I could stop him."

Kennedy's gaze was swinging back and forth between the two men and she was frowning.

"I thought you guys were PIs."

"We are, among other things," Weston started, and Jameson really wished his friend would keep his trap shut. Kennedy already looked freaked; he didn't want her more worried about his job. "In this case, our client's an attorney and hired us to track the guy down and serve him. Holden and Chasin are working a bond skip right now and are in West Virginia hunting. Nixon left this morning for Pennsylvania to haul a fugitive back to Maryland."

"That sounds dangerous," Kennedy muttered.

"It's really not. It's mostly boring and the majority of our work is done in the office," Jameson said.

"Really?" Kennedy tipped her head to the bloody shirt still on the table then over at the angry red welt on Weston's bicep before looking back at him with raised eyebrows.

"Most of the time it's not."

"You sure you don't need to go to the hospital?" she asked Weston. "Do you need antibiotics or something?"

"Nope. Got bags of them at home. 'Preciate it though."

"You should come home with me and Jameson, you need to put that arm up and eat something."

Jameson froze and sheer panic set in.

Home.

He didn't have a home, hadn't for a long time. He'd been given housing when he was in the Navy, then he'd rented crash pads, and now he was staying at a buddy's house—but it was not *his* home. He hadn't had one of those since before his dad had walked out and fucked his mom over. After his dad left, Jameson had lived in hell, the happy home he'd known was gone.

"Kennedy, darlin'," Weston started. "Can you do me a favor and run up to my office? There's a gym bag up there and if you open it there should be a clean tee."

"Sure." She smiled at him, happy to help.

"You know which office is mine?"

"Yeah, Jameson showed me."

Kennedy had left the room but Jameson barely noticed. He was too lost in his own head.

"Don't fuck this up and lock yourself away," Weston snapped.

"What?"

"Don't play dumb with me. I saw it happen. She invited me *home* and you closed down."

"I—"

"I know you, and I've never known you to be a liar. Don't start being one now. I'm gonna tell it to you straight. I like her." Jameson jerked at his friend's admission. "She's smart and funny and damn if she's not hot as hell. I'd jump at the chance to make a play. Let me rephrase that, I *would've* made my play and she'd be in my bed right now and I wouldn't be squandering the gift, if I hadn't known *you* were interested. Don't make me regret steppin' aside by fucking this up because she used a phrase that freaks you out. You know what she meant when she said it and you're making a big deal out of nothing."

Jameson heard Weston's words, but he'd stopped comprehending them after he'd heard that Weston would've made a move for Kennedy. It played into all of his insecurities. Weston was the better choice. The better man. But Jameson didn't have it in him to step aside, Kennedy was his. He'd felt it the first day he'd seen her in front of her mom's house. It was more than a spark of interest. It was more than her beauty. There had been a moment when Jameson saw the fire and determination in Kennedy's eyes and he'd known right then if he didn't run like a coward, she'd have the power to own him.

And he had been right.

"You're reading me wrong," Jameson growled and took a step toward one of his best friends. "I know what Kennedy meant. I just wasn't prepared for how much I'd like hearing it."

"Good." Weston held his eyes and made no move to retreat from a very angry Jameson.

"Now, you wanna talk about why you're thinking about being in my woman's bed?"

"Not thinking about it. Said I *would've* made a play. But I didn't. And you damn well know why I didn't. Glad to see you pulled your head out of your ass because you deserve this."

Before either man could say more, Kennedy came into the conference room holding a t-shirt. Her nose was scrunched and she handed Weston the bunched-up material.

"You need to wash that bag," she told him. "This was the cleanest tee I could find."

"Thanks." Weston chuckled and pulled on his shirt. "And thanks for the offer to feed me, but I'm gonna head home, shower, and hit the sack. Another time?"

"Are you sure you don't need help? We could go with you back to your place and get you settled."

Kennedy was speaking in "we's" and Jameson liked that, especially now having confirmation that at one time Weston had been interested in her.

"'Preciate your concern, but this isn't the first time I've had a little scrape and I'm sure it won't be the last."

Jameson was happy Weston had donned the tee and was no longer standing in front of Kennedy bare-chested.

The two men shook hands, Weston thanked Jameson again for sewing him up, said his goodbyes to Kennedy, and left.

Kennedy and Jameson followed suit, locking up the office, and then heading home. He was surprised when on the way home, Kennedy hadn't asked any questions about his job or commented on Weston's wound. They were almost to her house when Jameson decided to broach the subject.

"You okay with what happened?"

"Which part? Weston getting hurt? No. Finding out that your job is more dangerous than I'd thought? No. Finding out you know how to stitch up a wound and you're very proficient at it? No."

"So breaking that down, you're not okay with any of it."

"Not right now, but I will be. I have no choice, but it will take me more than an hour to process it. Never seen someone get their arm sewn without some sort of anesthetic or painkiller. And I've never seen anyone but a doctor give stitches."

Then Jameson did something he never thought he'd do in an effort to help Kennedy get past her fear.

"You can ask me anything you want."

"Where'd you learn how to do that?"

"In the Navy. I have basic med training."

"And you were a Navy SEAL?"

"Yes."

She shook her head and asked, "Does that happen a lot?"

"When we were in the teams and deployed, yes. But that's the first time it's happened since we started Gemini Group."

"The scar on your shoulder and the one on your torso?"

"The one on my shoulder was a bullet graze. Hurt like a motherfucker when the adrenaline from the firefight wore off. I'd wished the bullet had actually gone through rather than burning my skin off. The scar on my stomach is from a blade. We'd breached a house and were cleaning it when a man jumped out from inside a hidden closet. When he attacked, he stupidly went for center mass and hit my vest, but his last slash as he was going down, hit below my plates and gashed my stomach. Holden stitched me up when we got back to base. He's better at it than I am, his patch jobs rarely leave scars. It would look worse now if one of the other guys sewed me up."

"And your back? I saw a few puckered scars there."

"Shrapnel. We were rescuing an aid worker. When we got to the camp where he was being held, there was a second hostage we weren't prepared for. I gave her my vest and on the way out, the terrorists detonated a bomb. I was hit with some fragments."

Jameson pulled into Kennedy's drive and parked next to her truck. He was happy to see the newly installed motion light flooded the area nice and bright.

He unbuckled and turned toward her and asked, "What else do you want to know?"

Jameson had found that answering her questions wasn't as hard as he thought it would be.

"You've been shot at a lot." That was a statement but he still answered in the affirmative.

"And you've shot back."

"If that is your nice way of asking if I've killed someone, the answer is yes."

Kennedy was suspiciously quiet, and as much as he feared her censure, she had a right to know what kind of man she'd invited into her home and her bed.

"I told you I'm the way I am because of the things I've

seen and done. I'm not proud of taking lives but I am proud of my service." Jameson shifted in his seat. "I do not take joy in killing another human, but I don't feel remorse or sympathy for ending a warlord's life, or a terrorist's, or any other man or woman who meant us harm. I don't dwell on the people I've killed or the act of ending a life. I dwell on the knowledge that people are seriously fucked-up."

He looked out the windshield, thankful for the light. "There are men out there that will starve their people for power, they will rape their women for control. There are women who will sell their daughters for food, but more astonishing is that there are places in this world where a mother has to make that choice."

Jameson didn't dare look back at Kennedy as he went on. "Men who will strap bombs to their daughters because they know that Americans will grapple with the moral dilemma before we shoot a ten-year-old girl. They give their five-year-old sons rifles and hide behind them, because again, we will struggle with killing a child."

He shifted his gaze to his hands gripping the steering wheel. "That haunts you, knowing you had no choice, your decency and honor was stolen from you and you were forced to end a child's life. A child who should've been home tucked away and protected. Instead, their own flesh taught them hate and sent them out to kill and be killed."

Jameson hadn't realized he'd fisted his hands until Kennedy reached over and pried his fingers open and laced them with hers.

"There are times when I hate myself more than I hate the world. I fucking hate I'm not strong enough to bury it."

He hadn't meant to tell Kennedy his closely guarded secret. He'd never told anyone that. His friends all thought his bad attitude and general dislike for everybody was simply because he was an asshole. They had no idea it was because the person he despised most was himself for being weaker than them. The kernel of distrust his father had planted had blossomed into a forest and Jameson wasn't strong enough to stop it. He'd allowed it to take over his life and turn him into a cynical prick. And war hadn't helped, it had only reinforced his notions, there was no such thing as love. There was only evil in the world—and in an effort to protect himself, he'd gone into seclusion, only allowing those who proved themselves close.

"You can't bury it, Jameson," Kennedy spoke softly. "And it's not because you're weak, it's because you're a good man. A protector." She squeezed his hands in her tiny ones.

"You can't forget what you've seen because the things you've witnessed are disgusting and atrocious. They're unforgettable to you, because it's unfathomable that a man would harm his child. A woman would be put in the position to have to sell her child. But you did not do those things, they did. And yes, they took your control, forced you to do something or see something that burns your soul. And it burns because you are good person."

Kennedy searched his face. "I hope you don't think

that by you sharing that with me I think less of you. I may be just a girl from a small town living a simple life, but I'm not naïve to the fact we've been at war for a long time. And knowing that means I know that men like you exist. The men that are sent to keep us safe. Who face things that they should never have to."

She ran her thumbs over the tops of his fingers. "I'm grateful for what you've done. If it weren't for men like you that live with the burdens you do, I could be one of those women. I don't like that you carry the pain, but, Jameson, the alternative is that one day it may be my children or their children that are one of those women with no rights, no protection, living under the constant threat of being harmed."

Kennedy paused and squeezed his hand and shook it, bringing his attention from staring unseeing out the windshield to looking at her. Determination and compassion shone in her eyes, and the tight knot in Jameson's gut started to loosen.

"I'm not trying to diminish what you've seen, I'm telling you that you've made a difference and I hope that helps you just a little bit. I appreciate your sacrifice. You feel things much deeper than you let on and that does not make you weak, that makes you strong. It makes me proud to know you. It makes me thankful."

Jameson was at a loss for words. But just because he couldn't find his voice didn't mean he hadn't felt every word Kennedy had said—every single one of them had penetrated the fortress he'd built around his heart. She rocked the very foundation he'd spent years fortifying.

He would've bet his life that his walls were so high, so armor-plated, that no one would've been able to scale them. Yet there she was, standing on the other side, seeing Jameson for the man he was, not the man he'd pretended to be. It was both disconcerting and soothing.

He had no idea how to deal with the riot of emotions that had taken over. He feared in that moment anything he said would scare the hell out of her, because the thoughts racing through his mind scared him to death.

It was too soon to say he loved her, but damn if it didn't feel like it. Or at least what he'd imagined love would feel like. There was no denying what he felt went beyond friendship and attraction. It was soul binding. Unsettling and calming. He'd been honest with her and instead of condemnation she'd given him something he never thought he'd taste—peace.

"Come on, let's get inside." Her smile was small and tentative.

He nodded his acceptance, and when they made their way into the house, he took her hand and led her up the stairs into her bedroom, slowly stripped her clothes off, his followed, and he laid her down on her bed.

Then Jameson did one more thing he never thought he'd do in his lifetime. He made love to Kennedy Lane. No words passed his lips as they explored her curves, but they said everything he couldn't. His hands roamed her body, strong and sure, and finally when his body covered hers the magnitude of their connection was undeniable. Moving slowly inside of her this time instead of taking what she was offering, Jameson gave her everything.

And it was then that Jameson realized he'd lied to her. He hadn't meant to and at the time he had no way of knowing. But the first time they'd been together, he had held something back. Not his attention, not his lust for her, not his need. But he'd certainly held his emotions in check. And he knew that with a hundred percent certainty, because now he wasn't.

Yes, Jameson felt a hell of a lot more than he let on, and maybe it was time to be honest about that, too.

14

KENNEDY

Two days ago, something big changed, yet everything was still the same.

Peyton Marshall was still at large. The threat of Reggie was still looming over me, though I hadn't heard from him again. Jameson was going to work every day, the team trying to dig up some sort of dirt on Reggie while handling their other business. I still worked every day. And Jameson came home to my house each night.

He'd packed a bag and brought it over, instead of going back to his house every morning to get ready. That was one thing that had changed, though it seemed small, I sensed it was huge for him and a pretty big step for me, too. It said he planned on staying awhile and strangely I was more than okay with that. Yet, we didn't talk about it. As a matter of fact, since the night in his truck, conversation had been light.

I think after all the heavy we needed light. We were getting to know each other, the people we were now, not what had made us into who we were. It was like we'd slipped into this natural routine that was comfortable and exciting all at once.

I was in my truck when Jameson returned my earlier call.

"Hey," I answered.

"Where you at?"

"On my way to my mom's. She called to tell me her air conditioner's not working. It did this last year, too. Hopefully it will be an easy fix."

"Did she say what was wrong?"

I could hear a door slam shut in the background when I answered. "Honey, she doesn't know anything about her AC. All she said was when she turned it on, it wasn't blowing cool air. Last time it happened it was the run start capacitor. I'm praying it's the same this time and a forty-dollar fix and not a two-thousand-dollar new unit."

My response was met with silence so I called out, "Jameson? Did I lose you?"

"No. I'm here. I'll meet you at your mom's."

"You don't have to—"

"Is there a reason you don't want me to meet your mom?"

Yes!

"No. All I'm saying is you've been working all day and it should only take me a few minutes to figure out what's wrong and hopefully another thirty to fix it."

"Good, then it will only take you fifteen with my help."

Jameson ended the call without a goodbye and I spent the rest of the drive to my mom's in a panic. I'd never brought a man around my mother. Mostly because there had been no man who lasted long enough to meet her, but also because I didn't want to get my mom's hopes up. No guy lasted because he eventually got fed up with my work schedule and never having time to go out. That may've been a slight exaggeration—I could've made time, but I never had because I'd never been all that interested in a man enough to rearrange my life.

I was still having a minor freak-out when I pulled in front of my mom's house. I checked her mailbox which was empty, indicating Miss Janice had already done it, and made my way to the front door. It was unlocked as usual and I realized I'd have to find a way to tell my mom to keep her door locked from now on without telling her my house had been broken into.

Her doctor had said that not only did her diet have to change, but her stress level as well. My mom hadn't held a job since I was born. She'd been a stay-at-home mom and a farmer's wife. Both of those had been full-time work. Then after what happened to my dad she got his insurance money and it had been just enough for her to live on if she budgeted. When she bought her house in town, she'd used the money from the land to purchase it outright. But that didn't mean she was flush with cash, it meant she had to live on a budget and she did. So instead of finding a nine-to-five so she could make more money than just meeting her necessities, she over-scheduled herself volunteering.

She'd worked every fundraiser Kent County had, from the fire company's to the elementary school. If someone was trying to raise money, my mom had her hand in it and worked herself to the bone. It was her way of repaying her community for the support they'd shown when her husband was murdered.

She obsessively worried about the hospital downsizing, the elementary schools in the area closing, about a bridge that was proposed that would bring traffic from the western shore. Anything and everything she could worry about she did. Since her stroke she'd been curtailed, but that didn't mean she wasn't trying her best to get back to a hundred percent so she could go full-steam ahead.

The last thing my mother needed was to be worried about me. And thankfully this bridge business had her mind occupied to capacity.

"Hey, Mama," I called out.

"In the kitchen."

I walked through her living room, glancing around as I went. It was as tidy as it always was. She hadn't changed a thing since she'd bought the old Victorian. The three-bedroom house had been built around the same time our old farmhouse was, but the previous owners of this one had gone to great pains to keep everything original except for the kitchen. That had been upgraded and was fabulous. Though I thought the dark mahogany floors and ornate woodwork throughout the house was fabulous, too, I could've gone without the flower wallpaper. But my mom loved it. She said it added charm.

"It's hotter than Hades in here, Mama."

"Humid, too. Janice is going to have to take me to get my hair washed and set a second time this week."

I glanced at my mother's hair and it was perfect just like it always was. She'd taken to the beauty salon to get her hair washed and straightened after she declared I didn't know how to do it correctly. I hadn't known there was a specific way to straighten hair seeing as mine was bone-straight, something I'd thankfully inherited from my father.

"I'm sure Miss Janice won't mind, she loves to go in and gossip with all the old biddies."

"You know that's rude," she chastised. "I'm no spring chicken so you're talking about me."

"Mama, those women in the salon have twenty years on you yet. How long's your air conditioner been broken?"

"Three days."

"Three days? Mom, it's damn near a hundred degrees outside and it was hotter yesterday. Why didn't you call me sooner?"

"Because I knew you'd be getting everything ready for the market. It's the busiest time of the year for you and I was going to tough it out. But it got too darn hot today."

I sighed and hated that my mom had been sitting here in the heat because she didn't want to bother me. Then I remembered—had I not been so caught up with Jameson I would've come by to check on her and she wouldn't have had to call me. I was in the middle of mentally berating myself when I remembered Jameson was on his way over.

Shit.

"Mom, listen, a friend of mine is going to come by and help me take a look at your AC. Before he—"

"He?" Mom cut me off.

"Yes, Mother, he. I don't want you to get the wrong idea. He's just a good friend."

"How good of a friend?"

Damn, my mom didn't miss much.

"A good one. Can we please leave it at that? And don't say anything that will embarrass me."

"Embarrass you?"

My mom's face fell and I wanted to kick myself in the ass. Since her stroke she'd been self-conscious of everything.

"You know what I mean, Ma. Don't tell him any embarrassing stories about me when I was a kid."

"You never did anything embarrassing. You were a perfectly well-mannered child."

Except I wasn't.

"Right. Then I have nothing to worry about then."

I smiled sweetly at my mom and she gave me an over-exaggerated eyeroll.

There was a knock on the door and elephants started to stampede in my stomach.

"He's here," I unnecessarily announced.

When I opened the heavy front door, Jameson was standing on my mom's front porch looking out of place among the hanging flower baskets and white wicker furniture that decorated the entrance.

"Hi," I greeted. "Come in."

"You did a great job." He tilted his head to the side, motioning toward the new ramp I'd built.

"Thanks."

I couldn't stop myself from smiling, his praise felt good. No, better than good, it felt great. It always did when he admired my work. And he did it a lot, always telling me my garden looked great, or my cooking was awesome. He complimented my house and the renovations I'd done. Lots of little things throughout the day that made me feel like a million bucks.

I stepped aside and let him walk into the living room. He scanned the interior before looking at me and asking, "Did you remodel this, too?"

"No. Mom hasn't changed anything since she moved in. Come on, she's in the kitchen. Let me introduce you."

He nodded and followed me the short distance. My mom was sitting at the table and I knew the milli-second her eyes landed on Jameson. They widened in shock before her face broke out into a splitting smile and I wanted to tell her not to get her hopes up, but it was too late.

"Oh, my. You're a big fella," Mom murmured, and I wanted to crawl under a rock—or better yet turn and flee before she could say anything else.

Jameson's chuckle filled the room and I supposed he was used to it. After all, I'd pretty much said the same thing to him, only I hadn't called him a "fella."

"Jameson, this is my mom, Lola. Mom, Jameson Grant."

"Mrs. Lane, it's a pleasure to meet you."

"And that voice," she gasped. "Rich and deep." My eyes nearly bugged out of my head at my mom's proclamation. "A man with a baritone like that is a born leader, commanding attention when he enters a room."

"Mother," I hissed then turned to Jameson.

"Don't *mother* me. It's the truth. It's said that men with deep voices have higher levels of testosterone. Your father had a deep voice, so I should know."

"Ohmygod. Shoot me now. Mom, please stop talking."

"Since when have you become so square? We're talking about testosterone, not sperm count. And just for the record, higher testosterone does *not* mean a high sperm count, like one might think."

"Why is this happening to me?" I looked up at Jameson, hoping he'd somehow have the answer as to why my mother was talking about sperm counts.

"That is an interesting fact, I did not know," Jameson good-naturedly told my mother.

"I have this book, it was given to me by my friend, Janice. It's called *Why Do Men Have Nipples*. It has all sorts of interesting tidbits."

"Did my mom just say, 'nipples'?" I don't know who I was asking, perhaps God. Maybe He'd take pity on me and lightning would strike me dead so I would no longer be a part of this conversation.

Thankfully, Jameson was smiling and thought my mother's antics were amusing, because I did not.

"During my last deployment, a buddy brought along a book called, *Why Do Men Fall Asleep After Sex*. I believe it was written by the same author. There were some long, boring nights when we'd sit around and read the questions out loud for laughs."

"You were in the service?" my mom asked and sat a little straighter.

Oh, boy. Jameson was in for it now.

"Yes, ma'am, the Navy."

"Call me Lola. And I thank you for your service from the bottom of my heart. I'm a member of the VFW Ladies Auxiliary and The Red Cross, and before I had this damn stroke, once a month me and a group of ladies would head over to Walter Reed. Now the ladies go without me, but I'm hoping by Christmas I'll be ready to go back. I miss my boys, that's for sure."

Jameson's face lost all humor and I was worried she'd hit a nerve and wished she'd go back to talking about nipples.

"When Christmas rolls around, I'll make sure you get there."

"I'd like to be able to walk—"

"With respect, Lola, it doesn't make a damn bit of difference to the men and women who are lying in those beds if you go in there walking, rolling, or are being carried. All they need to see is your beautiful face and sweet smile. That's what matters to them."

With a solemn nod my mom announced, "You're

right. And normally I wouldn't accept such a gesture, seeing as it would take up your whole day. But I'm going to. Thank you."

"Now I see where you get it from." Jameson looked down at me and smiled.

"On that note, we're going out back to check your unit," I told my mom.

"It was nice meeting you, Lola." Jameson smiled at my mom and I swear my mom melted.

Her eyes shown with happiness and my heart squeezed. I hadn't seen a genuine smile on her face in a long time.

Jameson waited until we were in the small postage stamp-sized backyard and out of eyesight of my mother before he pulled me into his arms and kissed me.

"Missed you today, babe," he murmured against my lips.

"Missed you, too. Did you get a lot of work done?"

"Chasin got a lead on a skip and headed to Ohio and Weston's in DC for the next few days meeting with our contact at Homeland."

"Homeland Security?"

"Yep. There's a new contract. Nixon normally goes, but it's McKenna's birthday so he sent Weston."

Jameson scanned the backyard. Finally his gaze went back to the house and his eyes landed on the second story window. "Is your mom's bedroom upstairs?"

"No. Thankfully there's a room downstairs that was used as a guest room. After her stroke I moved her bedroom down and she insisted I moved all of the guest furniture upstairs."

"That's a lot of work."

"You're telling me. But she said, every good Southern woman always has a guest room made up. She's not from the South, by the way. She was born in Pennsylvania. But she loves herself some Southern Living magazine. I swear she reads it cover to cover every month and takes it as gospel. So I made up a guest room she'll never see." The truth of my words hit my chest and I prayed I was wrong and one day my mom would be able to climb her stairs again. "She hasn't been upstairs since her stroke."

"She'll get there. If she's anything like you she won't let anything stop her."

"I hope so."

We walked to the air conditioning unit and Jameson's eyes narrowed and he knelt to get a better look at the refrigerant lines and inspected the pipes before saying, "Found the issue."

His voice was tight and had taken on a hard edge like it did when he was angry.

"What is it? Did the line freeze and crack?"

"Not unless it broke in a perfect hole." He stood and let me look.

Sure enough, there was a hole in the refrigerant line. "How would that happen?"

"Considering there are copper shavings on the ground, I'd say someone drilled a hole in the line."

I was still balancing with my thighs to my calves, my

ass a few inches from the grass, and my hands went to my face and the heel of my palms dug into my eye sockets.

"What?" I whispered.

Jameson reached down and hauled me up, pulling me to his chest, and wrapped his arms around me.

"I don't know what I'm more pissed about. That someone was in my mom's backyard—and I have to tell you, that freaks me out. Or if I'm more angry Reggie's now moved on to fucking with my mom."

"Good news is, it's an easy fix. But we're not doing it tonight. After I fix the line, someone needs to come and refill the refrigerant. We'll head to the store now and get your mom a window unit so she doesn't sweat her ass off tonight."

I nodded, the side of my face rubbing against his solid chest. It didn't take a genius to know he was angry. His body was stiff—almost vibrating with it.

"I'm glad you're here."

"I am, too." He kissed the top of my head and pulled me back so he could look at me. "We're gonna nail Reggie. In the meantime, we're gonna keep you and your mom safe. But I think you should consider telling her what's going on." I started to protest but Jameson leaned down, silencing me with a quick, hard kiss before he continued. "Not right now, but just think about it. I know you don't want her worried, but, babe, she needs to know so she can stay vigilant."

"I hate Reggie Coleman."

"Know that, too."

An hour later we were back at my mom's with two new window units. Jameson had insisted on getting one for her bedroom and one for the living room. He'd also purchased locking devices to secure the windows so they couldn't be opened farther once the air conditioner was in the window frame.

My mom was not happy at the *unsightly*—her word—condensers hanging outside her house. She reserved her complaints for me and praised Jameson for his hard work, thanking him over and over again.

When we were done, we wandered back into the kitchen to say goodbye to my mom. She was standing at the counter precariously balancing on her right leg and I ground my molars. She had a walker and a cane—neither of which she was using—and I knew she wouldn't, not in front of Jameson. And if I called her out on it, I knew she'd tell me her physical therapist told her she needed to be up and moving. Which was true, but she was supposed to use the damn support cane to help her balance.

"Won't you stay for a glass of iced tea? I just made a fresh pitcher." My mom smiled brightly at Jameson.

"Love to. Thank you," Jameson answered, and my eyes cut to him.

Memories of the first time I'd met Jameson, when I, too, had offered him iced tea, flooded my mind. He'd swiftly declined my offer and fled like the hounds of hell were nipping at his ass.

I huffed and started for the counter to help my mom, when I was hauled back into Jameson's arms.

"Babe." He chuckled and kissed me full on the mouth in front of my mother.

Oh, shit.

I didn't have to turn and look at my mom to know she was beaming. It filled the room right along with her hope of a spring wedding.

15

JAMESON

After calling three repairmen, Jameson had finally found one that would replace Lola's line and refill the system for a reasonable price—and more importantly he could do it that afternoon. He could've replaced the line himself, but decided he'd rather use the time to investigate Reggie Coleman.

The man had decided a financial attack was the best way to get to Kennedy. He was draining her resources, forcing her into ruin so he could scoop up her land. It would also compel her to take whatever shitty deal he was offering.

Jameson tossed his phone on the conference room table and went back to his laptop when Nixon filled the door frame.

"You're in early," Nix noted.

Jameson glanced at the clock on the corner of his screen—ten after seven wasn't all that early but he sensed his friend had a point to make so he sat back and waited.

"How's Kennedy?" Jameson remained quiet. Nixon's question wasn't really an inquiry, it was a lead-in. "You've been spending a lot of time with her." There it was. But Nix had more to say so Jameson patiently waited. "You know her father was murdered."

"I know," Jameson finally spoke, not liking the direction of the conversation. "She told me."

"She did?"

"Yeah, she did. She also told me she was there to witness it. And told me about her mother's breakdown." Jameson stopped to take a breath and held his friend's gaze. Nixon had a point to make but so did Jameson. "She *also* told me about the night she got shitfaced and tried to get you to fuck her."

Nixon's brows hit his hairline and deep frown lines marred his face.

"She told you about *that*?" Nix scowled like he was remembering something dirty. "I never—"

"I know you didn't. And I know you never would, even if it wasn't Kennedy coming on to you and just some random drunk girl. I'm only bringing it up so you'll know she told me what she did and what you said to her that night."

"So she told you I was a dick to her."

"Yep. And she also told me what you said to her opened her eyes to the person she'd become and she didn't like what she saw so she changed."

"Could've taken more care, I regret being such an asshole that night. But I was young and my temper got the best of me. Kennedy and I were friends, I liked hanging around her, she was always sweet and funny and palled around like she was one of the guys. And she was pretty back then, but I never thought of her as someone I would date. We were too good of friends. But that didn't mean half the guys in school didn't see her as a challenge, and that's how they saw her because she turned them all down. Then her dad was killed and the change in her was immediate, a switch flipped and she was someone I didn't know. So that night, when she came on to me, I lost it. I was so fucking angry my sweet, funny, pretty friend had turned into..." Nixon stopped and shook his head. "I shouldn't've been so hard on her, I ruined our friendship. She avoided me for a long time after that. To tell you the truth, I was shocked to see her at the house. I knew she'd been close to my dad, but I was gone by then. It sucked losing her, first to the sadness of losing her dad, then again after that night."

"You shouldn't regret a thing. She avoided you because she was embarrassed about how she behaved. And I'm not breaking confidence when I tell you, she still to this day thinks of you as a friend. Her words were, 'a friend I can trust with my life.' You didn't take advantage of her that night, and she was so drunk, you know you could've. Instead you saved her from a life of misery."

Nixon nodded and continue to stare.

"What else is on your mind?" Jameson invited.

"Never seen you spend the night with a woman."

"Nope," Jameson unnecessarily confirmed.

"I take it you're not sleepin' on her couch playin'

sentry." Jameson didn't answer, he didn't need to, Nix wasn't stupid. "Right. And you're good?"

"More than." Jameson smiled and so did Nix.

"Suppose you are. Where are we at with Reggie Coleman?"

"Can't prove it, but either he drilled a hole in Lola Lane's AC line or he had someone do it."

"Hittin' her in the pocketbook." Nixon echoed Jameson's thoughts.

"Yep. And I'm not sure if Kennedy has drawn the correlation yet or not, but she told me the organic grocery store flat out cancelled their long-standing order to stock her honey. And there are two more smaller shops in town where she sells the candles she makes and some jewelry. They didn't ask her to take her stuff out but they moved it all the way to the back of the store and haven't sold anything in a while."

"Goddamn it," Nix muttered, then leaned back from the door frame and shouted down the hall, "Holden. Bring your shit down here."

A few seconds later Holden entered the room and both men sat at the conference room table.

"Who owns the property Nature's Choice rents from?" Nix asked.

Holden went to his computer and a minute later he had what he needed.

"Chester River Holdings owns the building. Willow Realty handles the rental."

"Who owns Chester River Holdings?" Jameson asked.

"Hold on, I'm looking."

"Kennedy also told me that sales have been down at the farmers market, too, but she's blaming that on the weather, says when it's hot attendance goes down."

"It shouldn't be this hard to find out who owns Chester River Holdings, but I can't find it. We can ask Micky—"

"Ask Micky, what?" She popped her head in the conference room and smiled.

"What are you doing here? I figured you'd spend the day sleeping off your birthday celebration," Holden teased, and McKenna's face flamed red.

"Eh, it wasn't—"

"Don't think you wanna go there." Nixon smiled at his girlfriend.

"You don't know what I was going to say." She continued to smile wide.

"It doesn't matter what you say, these idiots will take your words, twist them, and use them to bust my balls."

"Right. Wouldn't want your balls or my words twisted." She laughed. "What do you need me to do?"

Holden explained the searches he'd tried and asked her to find who owned Chester River Holdings, though Jameson already had a good idea who that search would show.

"What's the name of the other two stores?" Holden asked.

"Five oh Five Cannon and Betty's on the Bay," Jameson answered.

Jameson's phone rang and it was the AC guy. He excused himself to take the call.

"Grant," he answered.

"Mr. Grant, I'm sorry but I made a mistake this morning with my scheduling. I...um...thought my day was free but it seems I was...mistaken. I'm sorry but I have to cancel."

"Mistaken?"

"Yes."

"So when can you reschedule?"

"Not until...well...perhaps next month," the man stuttered.

The more the man lied the more Jameson's ire rose. He had no doubt that Reggie Coleman had somehow gotten to the man.

"You wanna explain the real reason you're cancelling on Lola Lane?"

"I'm just overbooked, that's all."

"But you weren't a half hour ago when I called."

"Well...I wasn't looking at my schedule then. I should've and that's my fault. But I'm backed up solid for the next month, maybe two."

"Right."

Jameson disconnected, not caring that the other man was still speaking.

"Need to head to Lola's and fix her AC. That was Sunbelt Air Conditioning. Seems he over-scheduled himself and is busy for the next two months."

Nixon frowned and turned to Holden. "See if

Sunbelt has ties to Reggie. Maybe he uses Sunbelt as a sub-contractor."

"Both businesses rent from Willow Realty and the property is owned by Chester River Holdings," Holden announced.

"And Chester River Holdings is owned by Reginald Coleman, Clifford Marshall, and Gary Earle," McKenna confirmed what Jameson had suspected.

"Clifford Marshall? Is that Peyton's father?" Jameson asked, remembering the punk that broke into Kennedy's house.

Nixon sat back in his chair and shook his head. "No. Peyton's first name is Clifford. For obvious reasons he goes by his middle name. Why would Coleman go into business with a fuck-up like Marshall? The guy's a tool. He can't hold down a job. Reggie Coleman may be a conniving asshole but he's not stupid. It doesn't make sense. Babe, can you see what percentage of the company Marshall owns?" That last question was for McKenna.

"All equal shares."

"Fuck, man, you got me." Nixon shrugged. "Unless Peyton has something on Coleman and wormed his way into owning part of the business, I cannot see Coleman willingly allowing Peyton near his business. And I don't know who Gary Earle is. As a matter of fact, I don't know any Earles, period."

"I'll look into Gary and see what I can find on Peyton."

"Thought you already did a search on him after he broke into Kennedy's?" Jameson queried.

"I did, but I was looking for places he's hiding and checking his criminal record. Now I'll crawl up his ass."

"What's this, 'No Bridge to Kent' business? I see signs saying that all over," Holden asked.

"Yeah, Lola Lane has one in her yard."

Nixon gave a quick rundown of the state's plan to build a new bridge over the Chesapeake Bay. There was already one bridge, but with more people than ever living on the eastern shore and commuting to Baltimore and the District, traffic was so bad a second bridge was needed. One of those proposed bridge sites would be in Kent County. A location that a lot of residents were opposed to.

"Why do you ask?" Nix gave Holden his attention.

"It seems Reggie Coleman is a huge proponent of the bridge going from the western shore to Kent County. He's quoted in the paper as saying the economic impact would do wonders for the community. He also formed a group in support of the bridge to combat the opposition."

"That would make sense," Jameson started. "I would assume property value in the area would go up if a bridge was built. People who worked in Baltimore could live in a nice quiet setting outside of the city and only have a twenty minute commute. Not to mention, all the housing developments that would pop up. Which no doubt he'd have his greedy hand in that pot, too. That's why he wants Kennedy's property. The land he owns behind her only has fifteen feet of street access. He needs her land which would provide more than five hundred feet so he can build a housing track."

"Holden, also check when Coleman started buying up all this property. Before or after the new bridge proposal was made public," Nixon instructed.

"By the way, if you need help working on Lola's AC, call Zack. He's savin' up to buy a car, so he's looking for all the work he can."

Before Jameson could answer Nixon about McKenna's soon-to-be sixteen-year-old brother helping him, an alarm went off on his phone at the same time one went off on Holden's and Nixon's.

Jameson snatched his phone off the table, tapped the app, and his vision blurred as he watched a man dressed in black with a ski mask covering his face cruise by one of the cameras in front of Kennedy's house.

"Fuck."

His chair scraped on the wood floor before it tipped back and landed with a loud bang.

He didn't bother righting the chair, he shot out of the office taking the stairs two at a time, and ran across the street to his truck. His wheels screeched as he gunned it away from the curb.

After his second call to Kennedy went unanswered, he tossed his phone in the cup holder and jammed on the accelerator.

The fury seeping into his bones shocked him.

Maybe he should've expected it—he was falling in love with the woman after all. However, he hadn't known. How could he have? Until Kennedy, he hadn't had the first clue what love was.

16

KENNEDY

My head throbbed like I'd been hit with a two-by-four. Which made sense because I think I *had* been hit by a two-by-four. That, or a baseball bat. I hadn't seen anything because I'd been checking on my hives and wearing my hat and veil. Either way, my head was spinning and I was dizzy. I pushed past the nausea and got to my feet.

I had bigger issues. My bee boxes were on fire, completely engulfed in flames and unsalvageable. I didn't have time to process what the loss meant for me or how upset I was that all of my bees were dead. It was summer and there was plenty of dried grass and other tinder that could catch and get out of control.

Moving as quickly as I could, I staggered away from the crackling fire toward my four-wheeler and wanted to cry when I found the key missing. I had to go back to my house to get a bucket of water. My hives were at the edge of my property and there was no well back there. I took off my gloves and reached into my pocket, thinking my best option was to call 911 and get the fire department out here, but came up empty.

Of all the days for me to forget my phone in the damn shed.

With no other choice, I started to make the mile walk back to the house. I had to pick up the pace—at this rate the back field would be on fire by the time I got to a phone. But my legs were wobbly and refused to move any faster. My stomach rolled and I had to stop to catch my breath. It was hot as shit outside and I was covered head-to-toe from tending the bees. I tossed aside my hat and veil and ripped my long-sleeved shirt off, not caring I was only in my bra, but it did nothing to stop the vomit I felt rising in my throat.

I bent forward and heaved, my head swam and my vision darkened.

No, *no*, no. I couldn't faint. I had to get home.

Sweat dripped down the back of my neck in rivers. My head spun. I plopped down on my ass, and gave into the hazy darkness.

THE FIRST THING I noticed was I was freezing, and considering the last thing I remembered was being burning hot, I was confused. And thankfully I no longer felt like I was going to throw up. I slowly opened my eyes, harsh light blinding me through the slivers and I quickly shut them again.

"Take it slow, baby." Jameson's large hand pressed on my forehead and I relaxed.

Then I remembered. "Fire," I croaked. My throat was dry and scratchy and it felt like I swallowed nails.

"Shh. Everything's been taken care of."

Thank God!

"I'm so cold."

A blanket was pulled up to my neck and I cuddled in.

A blanket?

I started to open my eyes again but all I could do was blink. The motion made me light-headed and my stomach woozy.

"Where am I?"

There was no smell of grass and wood burning. It almost smelled clean, like the scent of bleach hung in the air.

"The hospital."

"The hospital? Why?"

"Babe." Jameson's voice sounded strangely thick. Not like his normal deep, honeyed tone. Like he was wrought with worry. "You lost consciousness."

What the hell? I did? I remembered sitting down so I didn't fall forward and land in my own vomit, but I didn't remember passing out. And I certainly didn't remember going to the hospital.

"How'd I get here?"

Maybe one of my neighbors saw the smoke and called 911.

"I drove you."

I took one more chance and tried to pry my eyes apart

slowly, and finally Jameson's handsome face came into view, albeit blurry.

"Hey there," he whispered. "Welcome back."

Welcome back? What did that mean?

"I'm a little freaked out. I can't remember what happened."

"You were hit in the head and you have a concussion."

"I remember that part. It hurt so bad, and my boxes were on fire. I tried to get help but don't remember what happened after that."

Jameson's frown lines deepened and his thumb gently grazed my forehead.

"What's wrong?" I asked.

"Beyond the obvious?" His head tilted and his eyes roamed my face.

I started to nod but the tiny movement sent a shock of pain all over and I winced.

Good God, my head hurt.

"I need to ask you something," he started and his lips twisted in indecision. I wanted to prompt him to go on, but it hurt too bad to move. "Do you know why your shirt was off when I found you?"

My shirt was off? Panic started to bubble in my chest as I searched for an explanation.

Then I remembered. "I was hot. I cover up when I'm collecting the honey frames so I don't get stung. The key to my four-wheeler was gone so I started walking home to get water. I was sweating so bad, I took off my shirt."

Relief washed over his features and he leaned

forward to kiss my head. It hurt like a mother, but I wasn't going to complain. Jameson's touch was the only thing keeping me together.

"Who hit me?"

"Don't know yet. He had on a ski mask."

"How bad was the fire? Did it catch the hedgerow?"

"No. Holden got it under control and called the fire department."

"Holden?"

"I'll explain everything later. For now you need to rest."

"When can I go home?"

"The doctor said forty-eight hours after you woke up. I'm going to get the nurse to give you something for your head."

"No. Don't leave me."

Fear set in and I didn't want him to leave my side. I felt oddly vulnerable, both physically and emotionally. I needed Jameson next to me, to protect me, keep me safe, keep me from flying apart and breaking down. As long as he was next to me, no one could hurt me.

"I'm not leavin' your side, babe."

He reached over me and nabbed the plastic call button. A moment later a woman's voice came through the speaker and Jameson explained I was awake. The nurse's relief at the news hit me as strange.

"How long was I passed out?" I asked.

"Six hours."

"Six hours?" I gasped then regretted it.

"You scared the shit out of me, Kennedy. Worst six hours of my life."

Worst six hours of his life? Holy shit. The man had seen combat.

I didn't have time to process his statement. The door opened and an older woman in scrubs stepped into the room and smiled.

After that, there was a flurry of commotion. While the nurse was checking my vitals and preparing my meds, the doctor came in and explained I'd had a CT scan, three staples to the back of my head, and I'd be staying for observation for at least two days. Longer if I continued to experience dizziness and headaches. Jameson had asked about an MRI and more testing. He was frantic about making sure I didn't have a TBI or any long-term lasting effects. The doctor had spent more time explaining the CT results with Jameson than he had with me. Jameson was relentless, it wasn't until I squeezed his hand and told him I was okay that he calmed.

He agreed to table the MRI talk for a few days but threatened to revisit the topic if my headache wasn't gone by morning. I figured it would take more than a few hours for the pounding in my head to subside but I didn't tell him that.

A warmth I'd never known spread over my chilled skin. No one had ever taken care of me, not like this. Not with so much vigor and protectiveness. I'd never had someone so fully care about my well-being. I knew my mom loved me and wanted what was best for me but she didn't have the strength Jameson had. It had always been me looking after her.

Shit. My mom!

"Mom," I croaked.

"She's fine. Nixon took care of her."

I wanted to ask more but sleepiness from the pain medicine the nurse had given me started to pull me under.

If Jameson said she was fine, she was fine.

I trusted him.

17

JAMESON

Jameson was coming out of his skin. Kennedy was pressing to be discharged and it had been less than twenty-four hours since she woken up. She was grouchy, uncomfortable, and wanted her own bed. All of which Jameson understood. But he wanted her under the constant supervision of medical professionals. The thought of her going home made his gut clench for a variety of reasons.

There were too many what-ifs. Too many things that could go wrong. Her headache still hadn't gone away. She couldn't take more than a few sips of water before she felt nauseous. And every time she spoke, she winced. She wasn't ready to leave the hospital and thankfully her doctor agreed.

But Kennedy was, like always, determined.

With Weston still gone, the team was already down a man. And since Jameson refused to leave her side even when Nixon, Holden, and McKenna had said they'd stay with her while he went home to shower and rest, he was out of the search for who'd hurt Kennedy as well.

It wasn't that he didn't trust his team, he knew they'd protect her. It was the visions that plagued his mind of her unconscious body. He'd never forget finding her shirt-less, lying in the grass, unable to wake her up. He'd known he'd taken a risk moving her, but he wasn't going to wait for an ambulance to get to her.

He'd scooped up her lifeless body and held her while Nixon had driven them to the hospital. So many thoughts had been racing through his mind he couldn't remember the drive. He'd been scared out of his mind, a feeling that Jameson wasn't used to. He'd seen plenty of death and carnage over the years, had dealt it out when needed. But he'd never held the woman he loved in his arms while she was bleeding and comatose. Then he'd spent the next six hours in hell.

Even now, listening to her complain about having to stay in the hospital, he couldn't stop thinking about those hours. The minutes dragged on. The seconds had felt like an eternity. All Jameson could do was watch the steady rhythm of the monitors. The only sign that she was alive. She hadn't even twitched in those hours. Hadn't groaned or made a sound. The silence had been so deafening he'd turned up the volume on the machine. He'd needed the beeping to reassure him her heart was beating.

"That's enough, Kennedy." His tone was harsher than he would've liked but he'd heard enough.

"I don't want to be here," she complained. "I need to get home. And I have to check on my mom."

"There is nothing you need to do at home. And Nixon is taking care of your mom."

"But—"

"Stop. Please stop." Jameson's hands scrubbed over his face before they went into his hair and tugged.

"Jameson?" Kennedy called. "What's wrong?"

"What's wrong? You're joking, right?"

"I'm fine. Even the doctor said, it's just a concussion."

Christ—*just* a concussion.

"Yeah, a concussion brought on by a goddamn two-by-four to the back of the head. Do you have any idea how lucky you are? If he would've hit you just a little bit harder, he could've killed you. If you would've turned your head you could be in a wheelchair, drinking out of a straw for the rest of your life. There was a fucking rusty nail on the end of the board. If he would've hit you with that..." Jameson shook his head, trying to dislodge the image of Kennedy with a nail in her skull.

She had been so damn lucky the person who hit her hadn't meant to kill her, or she'd be dead. His woman would be gone and it would've been Jameson's fault for leaving her unprotected. His ass had been sitting in his office fifteen miles away from her while some fucker had attacked her. There was no excuse for his oversight. He should've been there.

"But none of those things happened."

"They could've," Jameson growled.

Hate and anger rose to the surface and threatened to consume him. When he found the man that hurt Kennedy, he was going to unleash his wrath. Hell was going to rain down on the motherfucker that hurt her. There was no doubt about it. The man would pay.

"You can't dwell on what *could've* happened. It didn't. And you found me and got me help. Of course, it could've been worse. The field could've gone up and I was lying in it passed out. But it didn't and you saved me. I'm fine, Jameson. That's all that matters."

"Maybe I could stop dwelling on it if I could forget holding the woman I love while her blood seeped from her head and soaked my skin. Maybe I could stop dwelling on it, if I didn't spend six goddamn hours praying for you to wake up. Maybe I could stop thinking about how fucking terrified I was when I saw what was happening, knowing I couldn't get to you in time, if I could forget the sight of you shirtless lying in a field. So please, cut me a little slack, stop bitching about wanting to leave and let the doctor monitor you. Please, Kennedy, I'm fucking begging you. Just stop."

"Okay," she whispered. "I'll stop."

"Thank you." Jameson blew out a relieved breath.

"I'm sorry. I'm being selfish. I just want out of this hospital bed. I want to be able to lie next to you and feel your arms around me."

"Soon, Kennedy." He sat in a chair next to her bed and gathered her hand in his. "You'll be home soon."

He hated to bring up her mom, but it was a topic they needed to discuss.

"Nixon's not real happy he lied to your mom." Kennedy's hand convulsed in his. "When he went over there to fix her AC and tell her what happened, she had a lot of questions. He evaded most of them, but he's unhappy. She's worried about you and I think it's time you told her."

"You're right. I'll call her."

"How 'bout I call Janice and ask her to bring your mom to the hospital?"

"No way. She'll—"

"She wants to see her daughter," Jameson cut her off. "She's stronger than you think. And we're all here for her to catch her if she starts to backslide. But you keeping her away is gonna make it worse. McKenna can come down, too."

"I don't want to meet McKenna like this."

"Too late. She's been in and out just like Nixon and Holden. All three of them were worried about you and wouldn't leave the hospital until you woke up. Weston pitched a conniption when Nix told him to stay in DC."

At first Jameson was pissed when his friend had called frantic for an update on Kennedy. And when Weston had threatened to come home to see her, jealousy had reared its head. But then he remembered Weston cared for Kennedy as a friend. But more than that, Weston was worried for Jameson.

"I'm glad they were there for you even if I wished they didn't see me passed out in a hospital bed. I hope I wasn't drooling while I was asleep. And if I was, you better have wiped it away so they didn't see."

Jameson smiled for the first time since he'd found Kennedy. He liked—no, *loved*—that she wasn't the slightest bit embarrassed around him.

"There was no drool, babe. You looked beautiful, like you were sleeping."

And she had. Jameson hadn't stopped staring at her the whole time she'd been passed out. He'd studied her every feature. He'd memorized the contours of her face. But the one part he'd wanted to see, her pretty green eyes with flecks of gold, eluded him.

But now they were staring back at him and he needed to hold on to that.

She was alive.

KENNEDY WAS WIPED OUT. Her mother had been furious she'd been kept in the dark about what Reggie Coleman was doing.

Jameson had been right; Lola Lane was stronger than he'd even thought. And he imagined if the woman had all of her faculties, she would've been up pacing the room before she stomped out to pay Reggie a visit. As it was, all she could do was ball her right hand into a fist and shake it as she declared she was going to kill the man.

Lola had also added some much-needed insight. Peyton Marshall was rumored to be Reggie Coleman's son. A child created from a well-known affair. Both Reggie Coleman and Deloris Marshall were married to other people but had carried on for years. It was also a well-known fact that Clifford Marshall senior was impotent. He couldn't even get it up, something that had happened as a result of a pelvic fracture that damaged the nerves. An accident that occurred on a job site when Clifford had worked for Reggie Coleman.

That explained why Peyton Marshall owned a third of Chester River Holdings when by all accounts he was an idiot. Whether Coleman had willingly included him out of parental obligation or Peyton had blackmailed him was still unknown.

Kennedy's mother also admitted that Reggie Coleman had approached her in the last month. She hadn't mentioned it to Kennedy because she didn't want to worry her. Reggie hadn't come out and made any threats, just a comment in passing about how hard Kennedy worked and it was a shame a beautiful girl like her didn't have time to give Lola grandchildren. His parting shot was to tell Lola that if Kennedy ever wanted to sell her land he'd be more than pleased to take it off her hands.

The woman also had a keen mind and had easily drawn her own conclusions about Kennedy's business suffering. She'd also directly asked if her air conditioning unit had been tampered with.

Lola was no dummy, she was sharp, just like her daughter.

Before Janice had come back into the room to take her home, Lola's chin had jutted out and Jameson bit back a smile when the woman demanded for him to take care of her daughter. It wasn't until Jameson had promised her Kennedy wouldn't be alone again until Reggie was stopped did she finally leave.

Now Kennedy was looking at him with so much

sadness she didn't try and stop the tear from rolling down her cheek.

"I hate that my mom is so worried."

"I know. But it's better that she knows. And she had a lot of information for us."

Kennedy nodded, not looking convinced.

"And Janice has agreed to move in with her, so she won't be alone. An added layer of protection."

"Miss Janice is older than my mom. What's she gonna do? Beat an intruder with a cane?"

Jameson smiled at the vision of the little old woman beating a man with Lola's cane.

"I have no doubt she would. But Holden's staying there, too." Which was huge, considering how much Holden valued his privacy and with good reason. "Tomorrow, him and Nix will install an alarm system and Weston will be home. He'll take over sleeping on your mom's couch."

"Maybe she should move in with me."

"Maybe you should close your eyes and get some rest."

"Will you lie next to me?"

Jameson glanced at the small hospital bed and shook his head.

"Babe, I'd barely fit in that bed alone."

"Please?"

Her big green eyes bore into him and he couldn't deny her request.

Jameson carefully eased his big body onto the bed, while pulling her mostly on top of him.

"Does anything hurt?" he asked before he settled in farther.

"No," she whispered.

He adjusted them so Kennedy's head was resting on his chest, their legs were tangled, and he was taking her weight.

"Perfect," she muttered.

He agreed but stayed quiet, not wanting to jostle her anymore than he had.

Jameson lay awake for a long time, his arms full of his sleeping woman. He stared at the ceiling, sleep evading him, when he heard it. The faintest of whispers.

"I love you, too, Jameson."

Just a feather-soft admission that floated through the room, but had slammed into his chest like a sledgehammer.

He closed eyes and drifted to sleep.

18

KENNEDY

I'd spent three full days in the hospital. After Jameson's plea for me to stop bitching about having to stay, I'd kept my mouth shut. I had forgotten how hard it was to see someone you cared about in a hospital bed. How difficult it was to watch someone you loved in pain and not know if they were going to make it.

It hadn't been that long ago I'd been in Jameson's shoes. I'd stood next to my mother's bedside and prayed she wouldn't die. I'd felt helpless and heartbroken. Even if it wasn't the same thing, it was close enough and I could empathize with Jameson.

Beyond that, I'd been behaving like a total brat. Who cared if I had to stay in the hospital? I was alive, relatively unharmed, and I would heal.

But now I was sitting in Jameson's truck on my way home and he was acting weird. I wasn't sure if he was being weird because I'd been released. He'd obviously wanted me in the hospital where I'd been under constant medical supervision or if it was something else. But he was definitely off—fidgety, lost in his thoughts, and distracted.

It was scaring me. Maybe he'd changed his mind about us. Since the day I'd met him, my life had been full of drama. It was a lot to take in and even more to ask someone to participate in when it had nothing to do with them. Perhaps I shouldn't have gone to Nixon and gotten them all involved. I had no idea Reggie would get violent and I'd be putting everyone in danger. If he found out I'd enlisted Nix for help, they could be in the line of fire. And there were teenagers involved, too. Everyone knew how much Nix loved McKenna and her siblings. They'd been through enough and it wouldn't be hard to hurt Nix through them.

We were almost to my house when I couldn't take the silence anymore. That, coupled with Jameson twitching his thumb on the steering wheel, was driving me insane.

"What's wrong?"

Jameson's jaw clenched and deep lines formed on his forehead.

Yeah, something was very, very wrong.

"Fuck. I don't know how to tell you this."

My heart sank and my eyes automatically shut. This was going to kill me.

"Listen," I whispered. "If you've changed—"

"Stop," he bit out and gripped the wheel tighter. "Nothing has changed."

That should've made me feel better but it didn't.

He pulled into my driveway and I scanned my front

yard. Everything looked the same. I don't know what I was expecting. It wasn't like I'd been gone long, but it was hard to rationalize that just a few days ago I'd been attacked on my own property, a place I was supposed to be safe. Not only that but before that, someone had entered my home uninvited. Suddenly being home didn't hold the same appeal it had while I was lying in a hospital bed.

I was getting ready to ask Jameson if we could go to his place and stay there for awhile when he spoke through gritted teeth.

"I knew this was going to happen. I can see the fear in your eyes. I didn't want to add to it but, fuck, you have to know before you see it."

Oh, no. What else?

"See what?"

"The best Nixon and the police can gather is, someone sprayed your garden with Roundup."

"What?" I wheezed, unable to catch my breath.

"There's nothing on the surveillance video, which means they had to have come in from the back. And the cameras don't reach the fields, only the house perimeter."

"How bad?"

"Everything's gone. Nixon had Mr. Adams, the man who rents his land, come over as soon as Nix noticed some of the plants wilting. They tried to neutralize the glyphosate but it was too late."

In three days, my livelihood had been stolen from me. Years I'd worked to build what I had and it had taken days for it to crumble. I was finished. The rest of my summer income was dead and my bees were gone. I had four cases of jarred honey, six boxes of candles, and not enough money in the bank to get me through until next summer. Land taxes would be coming up in ninety days and only three quarters of the money was set aside to pay them. Not enough.

"He wins," I whispered.

"The fuck he does."

"I'm done for, Jameson. I can't pay my taxes and still have money left to pay my bills and eat. He wins and the worst part is, it was easy for him to ruin me and he knew it would be."

"Kennedy—"

"No. No. It's fine. He can have it—all of it. I don't want it, not anymore. Take me to your house."

"Babe—"

"Get me away from here!" I screamed and ignored the enormous hammer that pounded my skull.

Jameson put his truck in reverse and backed down my drive. I watched as the house I'd grown up in, the home I loved, started to disappear from sight. I never wanted to see it again. It wasn't mine anymore. It was Reggie Coleman's.

I came awake in a strange bed and for a moment had forgotten where I was and why.

Then I looked around the stark white room with minimal furnishings and remembered.

Then I wished I hadn't woken up.

A glance out the curtainless window told me it was daylight and I wondered if it was still the same day or if I'd slept the day away. Either way it didn't matter, time wouldn't change my circumstances for the better. As a matter of fact, time wasn't my friend. Every day I didn't work was a day I'd lost money.

"Sorry, Dad," I muttered to an empty room. "I tried."

What was my mom going to think of me losing what was left of the land my dad had worked? Day in and day out he'd farmed that land providing for us. We'd already lost the majority of it, but now the house would go, too.

He loved that house. He'd bitch and complain about all the things that needed to be repaired or updated, then he'd lovingly go about fixing them. He'd hand me a tool-belt and put me to work. Him and me. The two of us working side by side. Even though he'd been gone a long time, every time I put on the old toolbelt he'd given me I still felt him next to me.

The last thing I had of my father's would soon be lost to me. Another family wouldn't move in and love the house the way I did, it'd be gone. Reggie would demolish it and with it all of my memories. It would be nothing more than rubble and splintered wood.

Shit! What had I done? I'd taunted Reggie and allowed my ego and attitude to egg him on. Instead of playing it smart, I'd been ridiculously stupid.

Now I'd pay the price.

"Oh, good you're awake," a woman's voice filled the room. "I'm McKenna."

My eyes went to the open door and there McKenna stood. My height, but that's where the similarities ended. We were opposites, she had long wavy brown hair to my blonde. Light brown eyes that sparkled to my plain green, and she had flawless skin. She fit Nixon perfectly.

Sweet Jesus, someone kill me now.

"Hey."

I tried to sit up but she stopped me.

"Please don't get up." Her hands were waving in front of her and she added, "Jameson will kill me."

"Really, I'm fine. And if I'm honest, I'm kinda tired of lying down."

McKenna smiled and the subtle movement made her even more beautiful.

Forget sitting up. I wanted to lie back down and pull the covers over my head so she wouldn't see what a mess I was. I didn't need a mirror to know I looked like a wet cat that had been dragged through the mud before it was plunged into a pit of horse shit.

Could my life get worse?

"I'm running to Procolinos to get dinner. Jameson asked me to pick you up some shampoo and stuff while I was out. I thought I'd check and see if you were awake before I left."

My stomach took the opportunity to grumble at the mention of food and why not? Nothing like weird stomach noises when meeting your friend's very pretty girlfriend for the first time while you're sitting in rumpled clothes looking like a hot mess.

"I would appreciate it. I think a shower is not only

much needed but it would make me feel better. Any brand would be fine, I'm not picky." My new financial situation rushed back and slapped me in the face and I quickly rushed out. "Whatever's cheapest will work."

McKenna tilted her head and squinted before she recovered and smiled. But I didn't miss the look.

Great. Not only did I *look* homeless, but she probably thought I was, too.

Which sadly was the truth. As soon as I signed the papers Reggie would own my home and I'd be out on my ass with nowhere to live. Well, I could live with my mom. Just what every thirty-one-year-old woman wants. Yippy.

"I was going to pick up a few large pizzas. Anything else you'd like?"

I would have killed for a cheesesteak, but considering I no longer had the money for it, I wouldn't ask.

"No. I'm not that hungry. A slice will be more than enough."

McKenna sighed and much to my dismay stepped farther into the room. I smelled like hospital antiseptic and God knows what else. *I'm sure the combination's attractive—not.*

"I hope you don't think I'm out of bounds saying this, but it's gonna get better. I know it doesn't feel like it right now but it will."

I bit my tongue instead of lashing out. McKenna was Nixon's girlfriend and Jameson's friend but she had no idea what she was talking about.

"You don't believe me," she murmured. "I don't blame you. Before I met Nixon, if someone had told me my life would get better, that things would get easier, that if I had patience everything would work out, I would've call them a liar, too. I didn't want to admit I was drowning, that I had no idea how to handle my brother and sister and guide them through their grief of losing our family while *not* dealing with mine. I was so determined to do it on my own to prove I could, I forgot I didn't have to. That when Nixon offered his help, it was okay to take it.

"I'm going to tell you something I'm sure you already know. Those men downstairs, they live and breathe to protect the people they care about. I can't say I know Jameson as well as you do even though I work with him fifty hours a week. That's because he doesn't let anyone see the real him. But I have a feeling, he's shown you. So, I don't need to know you, to know there's something special about you and you're someone I want to call my friend. That is, when you're ready.

"But in the meantime, don't turn down their help. It will be a useless battle you'll lose anyway. They won't stop fightin' in your corner. They won't let anyone bully you or hurt you. They'll fight until the death for you and I know that as fact. Accepting their help, and Jameson's in particular, doesn't make you weak, it makes you smart. It means you're self-aware and know when it's time to call in the cavalry."

McKenna gave me a lopsided smile and asked again, "Other than pizza what would you like from Procolinos?"

"A cheesesteak with grilled onions and ketchup."

Her smile was beaming and genuine.

"And your shampoo?"

"I use Joico but I doubt the supermarket will have that brand, so really anything is fine. I wasn't lying, I'm not picky."

"Great. I'll be back. Anything else while I'm out?"

I thought about everything she'd said and as much as I hated to ask, she was right. I needed help, down to the simplest of necessities.

"Is Nixon going with you?"

"Yeah."

"Then would you mind going to my house and picking me up some fresh clothes?"

"Already done. I went with Nixon a while ago and packed you a bag. I tried not to go through your stuff the best I could, but Jameson was adamant you had clean clothes. Sorry I didn't think to grab your shower stuff, but I did throw in your deodorant."

Of course, Jameson would've already thought about clothes. The man was forever making sure I was comfortable.

"Thank you."

"Anytime, sister. I'll be back in a flash and if you're up to it, I'd like to spend time chatting with you."

"I'd love that."

"Great."

With one last smile, McKenna left the room and I laid back down to think about everything she'd said.

Could I ask Jameson for more help?

19

JAMESON

Jameson stood in the hall outside of his bedroom and without remorse listened to McKenna and Kennedy's conversation. It had been mostly one-sided but he didn't need more words from Kennedy to know how she was feeling.

He also knew she wouldn't give up, but she needed time to process this latest blow and he'd give her a safe place to do it until it was time to remind her to bundle up, because the world was a cold place to be. But with him by her side, she may stumble but she'd never fall.

McKenna exited the room and didn't look the least bit surprised he'd been eavesdropping. With a pat on his shoulder and a smile, she walked down the hall.

He stood there a while longer debating whether or not to give her more time. Finally deciding he could no longer stand being away from her, he entered his room and closed the door behind him.

They both had queen-sized beds but his was softer,

and with the thick down comforter she was lying on, she looked like she was being engulfed in white. It felt bizarre being back in his room after spending so much time at Kennedy's.

Her room had personality, it was warm and inviting, just like the woman who'd decorated it. Jameson's was boring and cold. The same could be said for the man who lived there. At least before he'd met Kennedy.

Now when he crawled into bed, cold didn't seep into his bones. He didn't lie awake staring into the dark replaying the worst of his life. Instead, Kennedy's body pressed close to his, her arm would pin him to the bed— grounding him, her goodness surrounding him, and he could sleep. She warmed him from the inside out.

"Thanks for letting me stay here," Kennedy murmured as Jameson made his way across the room.

He sat on the edge of the bed and placed his hand on her hip. He was unable to keep from touching her. When she was close, Jameson craved the contact.

"You don't need to thank me for that," Jameson said, then reminded her, "You're not alone anymore."

"McKenna's nice."

"She is."

"And beautiful."

"Yep."

Kennedy looked away and Jameson didn't like the unsure look in her eyes.

"What's wrong?"

Jameson gently guided her chin back to him and waited.

"My life is a mess right now. I feel like crap. I look like shit. I guess I'm letting all of my female insecurities get the best of me."

Honesty. Jameson loved that she hadn't tried to hide from him.

"You hit a bump in the road. We'll get past it. And you could never look like shit, you're beautiful."

"A bump? I've hit a dead end. Game over."

Tears welled in her eyes and Jameson struggled to find the words to comfort her.

"Babe, the game is not over. We have many more moves to make. We're getting closer. This will all be over soon."

Kennedy swiped the tears away and winced in pain.

"I'm out of moves. Even if I went out tomorrow and got a job at the grocery store, I wouldn't be able to come up with the money I need to keep my house in time."

"Money is not an issue, Kennedy. You will not lose your house."

"I have to pay my taxes, Jameson. I could sell my truck, that may be an option."

"You're not selling your truck either. I'll cover your taxes and—"

"No!"

"What do you mean, no?"

"No way am I taking your money. I don't take handouts. Either I earn it or I don't have it."

Kennedy's voice was firm and absolute. Certainly he could pay her taxes behind her back, and avoid the argument all together but that would be shady, and Jameson didn't do anything behind anyone's back. It wasn't his style.

He thought about the best way to approach the situation to get what he wanted.

"I want to invest in your business."

Kennedy barked out a weak laugh. "There's not a business to invest in. Everything's gone. Even if I plowed my plants under and started over, it's too late in the season. Nothing would grow. And from what I saw, my hives burned to the ground. And there's the other problem, no one's buying my products anymore."

"I'm not investing in plants and bees, I'm investing in *you*. I'm investing in the future."

"I can't—"

"Shh." Jameson rubbed his thumb across her lips. "Just think about it. You don't need to answer right now."

Kennedy remained quiet for a while and Jameson sat patiently waiting for her to gather her thoughts.

"I'm not sure I want to ever go back there."

"You will."

"I freaked out just being in the driveway."

Jameson didn't need the reminder; he couldn't forget the look of terror and devastation on her pretty face.

"You're being too hard on yourself. I knew it would come. Your home is a place where you're supposed to feel safe. I'm actually surprised it hadn't come sooner, after Peyton broke in. You were violated twice. Two times, Kennedy. Cut yourself some slack. We'll stay here until you're ready to go back. And if we try it again and you're still not ready, we'll come back here and wait some more."

"I was wearing earbuds, listening to music. That's why I didn't hear whoever hit me approach."

"But you didn't have your phone."

"I'm still in the dark ages and I use an iPod. I'm too lazy to figure out how to transfer my music over. Between the earbuds and the big helmet I wear so I won't get stung, I didn't hear a thing."

"It's not your fault. You shouldn't have to worry about some asshole coming up behind you when you're working in your yard."

But even as Jameson said it he wondered what would've happened if she had heard. Would she have been able to run away or would she have been hurt worse? Knowing Kennedy, she would've stood her ground. She would've gone on the attack, and a man armed with a bat or a board could've done some serious damage.

The thought of her being beaten worse than she was made Jameson murderous. As it was he was fighting to keep his control. He wanted nothing more than to be hunting down the man who'd hurt her, but he knew she needed him more and his vengeance would have to wait.

"But—"

"No buts, Kennedy," he said firmly. "It's not your fault."

She changed the topic to her mom and Jameson told her he'd called and checked in with Lola. She and Janice were more than happy to have a man in the house to cook for. Holden had also called and confirmed both women were force-feeding him and if he had to stay more than one night Nixon was paying for a gym membership.

"That sounds like my mom. She believes a way to a man's heart is through his stomach. She always loved to cook and bake. But now, she has a hard time standing at the stove so she just bosses Miss Janice." Kennedy smiled. "She has physical therapy tomorrow. I'll have to go over and get her."

"Holden has it under control. He's going to take her."

"That's too much."

"No, it's not. Besides, he said he wants to watch what exercises the therapist has her doing."

"Why would he want to watch that?" Kennedy scrunched her nose. "Therapy is two hours."

"Holden was injured in training. He went to PT for three months and wasn't seeing any improvement. So he decided it was time for him to learn what he could and take over his recovery. He was obsessive about it and took online kinesiology and physiology classes. He knows a thing or two about the mechanics of movement."

"Really?" She looked shocked.

"What? Did you think we were all just dumb sailors?" He smiled.

"No, of course not."

Jameson heard boots stomping up the stairs. He stood, his hand automatically going to his hip, his hand hovering over his sidearm. Chasin came into view and Jameson relaxed.

"Jesus, you big gorilla." Chasin chuckled. "I would've

announced my approach if I would've known you were gonna draw on me."

"I didn't even unholster my weapon, you big baby," Jameson returned.

"It takes you under a second from holster to trigger pull. I was as good as dead."

"Do you ever not exaggerate?"

"Not when I'm trying to get sympathy from a beautiful woman." Chasin's eyes landed on the bed and all the humor left his face. "How ya feelin', Kennedy?"

"I've been better."

"How are the headaches?"

If anyone could empathize with Kennedy it was Chasin. He had what they called a soft head. It seemed like the smallest of hits would give Chasin a concussion.

"I haven't had one today. But if I move too quickly it feels like an ice pick is being driven into my forehead."

"That sounds like an accurate description," he told her. "It will take a few more days for those to go away."

"Everything go okay in Ohio?" Jameson asked.

"Yeah, found the guy getting a blowjob behind a bar. Worst part was having to wait until it was over, because I did not want to grapple with the man with his dick flopping around. And it took forever, either the woman gave shit head, or he has some serious stamina because it took her the better part of thirty minutes. I was thinking of offering the poor woman an ice pack for her jaw after she'd worked so hard. As soon as he was tucked in and zipped up, I took him into custody. He actually thanked me for letting him get one more BJ before he went down."

Chasin shook his head and smiled. "Dropped him off in Baltimore and came home with a check. All in all, I'd say it was easy money, except for the watching the blowjob part."

"That's gross," Kennedy announced.

"You're telling me." Chasin mock shuttered.

Chasin was still working the drama edge. But Jameson didn't care. He was too busy enjoying the smile on Kennedy's face.

"Talked to Jonny," Chasin announced. "He's officially inviting us into the investigation. He needs all of us at the station tomorrow to be temporarily deputized. After that he'll share everything they have so far. He did mention he had a tip, but wouldn't go into details over the phone or until we were official."

Jameson wanted to kick his friend. It was good news the sheriff's department was going to share what they had. So far it had only been a one-way street of them passing along what they'd found but that's where the flow of information stopped. Jonny couldn't reciprocate. But as welcomed as the news was, Kennedy was no longer smiling.

"I've been thinking. It's pretty hard for someone to hide in a town as small as this," Kennedy started. "And after my mom told us the rumors about Peyton being Reggie's biological son and you guys found that Peyton owns part of Reggie's business, what if Reggie's hiding Peyton on one of his properties? If Reggie's delivering provisions, Peyton wouldn't have to leave."

"Smart woman," Chasin praised.

"We'll start running down any property he's purchased that still has the electric turned on," Jameson instructed.

"And starting tomorrow, I'll tail him. If he is making deliveries to Peyton he'll take me right to him," Chasin said.

"Hey! We're home!" Nixon's voice boomed up the stairs.

"You wanna go down or we can eat up here?" Jameson asked.

"Go down."

Chasin left the room and Jameson got Kennedy sorted. She wasn't pleased when he carried her down the stairs and set her on the couch, but being Jameson was twice her size, there wasn't much she could do except complain.

They'd filled Nixon and McKenna in on Kennedy's suspicions and both had agreed she was on to something.

With her cheesesteak on a plate in her lap, Kennedy announced, "I want to help."

Before the three men in the room could protest, McKenna answered, "That'd be great."

"McKenna," Nixon warned.

"What? She can help me narrow down Reggie's properties. I could use the help."

McKenna did not need the help. As a matter of fact, Kennedy would slow her down. McKenna was their resident computer genius. She could easily hack into any computer system and get them any intel they needed.

"We've been digging into Reggie, but we've been

going soft sticking to legal parameters. I think it's time to—"

"No, McKenna. We need to build a case. We can't do that if the information is obtained illegally. And tomorrow you'll be deputized, you cannot break the law," Nixon told her.

"No one will know," McKenna huffed. "Besides, we don't have to use what I find, but it will point us in the right direction. I could hack his cellphone in two point five seconds and you know it. I could have his camera and mic on and we could listen. And if I do it tonight before I'm deputized, then Jonny won't be on the hook if I am caught."

"But you'll be on the hook," Jameson reminded McKenna.

Fire lit in the woman's eyes before she narrowed them on Jameson. "So? Do you think I care? Reggie Coleman is behind Kennedy getting hurt. I want him nailed down, now, before he tries something else. And all ye with little faith in my skills are assuming I'd get caught. Which you all know I won't."

"I don't want you to get into trouble, McKenna," Kennedy spoke up. "Actually I don't want anyone in trouble or hurt. Maybe—"

"Don't go there, Kennedy," Jameson started. "We are all in this with you. And McKenna's right. We've been playing by the rules and it's got us nowhere. We need to tap his phone, but I'm going to do it."

"You don't know how," McKenna snorted.

"You're right. But you can stand beside me and tell me what to do."

"That's ridiculous."

"No. That's me being culpable and you keepin' your nose clean."

"Whatever." McKenna shook her head.

Jameson sat next to Kennedy with his own plate piled high with pizza.

"I don't want you getting into trouble," she murmured.

"Babe, me hacking into Reggie Coleman's cellphone is the least of our concerns. When I get my hands on the fucker who hurt you...now that's when we need to start worrying." Kennedy's eyes widened and Jameson continued. "Eat your dinner. When we're done, we'll go upstairs and get you a shower and settled for bed."

Much to Jameson's surprise Kennedy didn't argue. She simply nodded her head and dug into her sandwich.

"I had no idea someone could hack a cellphone and turn on the camera. Here I thought by disabling the GPS on my phone so it couldn't be tracked, I was doing something," Kennedy grumbled.

"Not so much," McKenna returned and smiled.

McKenna chattered on about how much help Kennedy would be in the office. It finally dawned on Jameson what she was doing and Jameson smiled. The woman was brilliant. With Kennedy in the office, she'd be under constant guard and there'd be no argument. And by Kennedy helping, her mind would be occupied and she'd feel useful, leaving less room in her head to think about the attack or that her business had taken a hit. Now that the sheriff's office had requested Gemini Group's help, they'd be paying the bills. Tomorrow, Jameson was going to talk to Nix about putting Kennedy on the payroll.

That would be a hard sell, not on Nixon's part, but getting Kennedy to accept.

Jameson was feeling a little lighter. This would all be over soon and he and Kennedy could get back to their lives.

At her home, in her bed, where they both belonged.

20

KENNEDY

What a difference a shower and a good night's rest did for someone's disposition.

It may've helped that the shower had included Jameson climbing in with me and washing me from head to toe. Then he'd clothed me and put me to bed before he did the same for himself.

After he'd settled me in his favorite position with my head on his chest and my arm resting on his bare stomach, he told me stories about growing up in Eureka, California. Hearing stories about his childhood saddened me, but it also explained a great deal. He'd started working at a salmon factory before he was old enough for a work permit and had been paid under the table. Every weekend for years he put in as many hours as the owner would allow and gave his mother, who worked as a maid in one of the many historic hotels in town, all of his money.

What little he brought home helped, but not enough,

and he and his mother moved a lot, either after eviction, or when she missed the first rent payment and knew they'd be kicked out so she'd leave before it happened. The most heartbreaking part was when Jameson had said he'd gotten so good at moving he could have their belongings packed and ready in under two hours.

I couldn't imagine. I'd lived in the same house my whole life. The more Jameson talked the more I wanted to crawl on top of him and shield him from the memories. I knew it was crazy but I wanted to firmly plant him in my house and lock the door so he could never leave. I wanted him to have a home. A place where he wouldn't have to keep his stuff packed because the place he was staying was temporary. Even his room at Nixon's wasn't permanent. He lived liked he was a guest in that house.

The longest he'd stayed in one place after his dickhead father had bolted was his last year of high school. And that was only because he'd quit playing sports and got a job at a logging company making enough money to pay the rent on a two-bedroom apartment. They'd stayed there for eighteen months. Then he moved his mom into a one-bedroom when he left for the Navy and continued to pay her rent until she could afford it on her own. With Jameson gone, she could afford to live on her own.

Which only made things worse for him—thinking he'd been a burden to her all those years.

It was utter bullshit. A child is not a burden, but when I'd tried to explain that to him all he said was, 'babe' and I dropped the subject. It was painful for him to talk about, yet he'd shared it with me. I wouldn't push him into seeing the truth. Not yet. But one day, I'd convince him his mother didn't see her beloved son as a hardship or hindrance. They'd both caught a raw deal.

Now I was sitting in Jameson's office running down a list of properties that Reggie Coleman owned. We'd narrowed it down to the ones that had homes, and McKenna had taught me how to check if there was electricity being delivered.

So far, I'd gone through ten addresses since they'd been gone and five had power hooked up. I still had ten more to go.

How in the hell had Reggie Coleman amassed so many listings? Sure, some of them were junkers and according to mortgage records, he'd bought them each for under thirty thousand dollars, but that added up. Especially when you took into consideration he also had purchased land valued at a million dollars. I hadn't taken the time to do the actual math, but averaging what Chester River Holdings owned without the rental income, he'd acquired nearly fifteen million dollars in property.

Now that may not be a lot in the city, but for a small town land developer in Kent County, that was a whole hell of a lot. Reggie lived in a nice home, drove a brand-new pick-up, his wife always had a top-of-the-line model of whatever she drove, but I couldn't imagine him having fifteen million dollars at his disposal. He had to be in debt out his ass, especially because he was sitting on the properties and not flipping them.

And to think the bastard had only offered me half of

what my fifty acres was worth, like he was doing me a favor.

What a prick.

I heard beeping from downstairs and I reached for my phone. When Jameson had left, he'd said they would be gone about an hour. It had only been twenty minutes. Footsteps had me pulling up Jameson's number. My finger was hovering over the call button when Weston yelled if anyone was there.

I shrank back into the seat and tried to calm my racing heart. Nothing like overreacting.

"Hey." Weston popped his head into the office, both of his hands bracing him in the frame.

"Hi."

"You okay?" he asked, studying me.

"Yeah. You just scared me."

"The alarm was set," he reminded me. "It would've blared like a mother if someone came in."

"I know, Jameson told me. I'm just a little jumpy."

He nodded his understanding and his eyes went to the computer screen.

"What are you working on?"

"Checking which of Reggie's houses have electricity."

"Find any?"

I ran down what I'd found as Weston came in and plopped down in the extra seat.

"Good work. When you're done, we'll go check them out."

"How was DC?" I asked, taking a break from my search.

"Too long. It's always good to see Alec and catch up, but I don't understand how he lives in that place. The traffic alone is enough to make me crazy."

"Sorry, I don't know who that is."

"Alec Hall is our contact at Homeland. Good guy, former SEAL, he left the teams a few years before we did and went to DHS. I think he's regretting it now, working for the government means rules and red tape. Alec is a lot like us and doesn't play well with others. I'd be surprised if he lasts another three years."

I nodded as if I understood what he was talking about even though I really didn't. I knew nothing about Homeland Security or how the government ran.

"Jameson said you were there about a contract. Did you get it?"

Weston tilted his head and once again he was staring at me funny. "Jameson told you that?"

"Is that a problem?" I answered with a question.

"No. No problem." Weston righted his head and gave me what was supposed to be a reassuring smile but it did nothing to ease my discomfort. "Yeah, we got the contract. There's been chatter about drugs being trafficked using the Maryland waterways. I mostly sat through meetings with the Coast Guard and the Delmarva Pilots' Association."

"I take it you don't like meetings?"

"Not even a little bit."

Weston sat back and the chair squeaked from supporting his large frame. He crossed his leg, resting his ankle on his knee, and crossed his arms over his chest.

"Can I ask you something?"

"Sure." Though I wasn't sure I wanted him to ask me anything now that his expression was serious.

"Why are you here running properties instead of getting your ground worked up or building a new beehive?"

Jeez, nothing like a slap in the face.

"I'm helping—"

"No, you're not. You're hiding."

My back shot straight and as much as I wished I could conceal how much his accusation hurt, I couldn't. Mostly because it was the truth.

"I'm not trying to be a dick. You're Jameson's woman. You're obviously welcome here and at the house anytime. But this isn't you."

"How would you know? You don't know me."

He chuckled though it held no humor.

"I know you well enough to know you're the only person who can handle Jameson's gruff, asshole attitude. I know you're the only woman who's ever made him laugh. I've seen you take both Nixon and Jameson straight on when you don't like that they're trying to boss you. I know you take care of yourself and your mother. I *know* you're stronger than this. So why are you here?"

"Someone broke into my house—"

"Yep."

"And then someone attacked me—"

"Yep."

"They burnt down my hives and killed my crops."

"Know that, too."

"Can't I take a fucking minute?" I asked irately.

"Sure, you can take all the minutes you need as long as they don't turn into weeks, then months. Everyone needs to regroup, revise, and plan. Is that what you're doing, or are you giving up and hiding? Because I have to tell you, that would be disappointing. I didn't think you were a quitter."

Ouch. That hurt like a son-of-a-bitch. I wasn't a quitter. Never had been, not once in my whole life had I not tried and tried until I couldn't try anymore.

"I'm not a quitter," I said, even though that was exactly what I was doing and my stomach roiled.

"That's exactly what you're doing if you allow this setback to ruin you. So, take your minute, then get your ass back in gear. We all have your back. All you have to do is ask. Hell, even if you don't, none of us are going to let you go at this alone."

"I don't like asking for help," I admitted. "I don't like feeling like I'm taking advantage of my friends or taking handouts."

"Tough tits, sweetheart. You think I've made it through thirty-two years on this earth without needing help? You'd be wrong. You know what makes me, Nix, Chasin, Jameson, and Holden such a strong team? Know how we all survived when shit went to shit out in the field? Because we had each other's backs. We helped each other. We trusted each other. You never push your team away, you lean on them, you ask for help and trust they will come through for you."

"But you're—"

"If you tell me we're not your team, you're gonna seriously piss me off," he bit out.

"But—"

"You're Jameson's—that means you're one of us."

"I don't know what that means." I threw my arms in the air in frustration.

"It means that Jameson has claimed you. It cannot be lost on you that he avoids people like the plague. He doesn't trust anyone but us. He hides behind his bad attitude to protect himself. But when he lets you in, you have his loyalty for life. He tried, but didn't succeed in pushing you out of his life. He spent seven days moping and if you can believe it, his disposition was worse than his normal hateful insolence. He struggled with letting you go, thinking he was doing the right thing. He spent those days watching the video feed from the cameras outside of your house, like a hawk. And at the first sign you were in danger, he did what we all knew he wanted to do—he couldn't get to you fast enough. Don't forget to be the strong woman he fell in love with, because none of us have."

"He doesn't—"

"Not my business." Weston held a hand up.

But even as I tried to deny it, Jameson's words echoed in my head. *Maybe I could stop dwelling on it if I could forget holding the woman I love while her blood seeped from her head and soaked my skin.* And in the darkness of my hospital room while Jameson held me tight, I'd finally said out loud what I'd known for a while—I'd fallen in love with him.

"I'll let you finish your searches." Weston stood. "Think about what I said."

He left Jameson's office without me confirming I would follow his instructions. He was right, I knew he was, but I wasn't ready to admit that I was behaving like a coward. I wasn't ready to ask for help even though Jameson had offered it. There were a lot of things I wasn't ready to process, so I went back to searching Reggie Coleman's properties, and like a big, fat chicken I buried it.

21

JAMESON

They'd been back from being deputized for an hour and something was wrong with Kennedy. Jameson hadn't asked her because he had a feeling she'd lie and say 'nothing,' which would irritate him. He knew she wasn't tired because last night she'd slept like a rock.

And he'd know because while she snoozed on his chest, he'd laid awake. Every time he'd closed his eyes, he'd see her bleeding. So somewhere around midnight he'd given up sleep in exchange for listening to her breathe. But she'd never stirred in his arms. Her weight was comforting but not enough for Jameson to get some shuteye.

Kennedy had finished the searches she'd been working on and they'd split the list. Jameson and Weston took half, and Nix and Chasin the other. Holden was staying back in the office with McKenna and Kennedy.

He'd walked her back into his office and closed the door. Memories of the last time he'd had her pressed against the wall flooded his brain. He'd been a monumental dick. It was a miracle she'd forgiven him. He wasn't going to dwell on the whys and wherefores she'd allowed him back into her life, he was simply going to take it and be grateful—and not squander the second chance. He knew he'd never get a third if he'd fucked this up.

Jameson's hands went to the sides of her face and gently brushed the apples of her cheeks with his thumbs.

"You are so beautiful, Kennedy."

Her face heated pink and she whispered, "Thank you."

"I shouldn't be gone that long. Please don't leave the office."

"I won't."

Jameson leaned forward and brushed his lips against hers, desperately wanting to kiss her but knowing it would lead to him wanting to touch her, and with her concussion she wasn't near ready. He'd never do anything that would cause her pain or put her in harm's way. And him roughly taking her against the wall would be the very definition of harm's way.

"Be careful," she murmured when he pulled back.

"I will."

Jameson smiled and couldn't remember anyone other than his team telling him to be careful. The concern settled in his chest and another piece of solace clicked into place. She was fitting one jagged fragment at a time back together. Though he wasn't entirely sure he'd ever been whole, at least not after his father had abandoned him.

He took Kennedy by the hand and led her back to Nixon's office where McKenna was listening to silence as she waited for Reggie to make a call, or pull his phone out of his pocket so she could listen in.

McKenna hadn't allowed Jameson to hack Reggie's phone. She'd waited until Jameson had taken Kennedy to bed and she'd done it herself. No one was actually concerned she'd get caught or that Reggie would know they could now listen to his calls and access his camera. McKenna was good at what she did.

After saying goodbye, the team left and Jameson waited until Weston was pulling away from the curb before he turned to look at his friend.

"What'd you say to Kennedy?"

Weston's reaction was immediate. The corners of his eyes wrinkled and he scowled.

"Seriously? You think I'd go there with your woman?"

"Hell, no. But you said something to her. When I left, she was excited to track Coleman and when I got back, she looked like someone had kicked her puppy."

"I didn't tell her anything you wouldn't've told her if you weren't babying her."

"Babying her? What the fuck does that mean?"

"It means, I'm not the one that loves her. I'm not the one who's reliving finding my woman bloody. She needed to hear the truth, so I told her. Again, nothing you wouldn't have said yourself if your head was on straight."

Jameson was getting pissed with the round robin conversation and Weston's evasion tactics.

"Which was?"

"I told her she needed to pull herself together and not quit."

"What the fuck, Weston? She was hit over the goddamn head with a two-by-four."

"She was. And if you let her, she's gonna hold onto that thread—"

"Hold onto it? Are you fucking serious? She just got out of the hospital."

"She did. And you know damn good and well the longer she has time to think on it the harder it will be for her to go back. Rip the scab off."

"And what? Watch her bleed some more."

"Yep. Then clean her up and help her heal. You know I'm right. When Holden fucked up his knee, we didn't let him wallow in it for two seconds. We immediately started riding his ass to rehab it."

Weston had lost his ever-loving mind. Kennedy wasn't a Navy SEAL. She hadn't injured herself in an accident and needed to recover as quickly as possible before she faced a medical board. She was his woman, and he would not treat her to "The only easy day was yesterday" SEAL mentality.

"Not even close to being the same," Jameson settled on saying.

"To you it's not, because you're lickin' your wounds right alongside her. You didn't push her to go back inside her house and face what happened because *you* didn't want to face it. And I don't blame you. I wouldn't want to go back to the place where my woman was victimized either."

"She's not a fucking victim," Jameson growled and Weston smiled.

Bastard.

"You're right. She's not. So stop treating her like one. She needs you to be the man she fell in love with. The asshole who calls you to the mat when you want to crawl inside of yourself and not face reality. You're doing her no favors by letting her hide in your room instead of taking her hand and facing her shit head-on. Reggie Coleman thinks he has her on the ropes. He's probably sittin' back waiting for her call. Fuck him. She needs to shove the stick he already has up his ass through his throat until he gags on it. And right now, she's not strong enough, which means *you* better get to shoving, friend."

Jameson sat back in his seat and stared out the windshield. Damn if Weston wasn't right. About all of it. Jameson had been relieved when Kennedy hadn't wanted to stay at her house. Relief so strong it had washed over his skin like silk when she'd said she wanted to go back to his house.

His jaw ached from grinding his molars. To loosen the tension, he stopped and licked his lips.

"I'm scared if I push her before she's ready she'll bolt and go stay with her mom," Jameson begrudgingly admitted.

"Since when have you been afraid of a little backlash and resistance?"

"Since now," Jameson returned. "Since I've fallen in love with her and the thought of her pulling away from me physically hurts my chest."

"All the more reason to set her straight and get your head sorted. You're looking at this all wrong. There's a storm around you and all you see is debris. But what I see is, this latest incident has cleared your path and you're not taking advantage of it. Be what she needs you to be. Make this better for her. We'll all take Reggie down, but you're the only one who can make her stand when she wants to crumble. And we both know if she gives in, she'll regret it and hate herself for quitting. We've all needed a hand-up—don't let her use your hand as a crutch."

Jameson glanced over and studied his friend, not knowing when he'd gotten so wise. Maybe he'd always been, but Jameson never had an occasion to need a come-to-Jesus talk. He'd always kept to himself and been the one to offer support while dealing with his demons in private.

"Thanks," he muttered his appreciation.

"Anytime. And for what it's worth, she's perfect for you. Don't fuck it up."

Kennedy *was* perfect. Everything about her stirred something deep inside Jameson. He needed to get his shit straight because he would not let her stumble. And so far, he hadn't been doing a very good job at keeping her upright.

THEY'D ALREADY STOPPED at two houses and found them empty. Weston pulled down the driveway of the third and didn't bother trying to be stealthy. If Peyton was inside, there'd be nowhere for him to run without being seen. The modest one-story house was surrounded by an open field and he'd be easily seen if he tried to bolt.

As they got closer it was easy to see no one had cared for the home in a long time. The wood siding was peeling, and in some places, boards were missing. All of the windows had been broken and the screen door was off the top hinge and rested crooked against the frame. Yet, the power was connected. It made no sense, the house was in shambles.

Jameson kicked the front door in, the wood splintering under his boot.

"Why the hell would the door be locked when all the windows are busted?" Weston asked what Jameson had been thinking.

"No clue," Jameson said and looked around the room. "Someone's been here recently."

The walls inside looked just as bad as the outside, if not worse. Tattered old furniture that was probably left by the previous owners because there was no way someone would move this shit into the house willingly was scattered around the room haphazardly. The out-of-date wallpaper was peeling off the walls in sheets and there was a thick layer of dust on everything, except one table which had takeout bags littering the surface.

"Oh, yeah, he's staying here," Weston agreed and headed for the hall.

Both men had their weapons drawn as they searched the first room, coming up empty. The second room the same. They opened the third and there was a blow-up mattress on the floor with a sleeping bag unzipped on top of it.

A scraping sound from the closet caught their attention and Jameson lifted his hand and silently motioned to the door. Weston nodded his understanding and quietly got into place, waiting to open the door when Jameson was ready. With a lift of his chin, Jameson gave the signal and the door opened, revealing Peyton standing in a pair of boxers with his hands in the air.

Pussy.

He wasn't going to fight, which was a crying shame because Jameson had been looking forward to unleashing hell on the man. But the one thing Jameson wouldn't do, no matter how angry he was, was beat a man when he'd clearly given himself up.

Goddamn, morals suck.

That didn't mean when Jameson reached into the closet and yanked the man out, he'd done it carefully, and when he'd tossed Peyton on the filthy floor, he'd certainly knocked the wind out of him. With a knee in the small of the prone man's back, Jameson secured his wrists extra-tight with a zip tie hoping the plastic bit into his skin.

Weston already had his phone to his ear calling Jonny.

"You're a slippery motherfucker to find." Then Jameson remembered he'd been deputized and he wasn't acting as a bounty hunter chasing a skip. There were procedures that needed to be followed.

They had Peyton on a minimum of breaking and entering, which necessitated Jameson reading the piece of shit his rights and telling him he was under arrest.

By the time Weston had called Nixon to tell him they'd found Peyton, and Jameson hauled the man to his feet, they could hear sirens approaching.

Jonny and another deputy appeared in the hallway, both armed but holstering their weapons when they saw Peyton was secure.

"Found him hiding in the closet," Jameson announced.

"Did you search the house?" Jonny asked.

"Nope. We were waiting on you."

"Newton, take him out," Jonny instructed the deputy next to him.

Once Peyton and Newton were out of the house, Jonny turned to Jameson and Weston, his scowl set, and he asked, "Do I want to know how you entered the premises?"

Jameson looked at Weston before his eyes went back to Jonny's. "We got here and the door was open. We knocked and thought we heard someone in distress so we entered."

Jonny's gaze slid to Weston and he confirmed Jameson's story.

"Did you read him his rights?"

"Yep. I even pulled the notecard out of my pocket and read it word for word." That part was the truth,

Jameson had read the notecard Jonny had given them. "We didn't have gloves so we didn't touch anything."

"Found something," a man called from the other room and all three of them made their way back into the living room.

"Looks like a key to a motorcycle or a four-wheeler." The deputy motioned to a table with the leftover takeout trash.

Gotcha, motherfucker.

22

KENNEDY

"Thanks again for taking my mom to PT this morning," I told Holden.

He'd just gotten back from picking us up lunch and we were sitting around the conference room table. McKenna had her laptop open and the volume up so we could listen in on Reggie Coleman. So far, all we'd heard was static, which McKenna explained was the sound of the phone being in Reggie's pocket, and a muffled conversation with a flooring subcontractor.

The conversation had been painful to hear, because Reggie was a dick and had berated the poor man for fifteen minutes about a nick in the wood the man had finished laying. And by all accounts the mark had been small but Reggie had insisted a section of the flooring be replaced even after the subcontractor explained it could be buffed out.

What a jerk.

"Not a problem. I talked to her therapist and he

agreed to add TENS therapy to her PT. Studies show that electronic simulation can help a stroke patient regain muscle movement. The earlier you start the better chance there is for mobility and muscle control to return. Your mom's made great gains and she does have some movement on her left side, which is a good indication the TENS unit will help her."

For the first time, hope started to swell in my chest. My mom's doctor had never been all that confident she'd get back more than the small movement she already had. From the beginning he'd had the attitude that my mom should accept that she'd be partially paralyzed and learn to live with it. Lola Lane didn't learn to live with anything she didn't want to live with. But that didn't mean there hadn't been times when my mom had been depressed about it.

But she hadn't given up.

Of course she hadn't, because Lanes didn't quit. *So was I ready to?*

"I really appreciate it. The doctor never told us that was an option."

"I got your back, girl." Holden winked and tucked into his ginormous burger.

I'd been hearing that a lot lately, that people had my back. Yet it was still hard for me to believe that they'd all welcomed me into their circle. And my mom, too.

There was a loud rustling sound coming from McKenna's computer, then a clear voice.

"Is he okay?" a woman asked.

"For God's sake, Deloris, he's fine." We all sat up

straighter and strained to listen to Reggie speaking to Peyton's mother. "I didn't come all the way out here to talk about your boy."

"*Our* boy," she snapped.

"Yeah, yeah, whatever. Why you standing across the room instead over here greeting me?"

There was silence, then it sounded like heels clicking on tile. The sound stopped and finally Reggie said, "Get your ass in the bedroom. I only have ten minutes. Bend over the bed, pull your dress up, and leave those shoes on. You know how much I love fucking you in high heels." He stopped for a second and my stomach roiled listening to Reggie. "Better yet, bend over the couch. No sense in wasting time."

Gross.

I glanced at McKenna and her pale face told me she was thinking the same thing I was. Were we really going to listen to Reggie huff and puff while he had sex with Deloris? God knows I didn't want to hear it.

Holden had abandoned his burger and his lips curled. "Turn this shit down. He's already ruined doggy-style couch sex for me. Which totally sucks because it's a favorite of mine." I did not need to know that about Holden. "If I have to listen to him pump away at her he'll turn me off sex for eternity."

"What if he talks during sex?" McKenna asked. "We need to hear everything he says."

"Chasin can listen when he gets back. He has an iron stomach."

"Poor Chasin. He just had to watch a skip get a BJ. Maybe Weston should listen," I told him.

"Weston's too squeamish. He makes gagging noises when he smells something rotten. Besides, I doubt that man will have enough breath in him to talk. I've seen him. He's out of shape."

This was true. Reggie Coleman's gut looked like he was fifteen months pregnant with a giraffe.

McKenna turned down the volume and said, "We'll give him five minutes. He said he only had ten but I don't think he'll need that long."

The three of us were silent as we all watched the time on the corner of McKenna's laptop. I nearly jumped out of my chair when Holden's phone rang.

"Yo," he answered. "Great. Tell Chasin he can catch up with Coleman at Deloris Marshall's house. He's there fuckin' her now. But he better hurry. The festivities have started and he doesn't strike me as a man who takes his time." Holden was quiet for a minute before he nodded and said, "Right. I'll tell her."

He disconnected the call and set his phone on the table. When he turned to me, he smirked. "That was Jameson. He said for you not to listen to Reggie and Deloris going at it."

"Okay, why?"

Holden's smile deepened. "For the same reasons *I* don't wanna listen."

"Oh." His meaning dawning on me.

Jameson didn't want me turned off of sex for all of eternity. Which I would've been if I'd had to listen to a live action porn starring the man I hated with every fiber of my being.

"He also said they found Peyton and he's in custody. Coleman obviously has no clue, which is good news. He'll carry on with business as usual."

"Why didn't you start with that?" I huffed, feeling a hundred times better now that Peyton wasn't lurking around.

"Because I have Jameson's back, too, so I prioritized."

McKenna giggled and turned up the volume on her laptop. She quickly turned the sound off when a woman's over-exaggerated, very fake moan filled the room.

"Why do women do that?" McKenna scrunched her nose. "Don't men know it's not real?"

"Men who pay attention do. Men who are out to get theirs and don't care about takin' care of their woman eat that shit up. It feeds their ego. They don't care if it is fake —as long as she's moanin' he can pretend he's givin' it to her good and get off," Holden explained.

"That was kinda a rhetorical question, Holden," McKenna told him.

"Well, now you know." Holden tipped his chin and smiled. "And you're welcome for the clarification."

I couldn't stop myself from smiling at their banter. I'd been so busy working I hadn't bothered to cultivate new friendships, and the ones I did have I hadn't taken very good care of, so they all simply withered away.

I wouldn't make that mistake again.

McKenna turned up the sound again and we caught the tail end of a conversation.

"...okay, fine. Will you call me tonight?" Deloris asked.

"Can't tonight. Lois wants me to take her to the fundraiser at the firehouse."

"Fine," Deloris grumbled.

"Don't do that, DeeDee," he cajoled. "You know I'd rather be here with you. She doesn't ask for much. I have to go."

"I know you keep saying that. But I'm lonely and you've been promising for years you were done going back to her."

"It won't be too much longer, pussy cat," he sweet-talked, and Holden made a choking sound.

"I just miss you when you're gone."

"Give daddy some sugar before I go. I'll be back in the morning and I'll take care of your..."

"LaLaLaLa," McKenna chanted and covered her ears.

There were some slurping sounds before the line went back to static.

"Ohmygod," McKenna breathed. "I couldn't take another second of that. I think he was going to try dirty-talking her."

I grimaced at the thought. Good thing McKenna had started with her LaLaLas because I liked when Jameson talked dirty to me, and if I heard Reggie's version of it I'd be turned-off for life.

"Why do women fall for that shit? He's a lying cheating asshole."

"Women who have self-worth don't," McKenna

started. "They see through the lies men tell and they'd never take another woman's man to bed. But women who are starved for attention will buy into the lie and live the fantasy because the alternative is loneliness. And for some, it's the thrill. They want control, and making a man fall in love with them and divorce his wife or leave his girlfriend gives them the power they crave."

"That was a rhetorical question, McKenna," Holden deadpanned.

"Well, now you know." McKenna shrugged.

Holden threw his head back and roared with laughter. Nixon and Chasin walked in and looked around the room before they both broke out in wide smiles.

"Hey, babe," Nix greeted McKenna and made his way to her side and kissed the top of her head.

"You guys just missed the show," she told him.

"Before you tell them, I want it on record I had Chasin's back," I announced.

Chasin looked over at me and smiled. "Good to know."

"But she did throw Weston under the bus," Holden added.

"He's used to it. It's fun to watch him heave." Nix chuckled.

Holden filled in Nix and Chasin about Reggie and Deloris and Chasin put his hands up.

"No fuckin' way am I listening to that shit. I'm still recovering. Weston can review it. It's not like he has to smell anything, which is his issue. It's damn well his turn."

My phone rang and I fished it out of my back pocket. Seeing it was Jameson, I answered.

"Hey, Jameson."

"Hey, babe. Did Holden tell you?"

"Yes. Good news."

"It is. One step closer. I'm going to be a while at the station. You have a couple of options. Stay at the office until I'm done, Chasin will take you back to my place, or you can go with Nix and McKenna to their place. But I may be done in time to pick you up myself. Weston decided since we were closer to Deloris's that he'd go follow Reggie. But he'll be at your mom's tonight."

I noticed he didn't give me the option to go back to my house and I wasn't sure if I was grateful he hadn't pushed, or upset with myself for freaking out and tying his hands.

"I think I'll stay here for a while and keep McKenna company as she listens. It's mostly boring when he's not trying to get some...you know."

"Yeah, I know." Jameson chuckled. "I heard it was bad."

"So bad. And then at the end he totally sweet-talked her. The whole thing was like a bad porn movie."

There was silence before he asked, "You watch a lot of porn?"

"Enough to know the difference between the bad stuff and the..." I stopped and my skin heated when laughter broke out in the room.

Damn. damn, damn. How could I have forgotten I was in a room full of people?

"Right. We'll talk about that later when we're in private."

I felt the heat rise into my cheeks. "No, we won't."

"Yeah, babe. We totally will. Now I have to know what you think qualifies as good porn. Though I think I already have a clear understanding of what turns you on."

"I'm hanging up now, Jameson."

"Kennedy?"

"Yeah?"

I was met with a beat of silence before he exhaled and said, "Never mind. I'll be home as soon as I can."

Home.

"Okay. Be safe."

"I will. You, too."

Jameson disconnected and I looked around the room. "Not a word."

"Touchy, touchy." Holden laughed. "It's not like we were going to ask you to swap porn collections or anything."

"Speak for yourself," Chasin said. "Mine's pretty sparse. I was hoping she'd have some good recommendations."

"Don't look at me." Nixon shrugged. "I have no need to watch that shit."

"Good answer," McKenna mumbled, and once again the room was filled with raucous laughter.

McKenna caught my eye and shook her head with what was meant to show her annoyance. But instead all it showed was her adoration for a group of rowdy men who held nothing back. Not their loyalty, not their care and concern for their team, and not their inappropriate comments.

Nothing was off-limits. If they liked you, they teased you. If they didn't, you'd never get close enough to them to see them for who they really were.

A team of men who stopped at nothing to protect the ones they loved.

23

JAMESON

Last night, Jameson actually got a few hours of sleep. With Peyton Marshall behind bars some of the tightness in his chest had loosened. But until Reggie Coleman joined his son, Jameson couldn't fully relax.

He'd also fallen asleep thinking about what Weston had said to him. He was still grappling with the knowledge that he was going to have to push Kennedy today, but knowing his team had his back had made his decision easier.

Part of what had taken Jameson's time yesterday after Peyton's arrest was the phone call to the Eastern Shore Beekeepers Association. Originally Jameson had called to get information on the materials he'd need to build her a proper hive. But when he'd called and explained the situation, he found that Kennedy belonged to the group and had attended their bi-monthly meetings since she'd started keeping bees. The president of the club, Harold

Ward, was personally meeting him and Kennedy at her house later that day.

Harold had given him a list of materials Jameson needed to purchase at the lumberyard and Harold was bringing the bees. The man had explained that it was best to start a hive in the spring, but being as Kennedy's land was appropriately prepped for bees with its field of bee-loving wildflowers, it should work out with a little added glucose to help them winter over.

Yesterday when Jameson arrived at Kennedy's to clear the old burnt hives and drop off the lumber, he was happy he'd been alone. He hadn't expected such a violent reaction to the area. But when he saw the blood trail, his step faltered and it had taken him several minutes of reminding himself that Kennedy was alive and safe before he could continue.

His gut still rejected the idea that Peyton had simply been arrested and Jameson didn't get the chance to knock his head off and teach him a lesson. But Jameson could not bring himself to beat the man even after what he'd done to Kennedy. It would make him no better than the scumbags he despised. He prided himself on being a better man.

Kennedy stirred in his arms and he laid still, enjoying the feel of her pressed against him. Her thigh hitched higher and brushed his morning hard-on and he tried to adjust her leg away from his throbbing erection.

It had been the best kind of torture waking up with her half-naked form against him each morning. And showering with her, washing her from head to toe, not being able to take it further had been the true test of his self-control. But he wasn't going there with her until her doctor had given her a hundred percent clean bill of health. And after that he still might wait a while longer. It wasn't that he couldn't be gentle while he made love to her, but he knew she liked to test his limits and beg him to go harder, and he wasn't sure if he could deny her. It was better not to let the bird out of the cage, so to speak.

"Babe," he warned when she moved her leg over his dick again and started to rub back and forth.

"Jameson," she whined. "It's been long enough."

"You're not ready."

"I'm really tired of hearing that," she retorted.

Jameson couldn't stop the smile that formed at hearing her annoyance. He was happy to know she was as needy as he was, but he wouldn't dare let her catch him gloating about it.

"Soon, Kennedy. And I promise to make up for lost time."

"Yeah, sure," she grumbled and he gently reversed their positions so he was on top of her looking down at her sleepy eyes.

"I swear it's absolute torture for me not to be able to touch you the way I want to. The way you want me to. Not to be able to feel your breath on my neck when I'm moving inside of you, or hear you pant my name when you come for me. I need that connection with you—need it—not just want it. I crave the intimacy of us coming together."

He brushed back a lock of her hair. "But, I'm

enjoying a different kind of intimacy, having you in my arms every night and just talking until we fall asleep. I've never experienced this. I've never wanted to know everything about someone before. So while I can't wait to finally get to bend your tight ass over and take you from behind, I'm good with what we have. More than good, actually. I love getting to know more about you."

Kennedy was now wide awake when she groaned and said, "Please don't talk about bending me over. All I can imagine is—"

"Don't say it," he cut her off. "I've been dying to take you from behind so you're gonna have to find a way to get over hearing what you did."

"Well, I'm sure when the time comes, I won't be thinking about anything but what you're doing. However, *until* that time comes, we shouldn't talk about it. Because really, the images I'm thinking about are enough to make me need a shower."

A shower was exactly what they needed. They'd slept in and were now running low on time before they needed to get to Kennedy's.

"We should get up," he told her.

"'Kay."

"But before we do, I need to tell you something."

"Oh-kay."

"I invited your mom over for dinner." Kennedy started to smile and he hated to do it but he had to. "Her and Janice will be at your house at five." The grin that had been forming faded into a scowl and she started to shake her head. "Yes, babe. Today we're going to your house to sort your beehives. Then your mom and Janice, Nixon and McKenna, and Chasin, Weston, and Holden are staying for dinner. Your mom and McKenna are bringing sides and I'm grilling burgers."

"I don't want to be there," Kennedy protested.

"I know you don't. That's why I'm going to be there with you. Nixon and the rest of the guys will be there around noon. But I wanted you and I to have some time alone there first."

"Why are you doing this? I thought you said I could stay here for as long as I needed."

Her question sent pain radiating through his body.

"You *can* stay here until you're ready for *us* to go back to your place. But that doesn't mean you don't have to face what happened, and part of that is going back to the place where it happened."

"I don't—"

"Do you think I'd let anybody hurt you?" he cut her off.

"No."

Thank God, her answer was firm and quick. He hadn't realized how much he needed the confirmation that she trusted him, especially knowing he was about to make her do something she didn't want to do.

"Then trust me to take you home. We don't have to stay the night. We're going to go over there, get a new bee house set up, and see what needs to be done in your garden. Nixon said something about getting the ground worked up for a fall crop. I don't know jack shit about farming. But I'm willing to learn anything you'll teach me."

"I don't have the money to do that," she seethed.

"Your new investor does."

"Jameson, that'd be a bad investment."

"Says you. I happen to think it will be the best investment I ever make."

"Seriously—"

Her face was becoming redder by the second and she'd dug her nails into Jameson's side. Not exactly the kind of pain he liked when he was on top of her.

"Kennedy, stop and take a breath. You're getting all worked up for nothing."

"I can't breathe. I can't think. What if I do plant a fall crop and Reggie just comes and destroys it? Or what if it doesn't matter because no one will buy my produce? It wasn't like I was making a killing before; I was just making ends meet. That's how I live. Some years I make a little more and put money in the bank. Other years are lean and I have to skip where I can."

"One thing at a time. You're looking at the big picture instead of solving each problem."

"I have to look at the big picture. I'm going to lose my goddamn house."

Now she was pissed and trying to wiggle out from under him. He used his weight to pin her to the bed, the effort doing wonders to keep his temper in check.

"You really think I'd let you lose your house?"

"You can't stop it from happening."

"Kennedy, I'd pay off the fucking mortgage before that happened."

"We'd have big problems if you paid off my house. Or better yet, you'd be living in your brand-new house without me there."

"You think I give the first fuck you'd be mad? Either you'd get over it or I'd live my life alone knowing you had something you loved." Jameson felt no remorse when he pulled out the big emotional guns. "At least I'd know you still had a piece of your dad even if you hated me for making sure you didn't lose it."

She sucked in an audible breath and her eyes widened in shock.

"You'd do it, wouldn't you?"

"Damn right, I would."

"Even if you lost me?"

"I'd pray it didn't come to that, but yes. And every night when I got into a cold lonely bed, I'd know you were lying in yours in the house that you love, knowing you still had what your father worked hard to give you and your mom. And it might make the pain of losing you just bearable—maybe."

Tears leaked from her eyes and rolled down her temples. The sight was painful and Jameson struggled to find a way to make it better.

"I can't talk to you right now," she whispered.

"You don't have to talk to me but you do have to get up and shower. Harold Ward will be at your house in an hour."

"Harold Ward?"

"The president of the Eastern Shore Beekeepers—"

"I know who he is. Why will he be at my house?"

"Because he's helping us build your hive and he's bringing you five pounds of Buckfast bees. He said that's what you had before."

Kennedy stared up at Jameson wide-eyed and in shock. "I can't...I need to get up. Please."

Jameson rolled to the side and watched Kennedy walk to the bathroom attached to his room. She gently shut the door and when the lock snicked, he knew she'd locked him out. His bent arm rested over his eyes and he really hoped he hadn't just fucked up the best thing that had ever happened to him.

WHILE JAMESON WAS WAITING on Kennedy to finish in the bathroom, he went downstairs to find Holden already up and in the kitchen.

"Thank God," Jameson muttered and went for the already-brewed coffee.

"I take it Kennedy wasn't happy with today's plans."

"Unhappy would be an understatement," Jameson answered and took a sip from his mug.

"You know she has to rip the Band-Aid off. The sooner the better. We'll all be there."

"I know that, but man, you didn't see her. I just gutted her. She seriously doesn't want to go over there."

"Give it a few minutes. She'll understand."

"I sure fucking hope so because if she doesn't, I have a feeling I'm screwed."

Jameson heard the water upstairs turn off and wanted to give Kennedy enough time to dress in privacy. He didn't think now was the time to try to talk to her when she was wet and naked, even if he wanted to rush upstairs and tell her they could forget their plans and stay in bed all day.

When the hell had he turned into a pussy?

"Has Weston checked in this morning?" Jameson asked.

"Yeah. Lola and Janice made him pancakes, eggs, and sausage. He said he might be late because he could barely roll himself out of the kitchen. You have no idea, brother, those two women are like the food police. Only instead of telling you *not* to eat something they don't let you up from the table until you have three helpings. They're goddamn food pushers. And damn if the food's not good, so you wanna eat it, but you know they cooked it with a pound of butter so it's gonna sit in your gut and coagulate. And don't get me started on the sweet tea. Christ, there's so much sugar it doesn't all dissolve," Holden explained with a smile.

"Other than bitch about his food coma, did he have anything else to say?"

"No. Reggie Coleman took his wife to a fundraiser at the fire station then went home and didn't leave. It was after ten and Weston wanted to get to Lola's. She said she stayed awake until around eleven and he didn't want to wake her when he got there."

"McKenna hasn't called with an update?"

"Not yet."

Kennedy came down the stairs wearing a pair of jean shorts and a tank top. Before Jameson could remember she was mad at him, he moved in her direction but stopped when he caught the sad look on her face.

"I'm ready," she announced even though she didn't look anything of the sort.

"Let me grab my keys."

Jameson jogged up the stairs thinking he better figure out a way to fix this fast or he was going to lose her.

24

KENNEDY

Jameson was quiet on the way to my house.

I was quiet on the way to my house.

The air in the cab of his truck was murky, thick with tension, and it was my fault, but I still didn't know how to verbalize my feelings. While in the shower I'd tried to gather my thoughts but I couldn't stop the tears long enough to rationalize my emotions. But as Jameson pulled into my driveway, I knew I had to figure something out. He deserved to know I wasn't mad.

I waited for him to stop the truck and I reached for his hand, laced our fingers, and set them on my lap. I stared straight ahead at my old farmhouse. The brick exterior of the original structure was weathered with age. The wood siding on the addition had been replaced by my dad, but was coming up on twenty years old and needed a good scrubbing and to be repainted and repaired. But what had caught my attention was the wraparound porch.

My dad had put it in the year before he died. One of the many projects he'd enlisted my help with. I could remember him telling me to 'measure twice and cut once' when we were cutting the railings. Him telling me to always use screws to fasten the floor boards, never nails. It would be easier when you needed to replace one. We spent days staining and sealing all of the woodwork. And when we were done, Mom brought out a pitcher of iced tea. With no porch furniture yet, we sat on the boards, my dad on the steps, and we enjoyed the fall evening. My mom was beaming with happiness, my dad proud to give his wife what she'd wanted.

That was what Jameson wanted me to keep. My treasured memories.

"I'm sorry," I started. "I was mad at first. I let my pride take over and cloud my reasoning. But I wasn't mad when I told you I couldn't talk to you. I was overwhelmed. I can't explain with what. Maybe part of it was relief that someone was in my corner and would stand beside me. And it goes beyond just helping me keep my house. Maybe it was because since my dad died, I've felt like it was up to me to take care of everything on my own, and now I feel like you've taken some of the weight off my shoulders. Maybe because no one has ever understood me and you do." I took a deep breath and looked from the house to Jameson. He was turned in his seat staring at me. "If the offer still stands to loan me money, I'd appreciate the help. But I want a contract with a monthly payment schedule set up. Part of why I'm scared to borrow money from you is that I don't want it to muddy what we have personally. Basically, I don't want to lose you over money."

"If you need a contract to feel comfortable, then we'll have one drawn up. But I want you to understand, I'm not a bank." I started to speak but he continued before I could get my words out. "Meaning that I don't want or need a set monthly amount. That's not the way your business operates. You have busy seasons and off-seasons. During the off-seasons the payments are deferred and during the busy ones, you pay whatever you feel comfortable paying. I have the money, Kennedy. I'll open an account tomorrow and you use it as you need it."

"Thank you for believing in me," I whispered.

"No need to thank me for that."

"And thank you for helping me. And I'm sorry for treating you to my tantrum back at your house."

"You didn't have a tantrum. I should've handled that conversation better. I've never done this, any of it. I know I can behave like a stampeding bull and railroad people. I'll try to curb that, but I doubt I can change it completely. Especially when it comes to you."

"Why me?"

That had been a burning question in the back of my mind. Jameson was gorgeous and successful, why in the world would he be willing get mixed up with me and my metric shit-ton of problems?

"Because you are the only person that has ever made me think of my future. Made me hopeful. You're the only person that has ever made me feel whole. You quiet the voices in my head and soothe my heart. You showed me that love isn't something to be afraid of. Though the thought of losing you terrifies me, so in some ways falling in love is scary as fuck. Because for the first time in my life I have something *to* lose."

My eyes had drifted closed as I savored his declaration.

"Look at me, babe." I opened my lids and his hazel eyes glistened with purpose. They were resolute and the sight stole my breath. "When I told you I wanted to invest in your business, what I really meant was, I wanted to invest in our future. Before you, I never thought about having a home, or having a wife, and most especially about having kids. But now that's changed. Now when I see this house, I can see my kids running in the back field. I can see them tearing through the house you've fixed up. I can see us sitting on the back deck or the front porch watching them do whatever it is kids do. Hell, I have no idea what kids even do because I've never been around them. I never wanted or thought I'd be a dad because I was afraid I'd be a shit father like mine. But you showed me differently, I am not him. I know you want to repay the money, but what you need to understand is you've given me something, and you continue to give it to me, something money can never buy."

"I can't talk to you again, Jameson," I choked out, emotion clogging my throat.

I was drowning in happiness. My mind was fighting to keep up with everything he'd said, still trying to process him investing in our future. He should've stopped there, because now that he'd mentioned our kids running around the yard, that was all I could think about, making it difficult to speak.

Jameson smiled and squeezed my hand. "That's alright. I don't need you to say anything. The way you look at me says it all. We'll get through this, I promise."

I nodded because there was nothing else to do. I believed him and I was afraid if I tried to tell him how much he meant to me and that I wanted all those things, too, I'd turn into a blubbering mess.

HAROLD WARD WAS a plethora of knowledge. There was a reason he'd been the president of the Eastern Shore Beekeepers Association for as long as he had. He seemed to know everything there was to know about keeping bees.

It had taken us several hours to build the new bee boxes and when we were done, he'd suggested a new location for my hives. He explained that if I set the houses near the apple tree my dad had planted it would change the flavor of my honey. I'd had my original hives near my garden for pollination. Harold had suggested a separate hive for that purpose.

Jameson jumped on the idea and asked Harold to leave the plans we used so he could build the other hive later. He even asked Harold to explain 'bee space' again so he was sure to space the frames correctly. His enthusiasm was contagious. Maybe I'd be all right. Maybe after the dust settled, we'd come out on the other side stronger.

Nixon, McKenna, Chasin, and Holden had shown up as we were putting the new bees in the completed hive, and with a wave they promptly went into my house. It had been rather amusing seeing big, badass Jameson with a keeper's mask and gloves on. I could tell he wasn't a hundred percent comfortable being around a bunch of bees, but he powered through it and stayed. Even though Harold and I both told him we could finish up.

With the promise to return next week to check on the hive, Harold left me and Jameson to watch as the bees checked out their new home.

"Thank you." I wrapped my arms around Jameson's middle and rested the side of my face on his chest.

"I never knew how much went into beekeeping," Jameson told me. "They're interesting. I had no idea each hive could have twenty thousand workers all diligently working to serve their queen." I smiled against his chest. "Bees are smart, they know where it's at."

"That they do."

"You ready to get your garden sorted?"

I pulled away and looked up into his handsome face and I couldn't get over how lucky I was.

"I am. You know what's funny? It's like we have a complete role reversal going on."

"What do you mean?" Jameson tilted his head in question.

"Well, you're normally the one whose attitude is... how can I describe it..."

"Hateful," he supplied.

"That's a good word for it." I smiled. "And I'm the

one who's always taken it on the chin and did it with a smile. But when I was ready to throw in the towel, suddenly you had a sunshine attitude."

"Don't get used to it," he grumbled.

"I wouldn't dream of it. Besides, I love the grouchy, prickly side of you too much."

Jameson gave a small jerk, then his eyes softened. "You know I love you, right?"

"I do."

"Good." His smile was bigger than I'd ever seen it.

"You know I love you, too, right?"

"Yeah, Kennedy, I know."

"Good."

His hand went to my ponytail and he yanked it back so my face was tilted up. I lost sight of his eyes when his lips crashed onto mine. His tongue glided against mine and I groaned into his mouth. This was the first real kiss he'd given me since I'd been attacked.

I don't know how long we stood in my meadow, but with each stroke of his tongue he washed away all of the fear and bad memories I had from that day. And as the minutes passed, he gave me back my home. My security, my hopes, my dreams of a future filled with happiness.

Just like that—all I needed was Jameson.

CHASIN WAS CUTTING MY GRASS, smiling like an idiot while he mowed circles in the yard. I guess when you didn't have to spend an hour-plus on the mower every few days, zooming around on a zero-turn mower could be fun. It'd taken Chasin a few minutes to get the hang of using his hands to both turn and accelerate. But after he figured out how to use the handles, he was off zipping around.

Men and machines—I guess it didn't matter what they were operating or how old they were, they'd find a way to screw around.

Jameson and Holden had taken my chainsaw to the edge of my property to cut some branches that had fallen. Later I'd split the logs into manageable pieces and use them for firewood. But for now I appreciated them just getting them out of the way.

McKenna was in the house working, listening in on Reggie Coleman, and Weston was in his car following him. So far nothing exciting had happened.

Nixon and I were in my barn and he was looking at my Case tractor.

"It doesn't have an enclosed cab," he noted.

"Nope."

"At least it has a shade cover."

Nixon was still pointing out the obvious. Some tractors had enclosed cabs and even offered a heater, air conditioning, and a radio. My dad used to say those were for sissy farmers who were afraid of sweating. He only said that because we'd never been able to afford one. With price tags upward of a hundred thousand dollars they were out of our price range. Even when the farm had good years, and the prices of corn and soybeans were high, he still wouldn't have bought one.

"When Mr. Nickels died, Mrs. Nickels sold it to me. I replaced my dad's old John Deere," I told Nix. "My dad knew just what to do to make the old beast run but I never could. The Case has a straightforward diesel engine. And really, it's all I need. I'm working up forty-eight acres, not five-hundred."

"Yeah, but you have to be hot as hell running this thing." He banged on the tire and continued his walk around.

"So? I'm not afraid of hard work and sweat." I stood a little straighter and braced for the "you're a woman doing man's work" lecture, surprised it would come from Nixon. "What's bothering you? I've been running tractors all my life. Hell, I've picked up hay bales right alongside of you."

"You shouldn't have had to sell the rest of your land." His comment startled me and I steadied myself on the wall of the barn. "You work too hard. Your dad left that to you. He wanted you to work it. You should've been able to."

"I gave it my best shot, Nix."

"I know you did. That's why it pisses me off. You shouldn't have had to sell," he repeated.

"At least Mr. Nickels bought it. He worked the land until he died."

"Yeah, and now that fucking weasel Coleman owns it."

Reggie Coleman did indeed own it. When he bought the Nickels' farm, that included the acreage that had once belonged to my dad. It was a kick in the teeth thinking about it.

"I want you to have it back."

"No way." I put my hand up. "I can't manage the extra two-hundred acres. It's gone. I've made peace with it. As long as I still have the house, that's all that matters to me."

"You could rent the land out," he suggested.

"Really? To who? That's why Mrs. Nickels had to sell in the first place. No one would touch it. She was growing a forest of weeds. And you know how expensive it is to spray herbicides on the fields. She couldn't afford it."

"Fucking Reggie Coleman," he bit out.

"You can say that again. I know he put the word out so no one would rent her land. But I just can't understand why everyone bows down to him. What makes him so high and mighty? Why is everyone in this town so afraid of him? I can understand the shopkeepers who discontinued selling my stuff, he could raise their rent or even cancel their leases. I wouldn't put it past him to do some shady shit like that. But farmers? It doesn't make sense, but I know he did it somehow."

"I agree with you." Then Nix changed the subject. "What do you want to do? Plow the field now and get it ready for a fall crop or is it too early?"

"It's never too early to get a jump start on tomorrow's work," I told him.

"My dad used to say that." Nixon smiled, but it looked painful.

"Your dad taught me a lot about hard work. Him and my dad were cut from the same cloth. Men's men, but still had a soft hand and a kind word. I think my dad would be happy that your dad continued to teach the lesson he'd started. I loved your dad, Nix. He was a good man. And losing him was devastating."

Nixon looked thoughtful and took his time to gather himself. I knew how much he'd missed his dad when he was gone in the Navy. And having him pass away while he was gone had to be hard for him.

"He was proud of you," Nixon said and held my stare. "'That girl can work from sun up to sun down and show my men a thing or two and she does it looking as pretty as can be.'" Nix did his best impression of his father's gruff voice.

Wetness hit the corners of my eyes. I'd known Wayne Swagger was pleased with my work on his farm but I hadn't known he'd talked to Nixon about it.

"He was always a character. Coming up with some crazy saying that made no sense but weirdly it did. And he swore by that damn Farmers Almanac. Wouldn't plant beans until the moon was just right." I shook my head. "I'm really sorry you lost him. I don't know if I told you that already. But I hope you know how much he loved you and talked about you all the time. I think his favorite thing to yell at the guys when they slacked off was, 'You don't know Navy SEAL tough. Until you do, quit your bitching and get to work.' He was proud of your accomplishments."

"Thanks for that. I miss him."

"I know you do."

"Just one more time I wish I could hear him yell at me across the house to get my ass to work, then mumble under his breath I was as useless as tits on a bull. You know not very many people would understand why a son would miss his dad berating him. But you do."

"Hell, yeah I do. Your dad was a cantankerous old man, but damn if he didn't love hard. And he loved you the most, Nixon."

"If him working me to the bone equaled love, he did."

"You know it does." I smiled.

Nixon's expression darkened. "We need to clear the air about that night. Jameson brought it up and—"

"No, we don't. I was out of control and you were the only one who did right by me."

"I should've handled it better. Been gentle."

"I wouldn't have listened to gentle. You saved my life that night and let's leave it at that. You did what I needed you do to—you were the no-bullshit man your father taught you to be. And thank God for that or I wouldn't be standing here right now."

Nixon nodded and deep lines formed on his forehead. "I'm proud of you, Kennedy. You're a damn good woman, and don't you ever forget it."

"I am," I agreed. "But it's because of my dad and yours and you. Strong men, who taught me to value myself. And don't *you* ever forget that."

"I may've forgotten to include bossy." He smiled.

"You ain't seen bossy yet, friend. Now get your ass in gear and help me grease the PTO so I can get to work."

Nixon smiled, shook his head at my ridiculousness, and laughed so hard it filled the barn.

"Jameson is one lucky bastard," Nix said through his hilarity.

Nixon's approval meant the world to me, though I knew I was the one who was lucky to find a man like Jameson.

25

JAMESON

Jameson had found that Holden and Weston had been correct, he needed to double-up on his workouts if Lola and Janice were going to be around. The women pushed food like a dealer on a street corner.

"A good Southern woman never allows her guests to leave hungry," Lola announced when Nixon had declined a third helping of potato salad.

Which incidentally was the best thing Jameson had ever eaten and he would be begging Kennedy to make it again for him in the near future.

"Ma! For the five hundredth time, you were not born in the South."

"So? You don't have to be born in the South to be Southern," Lola bristled.

"Yeah, ya do. That's what being Southern means."

"Being Southern is not a location, it's a mindset."

Everyone in the room except Kennedy chuckled at Lola's declaration.

"Jesus," Kennedy muttered.

"Don't use the Lord's name in vain."

"I wasn't. I was looking for deliverance."

"Such a dramatic child," Lola returned.

Jameson was enjoying the banter between mother and daughter. He'd never experienced a close bond between child and parent. His relationship with his mother had been very different. They were more of a team, working together to get through life. Never really stopping to enjoy it. And there was no funny back-and-forth. His mother had always been too tired.

A familiar hatred filled him as he thought about what his father had taken from him. Could this have been his life? A loving and fun relationship with his mom? How different would she have been if she wasn't working herself half to death? Would she have smiled and teased him? Would she have tucked him in and told him stories? Goddamn, he hated his father.

Kennedy's hand on his thigh pulled his attention to her and she smiled.

Immediately the knot in his gut unraveled. That was all it'd taken—one smile from Kennedy and she could ease the pain and fill him with her shine.

Unbelievable.

Nixon pulled his buzzing phone from his pocket and frowned. "Excuse me, this is Jonny. I have to take it."

Nix got up from the table and walked out the back door. Jameson watched as his friend's body went stiff and one hand went to the back of his neck. Something was wrong.

"What's that about?" Kennedy leaned closer and asked.

"No idea," he answered. "I'll be right back."

He kissed her temple and stood. Holden and Chasin followed him out the door and the three of them waited until Nixon hung up.

"What's wrong?"

"Peyton Marshall was found dead in his holding cell."

"What?" Holden asked the question for all of them.

"Apparent suicide."

"Suicide? Over a breaking and entering and assault charge?" Chasin shook his head.

"Suicide if you take into account the note Peyton wrote, explaining in detail that he alone acted against Kennedy."

"Really? And what was his reason, did he say?" Jameson inquired.

"He sure did. Said he was holding a grudge since high school, fighting the need for vengeance but he finally lost control."

"They have problems in high school?" Chasin asked Nixon.

"Not that I know of. Peyton was always a dick. But I never knew him and Kennedy were even friends. They didn't hang out in the same circles. But the issue is, the manner of death doesn't add up to suicide. Peyton was stabbed five times in his neck and stomach."

"Jesus," Jameson muttered, even though in the

darkest places of his soul he was thinking it couldn't have happened to a better person.

Just because Jameson couldn't injure an unarmed man didn't mean he wasn't pleased karma hadn't wasted any time.

"Jonny is pissed someone was able to get to Peyton. The detention center doesn't have the room to separate the inmates, so Peyton was in general population even though he was awaiting arraignment."

"You know Reggie made a call to his business partner this morning. I think we need to listen to it again and find out more about Gary Earle," Jameson suggested.

"Absolutely. As soon as Janice takes Lola home, we'll talk," Nixon said and nodded for the house.

Twenty minutes later, McKenna and Kennedy were putting away leftovers and Jameson and Nixon were helping the ladies to the car.

"You'll make sure that nice young man eats when he gets home, right?" Janice asked.

"Weston is already at Lola's waiting for you two lovely ladies to get there. And he's already eaten dinner," Nixon told them, and Jameson chuckled knowing it would not matter if Nix stressed Weston had eaten, they'd still force-feed him.

"Oh, good. It's nice having a man around the house," Lola said and winked.

"I agree," Janice started. "If I were twenty years younger, I'd give him a run for his money."

Good God. Poor Weston.

"Even twenty years ago, I think he could still outrun you." Lola laughed.

"Twenty years ago he wouldn't've been trying to run away."

Janice wiggled her eyebrows and it was time to send the ladies on their way. Jameson wondered if he should call his friend and warn him the cougars were on their way home but decided it would be more fun to let Weston figure it out on his own that two old women were looking at him like he was a juicy piece of meat.

"You drive careful, Miss Janice," Nix said and closed the driver's side door.

The men stood in the drive and watched the women drive away.

"Those two are a trip," Nixon muttered.

"How much you wanna bet Weston calls within the hour?"

"You know he will. Good thing for him he can indeed outrun those two or I have a feeling they'd put it to him."

Jameson smiled into the darkness thinking how different his life was now. Five years ago he would've never imagined having that type of conversation. Hell, six months ago he would've never thought he'd be standing in his woman's driveway after helping her mother into the car. And not even two months ago would he ever have believed he'd fall ass over tea kettle in love.

What a difference one woman can make.

They were sitting at Kennedy's table listening to the conversation between Reggie and Gary for the second time. Jameson had been surprised at Kennedy's lack of emotion over hearing Peyton was dead. She expressed sadness that life had been lost but had followed it up with, *bad people reap bad things.*

"Listen to this part again," McKenna said and played back the beginning of the recording.

"I heard a new business agreement is needed." Gary Earle started the conversation.

"Not so fast," Reggie protested.

"I don't take risks. I need to know my investment is solid." Gary obviously didn't like Reggie's hesitation and continued. "I had the new papers drawn up this afternoon."

"That's not needed," Reggie rushed out his tone, missing his normal cocky attitude. "Give it a week. Everything will work out."

"No risks. That was the deal. Risks are to be eliminated immediately. You agreed to that. I can just as easily dissolve the partnership and run solo."

McKenna paused the conversation.

"Does that sound like Gary was telling Reggie he planned on killing Peyton?" she asked.

"If we assume Peyton is the risk," Nixon answered.

"Gary was clear risks are to be eliminated immediately," Chasin added. "But how would Gary find someone to take out Peyton so quickly? He was only arrested yesterday and this conversation happened less than eight hours before Peyton was found dead."

"A leftover from Sheriff Dick Dillinger's reign?" Nixon suggested. "I know Jonny and the sheriff have been working on making sure the department is purged of all the shit that plagued them. However, it's gonna take more than a few months. That's one thought, but we need to figure out who Gary Earle is. He could have his own connections and it may have nothing to do with Dillinger."

"I can help with some of it, but McKenna will have to work her magic and dig deeper." Holden started looking at his tablet screen. "Gary Earle was born in Dover, Delaware, and now lives in Wilmington. He's hella wealthy and made his money by going into slums and rebuilding. I found an interesting article about him accusing him of bribing local and state officials. Of course, all involved denied the claims, but a local community outreach organization is adamant. They even provide documentation that their requests to tear down dilapidated old row homes to build low-income housing and a community center was denied, citing historical preservation. But six months later Gary Earle obtained the land and the permits for demolition. The county came back and said they were misquoted that the outreach organization lacked funding. Yet the organization supplied original copies of the denial letters and bank statements with more than enough funding."

"So Gary Earle's the Reggie Coleman of Wilmington," Kennedy concluded.

"Sounds like it," Holden agreed. "Now the question is, how did the two scumbags come together to form a partnership? And why would Earle have any interest in a small farming community?"

"I'll work on it first thing in the morning." McKenna typed her notes and looked around. "Anything else?"

"Yes, can you find the link between Sunbelt Heating and Air Conditioning and Reggie? If not for anything else, we'll have confirmation Reggie ordered the man not to fix Lola's AC," Jameson requested.

"Wait. Then who fixed my mom's AC?" Kennedy asked. "She said it's working."

"Nixon and Zack," Jameson offered.

"What happened?"

Jameson gave Kennedy the abbreviated story and with each word he'd spoken her eyes narrowed with irritation.

"You know, Reggie really is an asshole. I mean, we already knew that but he's the king of all dicks. I just don't get why everyone does his bidding."

"I'll find that out tomorrow, too," McKenna told her. "And someone should go speak to Willow Realty and the agent in charge of his rentals.

"I'm on that. I'll go first thing in the morning," Chasin volunteered. "And I'll see if the shop owners will talk to me."

"Go easy on Jonas Brown, he's a total hippy and very sensitive," Kennedy advised. "And maybe I'm wrong. Maybe he just wasn't happy with my product."

"He ever complain before?" Holden asked.

"No. But he really is a nice guy."

"Right. A nice guy, who's being jacked around by Reggie. I'll go easy," Chasin assured.

"I'm headed home. Get the lead out, woman." Nixon smiled at McKenna.

"You talk to me like that again, Nixon Swagger, and you'll be the one getting my buckshot lead outta your ass." A perfectly-shaped eyebrow lifted and Nix chuckled.

"Noted. How 'bout I carry your computer and purse to the truck so we can get home before Mandy and Zack's curfew?"

"Shit, I forgot they both went out. Dammit, Nix, why didn't you remind me what time it was?"

"Yeah, it's totally my fault I forgot I was the designated timekeeper."

"Whatever," McKenna huffed and gathered her stuff.

Holden and Chasin both announced they were leaving, too.

Jameson and Kennedy walked the foursome to the door and said their goodbyes.

"You have more to clean up or are you ready to go?" Jameson asked.

"I think I want to stay here."

Jameson took a moment to study her features. She'd been relaxed all day, and had smiled and carried on through dinner. She'd shown no signs of hesitation or fear being back in her house, but that didn't mean now that the house full of people had left and night had fallen she wouldn't slip back into not wanting to be in her home.

"If at any time you change your mind we'll go back to my place," Jameson told her.

"Now you sound like my mom before my first sleepover. She promised to pick me if I got scared, she said she didn't care what time it was." Kennedy's innocent statement sent of pang of hurt to Jameson's chest. He'd never had a single sleepover. How much had he truly missed out on? "Thank you for everything. You've been really great helping me through this."

Her appreciation worked its magic and hurt was filled with warmth. He was pleased he could help even though he felt like he should be doing more.

Jameson led Kennedy up the stairs and into her room. His hands shook with pent-up need when he helped her undress and get into bed. He slipped in next to her, donning a pair of running shorts. There was only so much a man could take and with Kennedy only in a tee and panties, Jameson's limits were maxed out.

And she'd already proven to be devious when she wanted something. The thought of the first time they'd been together assaulted Jameson, doing nothing to help his dick stay soft. He'd never forget the way she'd lifted her hips and impaled herself on his dick. The wonderment in her eyes when he drove his cock deep. Fuck. There was nothing about Kennedy that wasn't hot. Nothing he could think about that would deflate his now-throbbing hard-on.

"Why are we wasting this?" Kennedy's knee brushed his hard dick. "Seems like such a shame."

Jameson reached down and grabbed her thigh,

hitching it up to his stomach. "Trust me, babe, it is a cryin' shame," he groaned. "But when you're better, I promise to never waste another one."

"But—"

"Please have mercy on me. I don't want to hurt you."

"We'll go slow."

"No, we won't. You know all it will take is you begging me to go harder and I'll fuck you silly. Please, Kennedy, let's just go to sleep."

"But—"

"It'll go down on its own as soon as I stop thinking about you sitting on my face while I eat your pussy."

"That's what you're thinking about?"

"I got one sweet lick before you fucked me on the couch. I'm looking forward to burying my face between your legs and watching you come in my mouth. I can't stop thinking about the sounds you make and how good you feel under me. But the thought of eating you out while your hips buck against my face is so fucking hot, Kennedy, I think I can come from just the thought alone."

"You should stop talking if you don't want me to start begging," she moaned and rubbed her pussy against his bare thigh.

"Fuck, you're wet," he grunted when he felt the damp material of her panties.

"Oh, yeah, I'm wet. You just told me you fantasized about eating my pussy."

"Fuck, don't say pussy," he growled.

"Why not? You say it."

"Because you saying it is turning me on more."

"What am I supposed to say? You talking about eating my vagina is hot? Or what about you eating my cunt? Though I will admit I don't like that word. I prefer pussy. It sounds sexier. Cunt sounds like a dirty word."

His head turned, and in an effort to make her stop talking about her pussy, he slammed his mouth on hers. Huge mistake. The sneaky vixen pushed her tongue passed his lips and his resolve snapped. He gently eased her to her back and his hand went under the material of her shirt, circling one nipple before he moved to the other and repeated the movement. Kennedy's back arched when he cupped her breast and rolled her nipple between his thumb and finger. Satisfaction bloomed when Kennedy moaned as he plucked at the hard nub.

His hand moved down over her stomach and over her panties until he stopped at the gusset and yanked it to the side. It would be easier if her panties were off but Jameson didn't want to waste any time. His finger gathered wetness as he circled her clit. Kennedy's hips bucked just like he'd imagined they would if it was his tongue flicking the bundle of nerves and not his finger.

"Don't move," he said, breaking the kiss. "Stay still or I stop."

She nodded and he took her in. Eyes half-mast and full of lust and need, lips red and puffy from his kiss. Neck flushed—seeing it had him changing his mind.

"Sit up." He pulled his hand away from her pussy and helped her take off her t-shirt and panties.

When she laid back down fully nude he had to take a deep breath and remember tonight was all about making

Kennedy feel good. Giving her what she needed. His cock would stay safely inside his shorts—the downside of not wearing underwear was there was only one layer of material between them.

Jameson resumed their position but this time he spread her legs wide and came up on his elbow. One hand went back between her legs and his mouth descended to her nipple.

"Jameson," she breathed.

He swirled his tongue harder and teased her pussy, running a finger up and down her slit.

"Please."

The whine in her voice made him smile against her nipple. He gave her a hard nip and pushed two thick fingers inside of her.

"Holy..."

Kennedy didn't finish her sentence, and with a stern reminder Jameson warned her to stay still.

"I can't."

"Then I'll stop."

"No. Don't stop. I'll stay still."

Jameson worked his fingers in and out of her pussy and continued to lavish her tits with attention. He licked and sucked on every part he could reach.

When Kennedy's hips started lifting again and her mews of pleasure were getting louder, he knew she'd had enough teasing.

He eased his body down onto hers and lifted both her thighs over his shoulders. He speared his tongue into her wetness and used his thumb to strum her clit.

"Jameson!" she shouted and ground her pussy against his face.

So fucking hot.

His hips pushed into the mattress, his cock throbbing to the point of pain. He knew he was going to come with her. He flattened his tongue and lapped up her excitement, then shoved his fingers back inside of her and sucked her clit until she screamed his name. Her pussy convulsed around his fingers and his balls started to tingle. He continued to fuck her with his fingers until the pulsing stopped.

Jameson quickly rolled to the side, yanked his shorts down his legs, came up on his knees between her splayed thighs, and took his cock in hand.

"Ohmygod," Kennedy moaned.

Jameson rubbed the length of his cock against her drenched pussy, coating it with her orgasm and started stroking.

Kennedy's hands went to her breasts and she pushed them together, massaging them while she flicked her nipples with her thumbs.

"Goddamn, that's sexy as hell," Jameson groaned. Feeling his orgasm quickly approaching, he stroked himself faster.

"You're telling me," she murmured. "Does that feel good?"

"Not as good as your pussy," Jameson answered. "But I have to say jerking off while you watch is hot as fuck. I'm gonna come, baby. On you or in you?"

"On me. I wanna watch."

Jameson groaned and a few pumps later, his thighs tightened, his balls drew up, and his come splashed on her pubic hair and lower stomach. When his orgasm finally waned and he was able to focus, he grinned at the sight.

"Are you happy with your aim?" Kennedy chuckled.

He hadn't thought of what she'd think watching him jerk off. And certainly, he hadn't thought about how he'd feel doing it. That was a first for him, he never would've allowed anyone in the past to see him vulnerable. But he couldn't deny that it was hot having Kennedy watch, and he definitely wanted to do that again.

"Oh, yeah. Seeing my come mark your pretty skin is off-the-charts sexy. But next time, I'm aiming for your tits."

Kennedy smiled at his perverted statement and she quickly retorted, "I'll make sure I close my eyes then. I've heard come in the eyes can sting."

"Really? And where'd you hear that? One of your *good* porn movies?"

"Maybe?" She giggled and the sound hit Jameson with the force of a sledgehammer.

It was safe to say that Kennedy was the only woman he'd ever bantered with about sex. The only woman who could make him come hard and laugh in equal measure.

It was insane how happy she made him.

LATER THAT NIGHT after Jameson had cleaned up

Kennedy and settled her back to his side, she was drawing lazy circles on his chest when she whispered, "I love you, Jameson."

And just like the time before when she'd told Jameson she loved him, he waited for the panic to come. But just like the first time, it never came. Only peace.

"Love you, too, babe."

His arm flexed and pulled her closer and he drifted off to sleep.

26

KENNEDY

"If it makes you feel any better, Jonas Brown likes you a lot and he genuinely looked sorry," Chasin told me.

I was at the Gemini Group office. McKenna had asked me if I would help her today and even though I'd planned on working on my garden I couldn't turn her down.

So I was using the conference room and extra laptop to do basic searches on Gary Earle. McKenna was doing the deep digging, but she explained she liked to have both public record and what she could find to paint the whole picture.

"I like Jonas, too. But I don't feel any better. Did he tell you why?"

"Nope. And when I brought up Reggie Coleman ownin' the building, Jonas looked like he wanted to flee."

"Told you he was sensitive."

"And the woman, Faye Cook, who owns Willow Realty and she's the rental agent for Reggie's property, she visibly paled and asked me to leave the second I mentioned his name."

"You need to listen to this." McKenna came into the room with her laptop.

"What'd you tell him?" Reggie's angry voice boomed from the computer's speakers.

"Nothing, Mr. Coleman. I asked him to leave."

"That's Faye," Chasin said.

"What's his name?"

"He said it was Chasin Murray. I've never seen him before."

"Did he tell you why he was asking about me, or who he works for?"

Chasin's face broke out into a wide smile.

"Yes. He said he works for Kennedy Lane. He's her personal bodyguard."

"You did not tell her that?" I laughed.

"Yeah, I did." Chasin chuckled.

"Thank you," Reggie clipped. "If he comes back, please let me know. And remember our business is confidential."

"Yes, Mr. Coleman."

"You better not forget it either." Reggie's voice had taken on a menacing tone. "Or I'll sink your ass and call my friends at Chesapeake Trust and have your parents' loan called in early."

Reggie disconnected the call and McKenna's eyes went wide.

"Well, there you have it, proof King Dick uses threats to get his way. Makes sense, but now we know he has ties to Chesapeake Trust. Let's see if he banks there as well."

A few keystrokes later, McKenna was squinting at her screen. "He banks there. But there's no line of credit or loans. But you know who does have one? Gary Earle. It's a construction loan." McKenna's eyes scanned back and forth on the monitor. "When did Reggie approach you about buying your land?"

"About six months ago."

"Same time as this loan. And when did he start putting on the heat?"

"Two months ago."

"I know why. This loan isn't paying out yet and the line of credit will close if it's not used in the next thirty days."

"Why would a loan expire?" Chasin asked.

"Because the construction loan disperses as the work happens. Reggie can't break ground on the land behind Kennedy's because he can't get a permit without adequate road access," McKenna explained.

"That's never stopped him before. He got permits to build condos on marshland," I told her. "The town had denied every contractor for years. But he got approved."

McKenna continued to tap on her keyboard. "And Reggie had several loans in his name that are coming up for payment. He's deferred twice. I bet they need the money from the construction loan to start paying out so they can pay the other loans."

"Robbing Peter to pay Paul," Chasin noted.

"That's what it looks like. In the last year he's leveraged himself to the max. We need to call Nix and see what he knows about the bank president." McKenna pulled out her phone and dialed.

"Yeah," Nixon answered, sounding out of breath.

"You alright?"

"Just got back into the car after a sweet old woman set her seventy-pound German Shepherd loose on me after I asked her about Reggie Coleman. Had to run for my life with the bitch nippin' at my heels. I think Duke needs a friend, we're getting you a shepherd."

"Duke does not need a friend and we're not getting another dog," McKenna told him.

"Babe, did you hear me telling you I was running for my life? I wasn't lying. Duke just licks people. You need a snarly bitch that's not afraid to bite."

"Maybe we should talk about this while you're not on speaker phone and Chasin and Kennedy aren't listenin'."

"For the record, I agree with Nix. Duke's a great dog, but damn if he's not friendly."

"Just sayin', McKenna, I'd feel a lot better when I have to go out of town knowin' there was a dog in the house that would actually scare someone off."

"Can we please get back to why I called?" McKenna asked, clearly over the dog conversation.

Though now I was thinking about getting a dog and wondered what Jameson would think of the idea. We'd never talked about animals or if he liked them. If I did get a dog, I want it to live inside. I didn't see a point of having one if I was going to make it stay outside. And I wouldn't want it to live in a crate in the house either.

"Oh, hell, now we have to wait. Reggie's making a call to Gary."

I glanced at McKenna's screen and in the corner, there was an open application displaying the number Reggie was calling. I still couldn't believe how easy it was for her to hack into his phone.

"Yes?" Gary answered.

"We have a problem," Reggie announced.

"No. You have a problem and by the call I'm assuming you're making it mine."

Gary did not sound happy.

"I can assure you it is our problem. His name is Chasin Murray. Kennedy Lane is ready to sell and the only thing standing in our way is her boyfriend who's now playing bodyguard."

"He thinks I'm Jameson. Idiot," Chasin noted.

"I told you he was a problem the first time he was at that bitch's house. I'll handle him. But next time I tell you something, fucking listen. And you'd better have her signature by business end tomorrow!" Gary shouted.

The call disconnected and I was stunned.

"Did Reggie just order a hit on Chasin?" Nixon asked.

"Sure did," Chasin answered.

"Why are you smiling?" I snapped.

"Because he played right into my hands. I could've told Faye anything. Instead I told her who I was and that I worked for you, knowing Reggie was a dumbass and he'd bite," Chasin explained.

"Gary is going to try and kill you!" I screeched.

Jameson walked into the conference room back from wherever he'd been working, made his way to my side, and put his arm around me.

"What's going on?" he asked.

"Chasin's crazy, that's what's going on," I told him.

My heart was thundering in my chest. The thought of anyone getting hurt because of me hurt my heart. I couldn't live with myself.

Chasin filled Jameson in and when he was done, Jameson was smiling, too.

"Good work," Jameson commended.

"Are *you* crazy?" I asked.

Jameson didn't answer, but his entire body went rigid, then his arm around me tightened to near crushing. When I tried to wiggle away, he held firm.

"Nixon, get to the office, now!" Chasin growled, then for an odd reason he stepped toward me and Jameson. "Lock it down, Grant."

"What's—"

"Fuck!" Jameson roared and my body jerked with the force of his yell.

I turned my head to follow Jameson's gaze to McKenna's laptop. Her hands were nowhere near the keyboard but pictures were scrolling.

"What is that?" I asked.

"Reggie accessed his cloud." McKenna's answer was barely above a whisper.

I watched in horror as images of me and Jameson in my house scrolled down the screen. Some of them had an arrow in the middle of the image indicating they were movies.

"How did he...I don't understand..." I stuttered.

"Peyton Marshall didn't take anything, he set up cameras," McKenna explained.

My knees buckled and I was grateful Jameson had an iron grip around my waist or I would've hit the floor.

Reggie continued to scroll and when an image of me naked on the bed with Jameson's head between my legs filled the screen, I felt sick.

"Turn the fuck around," Jameson barked.

"Already did, man," Chasin answered.

"I'm gonna throw up," I announced but Jameson didn't let me go.

"Fuck. Goddamn," Nixon barked from the doorway.

"Jameson. I'm going to throw up. Let me go!" I shouted and wrenched my body away from his.

I pushed past Chasin and when I was halfway to the bathroom I heard him say, "Lock his ass down and don't let him leave. I'll call Weston and see to Kennedy."

I didn't have time to shut the door before I was on my knees heaving into the toilet.

"Weston. Get to the office now."

I heard a clatter on the sink basin, then a wet cloth was pressed to the back of my neck.

"Everything's gonna be okay, Kennedy." Chasin tried to soothe.

"No, it's not. He has naked pictures of me and Jameson. Oh, God." My stomach roiled again and if I'd been in the right frame of mind I would've kicked Chasin out.

Sick.

Reggie Coleman was a sick fucking bastard. Oh my God, he'd seen us have sex. He'd seen me naked—having sex. No. This couldn't be happening. That did *not* just happen.

"Kennedy. Try to take a breath and hold it, you're gonna hyperventilate."

"So?" I panted.

"You'll pass out, sweetheart. Slow your breathing."

"At least I would stop thinking about that fucking prick seeing us... seeing...holy shit, Chasin. He saw."

I must've been delirious because one second I was on the floor in front of the toilet emptying the contents of my stomach and the next I was sitting on a counter and Chasin was washing my face like a child. I had no recollection how I got there.

"My mom," I cried.

"Will never see them. No one will. McKenna will make sure everything is wiped clean."

"But once it's on the internet it's there forever."

"No, it's not. McKenna can delete everything."

Chasin looked to the doorway and took a step back before he nodded to Jameson and the men switched places.

Jameson's hand went to my face and he wiped the tears off my cheek.

"Kennedy, look at me." I lifted my eyes to meet his and I flinched at the anger I saw. "I'm going to fix this."

I nodded because I believed he would, even if I couldn't see how.

"I'm sorry," I sobbed.

"You have nothing to be sorry about."

"He has pictures of you and it's my fault. If...if...you weren't with me, he'd never—"

"I don't give the first fuck he has nude photos of me. I care he has them of *you*," he growled. "Don't bother me one goddamn bit he wants to look at my dick swinging in the wind, but knowing he's seen you and how he violated your privacy makes me want to rip his fucking head off. And, babe, that option is still on the table."

That I *didn't* believe—he did care, anyone would care that someone had pictures of them naked. Images of last night flashed in my mind.

"Don't go there, Kennedy. Don't think about it. We have a plan, and it needs to happen now so McKenna can get to work. We can't delete those pictures until Reggie is arrested. And unfortunately, how we saw them is illegal. So we need to set Reggie up. That way Jonny can get a search warrant, and McKenna can just happen to *find* his cloud server."

"The police have to see those?" I asked in horror.

"Yes. I want his ass nailed on every charge we can get."

"Ohmygod, I know Jonny and most of the deputies. How will I ever look at them again knowing they saw those pictures?"

I wanted McKenna to delete them now. I didn't want to press charges.

"You'll look at them knowing you did not one thing wrong. That fucking pig Reggie infringed on your privacy and invaded our private time. We're gonna nail his balls to the wall."

"Get in here!" Nixon yelled from down the hall.

"You ready to go back in?"

"Did they see?"

"I'm not gonna lie to you. Chasin and Nix both caught a glance but McKenna had to watch what he was doing on the screen. I think she's more disturbed that she had to see *me* but she was more focused on the URL paths than the pictures." Jameson's lips formed two flat lines and his face was set in stone.

Maybe Jameson didn't care that Reggie saw him naked, but he did care that his friend's woman had. He cared that McKenna was forced to advert her eyes the best she could but still watch what Reggie was doing. And Jameson allowed it, because the alternative was one of the guys would've had to and that meant they'd see me.

Fucking Reggie! Stupid dick. He'd gone from hurting me to mentally scarring my friends. I was done. I was beyond the shock that he had pictures of me and I'd firmly slipped into thermonuclear and would do anything I had to do to take Reggie down.

I'd simply wanted dirt on Reggie to make him stop bothering me, now I wanted to take him down—permanently. I wanted his ass rotting right next to his bastard son who'd planted cameras in my house.

"I'm ready," I told Jameson. "So ready."

Jameson dipped his chin before he helped me down.

When we went back into the conference room, Nix and Chasin were pacing back and forth. Weston had arrived at some point and was scanning documents spread over the table.

No one said anything to me about the pictures, which I appreciated. They knew I knew they'd seen them, I didn't need to be reminded.

"So this is how this is going to go down," Nix started. "You're gonna call Reggie, tell him you're ready to talk to him about the terms of the sale. I don't know how much he'll say over the phone—if we're lucky, he'll talk. If not, you're gonna have to meet him in person. You'll be wired so we'll hear the conversation."

"Okay. What am I trying to get him to say?" I asked.

"Anything that will incriminate him. We need him to admit he sent Peyton to your house to intimidate or hurt you, or that he damaged your mom's AC, damaged your crops, burned down your hives, anything. Jonny needs something to present to a judge for a search warrant. For once the small town, good ol boys' shit is going to work in our favor. Judge Price is an old man with five daughters, I can't see him takin' kindly to a man threatening a woman or causing her harm. He is also adamantly against the development of Kent County. He comes from generations of farmers. But we still need something to present him."

"All right," I agreed.

"You understand we can't show or even tell Jonny about the pictures. I obtained them by illegally hacking his phone. If we present them now, they'll be thrown out of court and I'll have to explain how I came to find them," McKenna added.

"I understand. I won't mention the pictures. And I won't say anything about Gary Earle, either. We're not supposed to know about him, right?"

"Smart, girl," Chasin praised. "You're correct. Keep on the topic of him harassing you and using Peyton to do it," he coached.

"Got it."

"Hold on, Reggie's just texted Gary a picture of Kennedy and Jameson. We'll let this play out, then you can call." McKenna nodded to her screen, and thankfully it was a picture of both of us fully dressed and standing in my living room.

"Why is Reggie sending Gary a picture of me and Jameson?" I asked.

"He thinks I'm Jameson," Chasin answered. "Jameson confronted him but didn't give his name."

"The camera has to be on the fireplace mantel," Jameson noted. "That's the only place it could be to get that angle."

He was right. I didn't have any other shelving on that side of the room. I quickly thought about what knick-knacks I had on the mantel and couldn't for the life of me remember. Damn, why wasn't I a better housekeeper? If I had dusted every once in a while, maybe I would've found the fucking camera.

"Gary texted back," McKenna announced, and I read what was on the screen.

Gary: What did I say about sending pictures, idiot.

"This oughta be good," Nix mumbled. "Reggie doesn't look happy Gary called him an idiot."

McKenna's screen had three applications running. One box was the cloud service with the pictures. One box looked like a messenger service displaying the text string Reggie had started. And the third was live-streaming Reggie. And he indeed looked irate.

"Is it just me, or is it totally creepy that it looks like Reggie is watching us?" I shuddered.

"It is," McKenna agreed. "He's looking at his screen, scrolling through the images. Look at the other box, you can watch what he's doing."

Thankfully Reggie was no longer in the folder with the pictures of me. He was now scrolling through images of an older man with gray streaking his dark hair.

"That's Gary Earle," McKenna told the room.

Reggie stopped on an image and my heart thudded in my chest.

"Gross." I diverted my eyes.

I didn't need to see Gary Earle getting a blow job from a girl who appeared to be very young. Not that I could see the girl's face clearly with it buried in his crotch.

"How much you wanna bet that is not Gary's wife?" Jameson snarled.

Oh, boy. He was pissed.

"Reggie's about to make a bad play," Nixon warned as the image of Gary and the girl popped up on the message string.

"Fuck. This is not good," Chasin said.

"Maybe it is." Nix stood back and crossed his arms

over his chest. "After that, Gary just might do the dirty work for us."

The room fell silent as we waited for Gary's response.

Gary: Wrong move.

"What does that mean?" I asked.

"That means there's a war coming. Reggie's a dumb fuck and took it too far. Now we know how he got Gary Earle to invest in his business. Bet there's more of that kind of shit in those files," Weston said.

I didn't know what war meant, and I didn't think I wanted to know. I just wanted this done and Reggie out of my life. However that came to be, I didn't care.

27

JAMESON

Jameson had completely detached from the situation. It was the only way for him to function at that point. In his mind, the pictures and videos were no longer of him and the woman he loved, they were strangers. He'd locked down every emotion in an effort to keep himself from committing murder.

Jameson wanted nothing more than to strangle Reggie Coleman with his bare hands and spit on his lifeless body.

The devastation in Kennedy's eyes had been too much for him. He knew if he didn't shut down he'd do something that would land him in prison for the rest of his life, and Kennedy would be lost to him forever.

A few months ago, he would've acted on impulse and damn the consequences, now he had too much to lose. He finally had a future and he wouldn't jeopardize it, not even for sweet vengeance.

"Now's the time to make the call." Nix nodded to

McKenna's laptop. "Reggie's pissed and backed into a corner. He needs to feel like he's in control, and having Kennedy push him right now, will piss him off more. He'll want her to know he's superior."

Kennedy pulled her cell phone out of her pocket and the sight of her shaky hands had Jameson grinding his molars.

"I'll make the call from upstairs. You'll be listening, right?"

"You give me permission to tap your phone, right?" McKenna smiled.

"Yes." Kennedy nodded.

"Perfect. We're ready."

"Come with me?" Kennedy turned to Jameson. For the first time, her request for support did nothing to calm his fury.

They made their way upstairs and he closed his office door behind them. Kennedy sat behind his desk and looked up with worried eyes.

"I'm really nervous. I don't want to screw this up."

Jameson snapped out of his funk and walked to her side. He crouched in front of her. Taking both of her hands in his, he rubbed some of the chill from her skin.

"You're gonna do great. Just be yourself. And you can't screw up, babe. Reggie's fucked and you have the upper hand. Remember that. He can't hurt you, he can't take your land, he's a pissant that's getting ready to go down."

"The pictures—"

"Are meaningless. McKenna will have them destroyed within seconds if he does anything with them."

"You're right." Kennedy sat up straight and steel infused her spine. "Fuck him. I have nothing to be afraid of."

Kennedy picked up her phone, dialed Reggie, and put the call on speaker.

"Kennedy Lane. Have you finally come to your senses?" Reggie answered, but some of his bravado was missing.

"I'm willing to negotiate."

"No—"

"Reggie, your offer is bullshit and we both know it. I checked around and I have a buyer that's willing to pay fair market value, which, as you know, is two hundred thousand more than your offer," Kennedy expertly lied.

"You're full of shit. No one will touch your land."

"Why's that?"

"Because they won't."

"Is that right? So, kinda like when Mrs. Nickels couldn't find anyone to rent her land so she was forced to sell it to your weasel ass? Like that, Reggie?"

"Exactly like that. And I'd watch your attitude, before I take another fifty K off the table," Reggie seethed.

Jameson nodded his encouragement. Kennedy was doing great getting him angrier by the second.

"Unfortunately for you, I'm not an old woman with no options. I knew you'd make it so I couldn't sell to anyone in Kent County so I contacted a few agents in

Baltimore. And guess what? They found someone who wants to buy it immediately."

"I'm warning you—"

"Warning me? You're hardly in the position to warn me, you idiot. I hold all the cards. And now I'm thinking, if you want to purchase my land, not only will you pay me market value, you'll tack on an extra fifty K for my troubles. After all, I now have that much in medical expenses, thanks to you."

"Watch who you're calling an idiot, bitch, or next time you'll have more than a bump on your head."

"Whatever, Reggie, your threats don't bother me anymore. I'm used to them. And really, you're like a little boy who cries wolf, always telling me I'll be sorry but never following through."

"I should've had him kill you," Reggie growled.

Christ, she'd done it. They had enough to get their warrant.

"Well, you didn't, dumbass, and now here I am telling you, you'll come up with two-hundred and fifty thousand dollars more on your offer or I sell to someone else."

"Tell me, Kennedy." Reggie's tone had taken an edge that sent chills up Jameson's back. "Is the extra money worth your crippled mother's life? You know how insecure her house is. Think how easy it would be for me to slip back into her yard and take out more than her air conditioning."

Kennedy started shaking and Jameson shook his head and motioned for her to keep going. Then he mouthed, "Holden," hoping she'd understand her mother was safe.

"About that," Kennedy's voice started to wobble and Jameson tightened his grip on her hands. "You owe me the thousand dollars it cost me to repair that as well. You have thirty minutes to call me back or the offer's off the table."

"Don't you—"

Kennedy disconnected the call, cutting off Reggie's threat. Not that they needed it, he'd thoroughly fucked himself.

"You did great." Jameson stood and pulled Kennedy up into his arms. "So proud of you, babe. So damn proud."

"My mom," she whispered.

"Holden's there now. Your mom and Janice are both safe."

Kennedy nodded against his chest and held on to him like he was her lifeline. Finally some of the tension started to ebb away.

They stood in silence, holding onto each other for a long time, Jameson content to give her all the time she needed to compose herself. On a heavy exhale she pulled away and looked up at him.

"Thank you. I wouldn't've been able to do that without you."

Jameson didn't believe that, Kennedy was so much stronger than she gave herself credit for. But he'd take her appreciation and store it, right next to all the other times she'd made him feel like he was ten feet tall and could take on the world, so he could recall it when he needed.

The couple made their way downstairs and back to

the conference room. Nixon was on the phone with a smile and he waved them in.

"Right. Thanks, Jonny. 'Preciate your help on this." Nixon disconnected the call and unnecessarily said, "That was Jonny." He tossed his phone on the table and continued. "He's personally walking the recording into the courthouse now and thinks he'll have a search warrant within the hour. Once he has it in hand, he's going to arrest Reggie, and McKenna can find." Nixon used air quotes. "The cloud account and we'll turn everything over to Jonny."

"What about Gary?" Kennedy asked, her voice small and unsure. "He's still after Jameson."

Jameson pulled her closer and kissed the top of her head. "Nothing to worry about."

"Legally we can't do anything about Gary," McKenna told Kennedy with a frown. "Unless there's something on that cloud server. But I've been through all of Reggie's emails and there's nothing in there. And we've yet to have access to his house and office. Hopefully, Reggie will have something that will compel Jonny to call in the Delaware authorities."

"Getting Reggie behind bars is the most important thing. As soon as he's there, McKenna can yank those pictures off the internet," Chasin added.

Nixon's phone rang and he quickly answered.

"That was fast," Nix greeted. "Right. Perfect, thanks." Then Nixon smiled. "Judge Price didn't even need to hear the entire recording before he signed the warrant. Price also said, he'd heard the rumors for years and has been waiting to take down Reggie Coleman. Jonny has deputies outside of his office and his home waiting for the go-ahead. McKenna, do your thing."

"What are my search parameters?" she asked, cracking her knuckles over her keyboard.

"Go crazy, baby. Whatever you can find."

"Awesome." She picked up her laptop and headed for the door. "Give me twenty minutes and you can call Jonny back."

Nixon nodded and Chasin stepped out of her way as she passed.

"Do you think Jonny will look into all of his purchases over the years?" Weston asked.

"I'd assume so," Nixon answered. "Why?"

"There's a lot here that doesn't add up. Someone at the bank is helping Reggie. I found two loans using nonexistent properties as collateral. Look at this loan document." Weston handed it to Nix. "The address is 123 Baker Street. There's no such address in Kent County. And Jonny's going to want to look into his building inspections. Kennedy said something about Reggie building on marshland after no one else could get a permit. There have been several grievances filed by the homeowners of those condos. Planning and Zoning has ignored the complaints."

"I'm almost afraid to see what Reggie has on the rest of that cloud. I can't imagine what he's blackmailing these people with." Chasin shook his head in disgust. "He'd never get away with this shit in the city."

Twenty minutes later, McKenna came back into the conference room looking haggard and thoroughly disgusted.

"I'm ready to talk to Jonny," she announced.

"What'd you find?" Jameson asked.

But when McKenna's gaze came to his, he was rethinking his question.

"We need to find that girl in the picture with Gary," McKenna stated.

"Why?"

"She's the key. Reggie's a sick bastard."

"We knew that, babe. What'd you find?" Nix waded in.

"Pictures. Lots and lots of pictures. And a few videos." McKenna's lips twisted. "The president of the bank. A loan officer at another bank. Peyton Marshall. A building inspector. A county commissioner. And three other men I haven't been able to cross reference to get their names. All of them in various sex acts with the same girl."

"Can you run her through facial rec?" Jameson inquired.

"Tried but there's no clear shot of her face, due to the...*sex acts*," McKenna spit out.

"Fuck," Nix clipped. "Do you think she's underage?"

"I think she's young, but with the makeup and boob job, it's hard to tell. Take a look. I isolated an image."

McKenna placed her laptop on the table and pulled

up a picture of a very young-looking blonde. Her face was in semi-profile, with her chin tilted up, and her mouth was open, looking like she was mid-moan. Thankfully, the image was from the neck up, Jameson did not want to see anymore of the woman—he could imagine she was taking someone's dick, pretending to like it, and doing it naked.

"Son of a bitch. She may not be a minor but she's no more than early twenties," Nixon sneered. "Come here, McKenna."

Nixon waited for his woman to get within reaching distance and he tagged her around the waist and tucked her close. "Sorry you had to see that shit."

"As long as Reggie goes down, it was worth it. Jonny needs to see this so I can wipe the cloud server," McKenna mumbled against Nixon's chest.

"I'll call him," Jameson offered and pulled his phone from his back pocket while keeping Kennedy pressed to his side.

Jonny picked up in two rings.

"Spenser."

"Jonny, it's Jameson. McKenna's got something for you. Do you want us to meet you at the station or do you want to come here?"

"She can't email it?"

"No."

"I'll come to you. Reggie's in custody and I don't want to take the chance of him seeing any of you. He's shoutin' and carryin' on, typical dumbass shit diggin' his hole deeper. Can it wait an hour?"

"No. You want this information. Plan on some more charges and you'll wanna brace yourself, Jonny—the information McKenna found is going to make a lot of people in this county uncomfortable."

"Christ. Just when we were starting to recover from Dillinger."

"This may be worse than Dillinger's bullshit."

"I'll be there in five. I'm already on my way."

Jameson hung up and told the rest of the team Jonny Spenser would be there soon.

"You want me to run and get you a coffee, babe?" Jameson asked Kennedy.

"No!" Kennedy's hand fisted Jameson's tee and held fast.

"Reggie's in custody and even if he wasn't, you're safe here."

"But you're not. Please don't leave."

Jameson's eyes drifted closed and the knowledge that she was worried about his well-being burned a trail of happiness. How the fuck he could feel any sort of contentment on a day like today was beyond him.

But that was pure Kennedy—sorceress. It was all a part of her appeal and charm. She could tame the beast that lived inside of him with a touch and soft word.

28

KENNEDY

I'd known Jonny for a long time. He was a hell-raiser in high school and I'm pretty sure everyone was shocked when he chose a career in law enforcement. He wasn't *bad* in high school, per se, but he pushed the limit on good old fashion teenage fun.

But in all the years I'd known him, I'd never seen him angry or lose control.

Until he saw the pictures Reggie had of me.

Nixon had to step in front of him to prevent him from leaving the office and going off half-cocked.

After Nixon and Jameson had taken Jonny upstairs for a word in private, Jonny'd come back down no less pissed, but he seemed to have a grip on his anger.

Before he left with the flash drive McKenna had made for him, and a stack of files the team had put together over the weeks, he stood toe-to-toe with me. His eyes bore into mine and he promised he'd make things right for me.

Then he left.

Jameson promptly declared we were leaving and I was done for the day. Chasin followed us out the door and when Jameson started for his house, I told him I wanted to go to mine.

I wasn't hiding again.

As soon as we'd walked in, I went straight for the living room and easily found the wireless camera. Jameson stopped me from throwing it on the floor and stomping it into a bazillion pieces. Instead, he put on a pair of blue latex gloves and placed it in an evidence bag and did the same to the one in my bedroom.

Then we spent the next hour searching my house from top to bottom, not finding anything else. Chasin had called McKenna and she confirmed there had only been the two cameras. But two was bad enough.

With the cameras outside in Jameson's truck waiting for Jonny to send a deputy to pick them up, I went about cleaning.

Jameson and Chasin sat at my kitchen table and worked, leaving me to my endeavors. I needed to do something with all my pent-up anger and energy and I didn't think Jameson would agree to let me use sex as a way to work it out. And I wasn't sure I ever wanted to have sex or undress in my house, or anywhere else again, for that matter.

Both bathrooms were spotless. I washed, folded, and put away all my clothes. I polished and dusted the living room. My kitchen floor was so clean you could eat off it. I was in search of more to do when Jameson grabbed my bicep, halting me as I walked by him.

"Enough, Kennedy."

"But—"

"You've been at it for hours. No more. Come sit with us."

"I can't sit. How 'bout I make dinner?"

"Nope. Chasin already called in food and Weston's picking it up on his way over."

"Holden still at my mom's?"

"Yep. And everything is fine, just like it was thirty minutes ago when you called and talked to her."

I knew I was being crazy about my mom but she literally couldn't run away if someone broke into her house. And I was so worried with everything going on she'd be overly stressed and have another stroke.

"Reggie's in a jail cell, Kennedy. He cannot hurt her or you."

"But Gary's not. What if he's pissed now—"

"No doubt he is. At Reggie. Gary's retribution will be aimed at Coleman. Not you. Gary's going to be more concerned about the pictures Reggie's been blackmailing him with. And don't forget, Jonny called in the Delaware State Police. Gary is in Wilmington. We'll be notified if he heads south."

Jameson was right. My nerves were shot and I was being paranoid. Everything was going to be fine.

It was finally over.

Reggie Coleman was in jail. No one thought he'd get bail because he was a flight risk. And Jonny had already

302

started questioning the men Reggie had been black-mailing and they were rolling over on him fast. They didn't want those pictures to get out on top of the crimes they'd committed. The State's Attorney was making deals left and right and likely would be doing it through the night.

Finally I could breathe without the threat of Reggie looming over me.

He'd been harassing me for so long it was like I forgot what it was like to just live. Not that I was out of the woods, I still had to recoup my business, but Jameson would help with that. And with him by my side, I could do it faster than I could going at it alone. Not that I *couldn't* do it by myself, but I no longer *had* to.

I sank down to Jameson's lap and wrapped my arm around his shoulder.

"Thank you. Both of you."

"No need—"

"Thank you, Chasin," I told him solemnly.

"We should be the one thanking you," Chasin said, blowing off my appreciation.

Jeez, could none of these guys take some credit?

"I don't know what kind of voodoo you're practicin', but never stop. I've never seen this asshole not be a, well... asshole." Chasin smirked before he continued. "None of us even knew he could laugh. We all thought he had some kind of vocal cord damage that prevented the sound. We knew he could bark orders. But laugh? No way."

"You're hilarious, Chasin," Jameson quipped. "So funny I forgot to laugh."

"You didn't forget shit and you never will as long as Kennedy's around."

Jameson's wide smile stole my breath. Damn, he was good-looking.

"You're right about that," Jameson agreed.

WESTON BROUGHT OVER MEXICAN TAKEOUT. After everything that happened, I didn't have an appetite and politely declined the food. But Jameson insisted I needed to eat something. Two bites into my first crunchy taquito, I was suddenly starved and woofed down all four, plus all the rice, before the three men were done with their plates.

Thankfully, all four of us were wiped out and needing sleep, because without a TV in my living room, there wasn't much to do. Chasin took the guest room upstairs but Weston refused the room I used as my office, even though there was a futon.

He wanted to sleep downstairs.

No one said anything but I understood why. It was the same reason Jameson had told me to get my shotgun out of my safe and why all three men had their weapons clearly visible on their hips.

I quickly changed into pair of pjs, something I'd never worn to bed while sleeping next to Jameson. But if I had to make a hasty retreat or possibly shoot someone, I preferred to be in more than one of Jameson's tees and my panties.

Not that I wanted to shoot someone—but to protect myself and the guys, I would.

"Tell me how you're holding up," Jameson requested once we were both in bed.

"I think I'm in shock. I'm almost numb, like today happened to somebody else. I don't know how to explain it. I'm horrified Reggie has pictures of us and they're now evidence. Beyond embarrassed Jonny and the State's Attorney and God knows who else will review them." I stopped and shuddered at the thought. "It's so disgusting I can't even think about it. But I think what's most unbelievable to me is that it's over. I'm not even surprised at the level of corruption or the blackmail. I didn't think it was *that* bad. I thought Reggie was a part of the good ol' boy crowd, and his cronies were givin' him a leg up for some cash."

"Money and greed make people do fucked-up things."

Jameson would know more about that than I would.

"I really hope Jonas Brown isn't one of the men that McKenna couldn't identify. I would be so disappointed. He seems so nice, and his wife, Lavender, I don't think that's her real name, but they're total hippies so I don't question her name. Anyway, Lavender is so sweet and all love, peace, and flowers she would be crushed," I sighed.

"I think Jonas is a victim in this. Just like the owner of Willow Realty."

"I hope you're right." Jameson tightened his arm

around my back, settling me closer, and for the first time in over six months I could breathe easy. "So now what?"

"Now, we relax, and just live."

"Sounds kinda boring."

"Boring is great."

"How do you feel about getting a dog?"

Jameson's body went solid and I wasn't sure what I said that upset him.

"If you don't—"

"Never had a dog but I always wanted one." His gruff voice was laced with sadness. "We couldn't afford another mouth to feed when I was a kid. Then I was gone too much when I was in the Navy."

"So? You wanna get one?"

"Yeah, babe, I want one."

"I want it to live in the house and I don't want to put it in a crate."

"No point in having a guard dog if he's locked in a cage," Jameson agreed.

"Can we look at German Shepherds?"

"As long as it's not a little ankle-biter, we'll get whatever you want."

"Can we name it Petal?" I teased.

"No. He needs a tough name like Killer or Cujo."

"Um, no. How 'bout Tank or Zeus?"

"Tank."

"Tank." I smiled. "I can't wait to get him. Can we look this weekend?"

"Whenever you want."

"'Night, Jameson."

"'Night, babe."

I closed my eyes and I was still smiling. I liked this agreeable, easy side of Jameson. But I also liked his gruff, bossy side, too. He was the perfect mix of hard and soft.

Maybe boring was great. I couldn't wait to find out.

29

JAMESON

Jameson's phone ringing on the nightstand pulled him from a dreamless, peaceful sleep. Something that only started happening since Kennedy had started sleeping next to him. Just her body next to his beat back the nightmares that had plagued him for years.

Jameson glanced at the table and watched the clock tick to five a.m.. Kennedy's alarm started blaring, accompanying the ringing from his cell.

Now fully awake and alert, he reached out with his free hand and slapped the clock, stopping the annoying buzzing, and tagged his phone.

"Yeah."

"Jonny called," Nixon started, and Jameson started to roll Kennedy off his chest, but she shook her head, obviously awake. "Gary Earle crossed the state line into Maryland ten minutes ago."

"Fuck. What's the plan?"

"Everyone to the office, now."

"What about Lola? She can't climb the stairs."

"She's five-foot nothing and weighs less than the iron you bench press. I think you can carry her."

If Jameson had been firing on all cylinders he wouldn't have asked. Of course he could carry her up to the office.

"Right. Is Holden bringing them over?"

"Yes."

"See you in ten minutes."

Jameson tapped the disconnect button and dipped his chin, looking down to his chest but only seeing the top of Kennedy's head.

"Did you hear that, babe?"

"Yeah."

"We need to get up and wake the guys if they're not already up."

"It's not over," she whispered.

Jameson rolled, forcing Kennedy to her back. He came up on an elbow and stared down at her.

"Look at me, Kennedy." Her focus came to him and his gut clenched at the worry in her eyes. "It *is* over," Jameson proclaimed.

"But—"

"We don't know why Gary Earle is coming to town or even if he is. But we're going to take precautions."

"We know why."

"No, we're assuming he's coming here to tie up loose ends. Which if you think about is a good thing. Now Jonny has access to him. He'll pick him up and question him."

"He's here to kill you or me. We fucked up Reggie's plan, which means I screwed him over."

"Not gonna happen. He won't even see one pretty hair on your head. You and your mom will be at the office tucked away nice and safe."

"And you? Where will you be?"

"Hunting." A wolfish smile spread across Jameson's face. "Holden will stay with you and the rest of us will help Jonny track Gary."

"He wants to—" Kennedy's voice had raised in both volume and octave.

"First, I'm not worried about some cocksucker getting the drop on me. I have years of experience on him. And, second, do you think Weston, Chasin, or Nixon would let him get close to me?"

"Bullets don't care about experience, Jameson. I won't...I can't lose you."

"You. Are. Never. Going to lose me." Jameson punctuated his words. "Jonny needs help. That's why he deputized us, remember? The sheriff's office doesn't have the manpower. He needs all hands on deck."

"Promise you'll be careful?" Kennedy still didn't sound happy or convinced.

"I promise. Get dressed."

He leaned down and gave her a hard and fast closed-mouth kiss and rolled again to get out of bed.

If Gary was headed to Kent County, they had forty-five minutes before he'd arrive. Ten minutes had been shaved off that before Jonny had called, and five more talking to Kennedy. They only had thirty minutes to form a plan.

Piece of cake. They'd adapted mission objectives in less time than that.

"McKenna has the monitors off, right?" Jameson triple-checked.

"Yes," Nixon answered on a frustrated grunt. "Three times I've confirmed."

Jameson ignored his friend's irritation and fought the urge to verify that McKenna was clear she wasn't to turn them on.

Weston, Nixon, Chasin, Jonny, and Jameson were back at Kennedy's. They'd left Holden at the office to watch over Kennedy, McKenna, Lola, and Janice. Just in case they were wrong, the women needed protection. What they didn't need was to be watching the camera feed from Kennedy's house. Jameson knew Nixon didn't want his woman watching what was about to go down anymore than he did. Everything should run smooth and be over in a matter of minutes, but Jameson knew shit could go sideways as quick as lightning.

"You're sure Gary's gonna show up here?" Jonny asked.

"It's six in the morning," Jameson reminded him. "Where else would he go? Gary has no ties to KC expect for Reggie who is locked up in the detention center.

Visiting hours don't start until three. The banks don't open until nine. And his lawyer who drew up the business agreement is in Delaware, so he's not seeking legal counsel. You have a deputy parked down the street from Lois Coleman's house and Deloris Marshall's in case he pays them a visit."

"What about one of the men Reggie was blackmailing?"

"Reggie was blackmailing. Not Gary," Weston took over the clarification. "Gary's scot-free on that charge. There's no proof he had any involvement. But, if he wants to salvage the business he still needs Jameson out of the way and Kennedy to fold. Besides that, Gary's pissed. No doubt he wants a little revenge, too. And you read McKenna's report on Earle, people around him who deny him what he wants mysteriously wind up dead. He's coming here."

Jonny nodded his understanding and Jameson looked back out the window, scanning Kennedy's front yard. His truck and hers were the only two in the driveway. All the lights were off in the house and by all accounts it would look like the occupants were still sleeping.

A black Cadillac CT6-V pulled into Kennedy's drive and Jameson tightened his jaw. The driver exited the vehicle and silently closed the door. It wasn't surprising the short, slightly rounded man drove a ninety-thousand-dollar Caddy with blacked-out windows and five-hundred and fifty horsepower under the hood. Power. Class. And wealth. He'd need his car to convey all of the things he lacked in stature, build, and looks.

He was a fraud. A bully who was used to getting his way.

Silently, the men all slipped into their hiding places and waited for Gary to make his move. They'd made it easy for him and had left the front door unlocked. No sense in wasting time seeing if he could pick it or spending money if he damaged the door.

Breaking and entering was breaking and entering, even if you didn't actually break something to enter a home that was not yours.

The door creaked open and shut with a click. Jameson couldn't help but think what an idiot both Reggie and Gary were. If the car pulling up wouldn't have woken him up, the door would've. Like amateurs they'd not done their homework on Jameson. A simple background check on him would've shown he'd served in the military—even if his affiliation with the Special Warfare Command was suppressed, they'd still know he was dangerous. Yet, they were cocky and stupid.

With the curtains closed the room was mostly dark. Gary's frame was still in shadow and Jameson itched for the man to hurry. They couldn't move until they had a clear view of the man to see if he was armed.

Too soon, Jonny stepped out of his hiding spot and yelled for Gary to put his hands up. The next thirty seconds played out like a slow-motion horror film.

Gunshots rang out and to Jameson's left, Jonny stumbled back and hit the floor with a thud.

Shit hadn't gone sideways, it was FUBAR. Completely and totally fucked beyond repair. Without hesitation, Jameson leveled his weapon and fired one shot. The back of Gary's head exploded, brain matter and blood splattered in every direction and the man was dead before his body crumpled to the floor.

Weston and Nixon were already crouched over Jonny's prone body and Chasin was on the phone with dispatch for an ambulance.

Fuck, goddamn, shit. What a clusterfuck of a mess.

FIVE MINUTES later Kennedy's living room was overrun with deputies and EMTs. Outside, fire trucks, ambulances, and squad cars with lights still flashing filled her driveway and yard. The medical examiner was pulling in and Jameson couldn't figure out where one more emergency vehicle could park.

"I fucked up," Jonny wheezed and rubbed his chest.

He had. He was also lucky he was wearing a vest. Gary's first shot had gone wide but his second had hit Jonny center mass.

What's one more hole to patch in Kennedy's house? And Jameson couldn't forget the blood and brain matter that now stained her walls, curtains, and floor.

"You need to ride to the hospital," an EMT told Jonny.

"I'm fine."

"You have at least one cracked rib," Sheriff Baker noted sternly. "You're going to the hospital."

Jonny didn't argue with his boss but he didn't look

happy. With two EMTs flanking him, Jonny stood and looked at Jameson. "Fuck. I'm sorry."

Jameson gave the man a chin lift and slapped his shoulder. "I'm just glad you're not dead. The rest can be cleaned up."

"But you—"

"Not the first time, Jonny. Hope it's the last but I gotta be honest, I feel no remorse for protecting a friend."

Jonny's face went taut and the lines in his forehead deepened. Without another word he walked out the door.

"You gonna tell Kennedy about all of this?" Nixon asked, waving his hand around the room.

Jameson thought about his friend's question. His first instinct was to protect her and not let her back into her house until it was cleaned and the holes were patched, and pretend the whole shitshow happened in the front yard and not in the living room of the house she loved. But shielding her from the truth would be a lie. And he hated liars.

"Yeah, I'm gonna tell her. Though she doesn't need to see this shit, so I'll have it cleaned before we come home."

Nixon's grin turned into a smile Jameson had only seen directed at McKenna and he said, "Happy for you."

Jameson was happy for himself, too. He'd be happier, however, when the mess was cleaned up and he and his woman were home sitting on the couch watching their new puppy run around.

30

KENNEDY

Jameson had kept me away from my house for almost two weeks. He'd told me what had happened that morning and he'd already called two different cleaning services by the time he'd made it back to the office. I'd thought two was overkill, but when he'd started to explain the mess, I simply put a hand up halting the details and told him he was in change. Whatever he felt was necessary, he should do. While I appreciated the honesty, I did not want to know what brain matter looked like.

After the living room was thoroughly scrubbed and the holes were patched, we'd gone back to my house. When we walked in, I waited for fear or panic to take over. But it didn't. Jameson and I stood in the room, and as I looked around, I felt nothing. It was just home. No creepy feeling someone had died, no lingering terror from Peyton or Reggie.

Nothing.

All I'd felt was relief.

We'd been back in the house for two days and I had more than enough work to keep me busy. The jumpstart on working up my garden and planting had dwindled substantially. As soon as Jameson had left for work, I'd started plowing and had finished tilling the ground by lunch.

I was in the house making lunch and making calls to order fertilizer and the seeds I'd need when Jonas Brown called.

At first the call had been awkward and strained as Jonas apologized profusely and told me what I'd already known—Reggie had threatened to renege on his lease. The conversation turned when I happily accepted his apology and told him I understood.

Then he asked me to bring all of my stock to his store. His customers had been ready to riot when he'd told them he'd no longer stocked my honey. He also asked me to bring all the candles I had made as well. He wanted to make a special display with products. Of course, I immediately accepted his offer and was on cloud nine as I showered and loaded the boxes into the back of my truck.

I was pulling out of my driveway when I called Jameson.

"Babe?"

His deep rumbling voice filled the cab of my truck and I couldn't help smiling. I loved it when he answered the phone like that. It was a greeting *and* foreplay and always made me shiver.

"Guess what?" I asked, but rushed to tell him before

he could guess. "Jonas Brown called. He asked me to bring *all* of my honey *and* candles to his store."

"Good news."

"Great news. I'll be able to start making payments to my angel investor soon."

"Kennedy," he growled, and that made me shiver, too.

Jameson had opened a joint account and had deposited thirty thousand dollars. Then he'd told me if we needed more, he'd transfer it. I didn't know how he'd saved up that much money and I didn't ask. Money complicated things, and I didn't want to take any risks with our relationship.

"Kidding. Kidding. Anyway, I wanted to let you know where I was going. After I drop this stuff off to Jonas, I'm heading to Southern States to pick up what I need to start planting tomorrow."

"I told you to wait until Saturday and I'd help."

"No sense in wastin' daylight. And besides, I have it down to a science. It will only take me two days."

"I still can't believe you plant each seed by hand."

"Gives a whole new meaning to homegrown, doesn't it?"

"Gives a whole new meaning to how much vegetables cost," he grumbled.

Large farms would not hand plant each row, but my garden was too small to use a tractor and machinery to plant. And besides, I enjoyed working in my yard.

"I'll call you when I'm at the grocery store, think about what you want for dinner. And don't say whatever you want or you're eating liver and onions tonight."

"All right, babe, I'll think about it." He chuckled.

I listened to the sound and wondered when it stopped sounding rusty. Over the last few weeks his smiles were coming easy and his laughter was frequent.

I let that thought slide down my chest and warm my belly. Jameson was happy.

"Love you, babe."

"Love you, Jameson."

Yeah, my man was finally happy. And we'd have our new puppy next week, one more thing Jameson would finally have. A dog and a home. Both I'd get to share with him.

———

JONAS AND LAVENDER had been all smiles when we set up the new display they'd placed at an end cap. It was front and center when you walked in the door. When we were done, we chatted for a few minutes, avoiding any talk of Reggie or what had happened. Before I left, I purchased the essential oils I'd been eyeing the last time I was in the store and a box of my favorite tea.

Jonas waved away my money with sadness clear in his eyes and I didn't push. If the man needed to give me fifteen dollars' worth of free products to make himself feel better, for once I would accept the offer and not quibble.

I was walking through the parking lot behind Nature's Choice thinking about how my life was looking up. I'd made it to the other side and now I could concentrate on Jameson and the life we were starting. He'd all but moved in—it had just happened, but we hadn't talked about it. He didn't even have his own key, even though he was there every night.

Why didn't he have one?

I made it to my truck and added a stop to the hardware store to make him a copy. I opened the door, excited to watch Jameson's face when I gave him the key to his very first house. He'd love it. I knew he would. His eyes would go soft and he'd grunt my name before he'd kiss me.

There was a pinch on the side of my neck and I swatted away whatever had bitten me.

Damn, that stung.

I braced myself on my open door and tried to stay upright as my vision blurred and I started to sway.

What the hell was happening?

I vaguely felt my knees scrape the asphalt as my eyes closed.

WHAT THE HELL was going on? Why was I moving? I cracked my eyes open and all I could see was the back of a car seat. My stomach churned and all I could think was that I'd had some sort of an allergic reaction to whatever had stung me. Thank God, someone had seen me pass out and was taking me to the hospital.

"Thank you," I murmured to the good Samaritan and

closed my eyes. The pain the light caused was unbearable.

"Oh, it's my pleasure."

I knew that voice. My eyes flew open and I fought to sit up but I couldn't move my hands. Tied. Why hadn't I noticed that? Because I was a naïve idiot, always thinking the best of people.

"Let me out," I demanded.

"Not yet."

I rolled the best I could, trying to sit up, when my cellphone dug into my hip.

Yes! Please God let McKenna find me before I lose service or my battery dies. How long before Jameson figures out I'm missing?

Hours, and I could very easily be dead by then.

Why was I so damn stupid, always living in a bubble of sunshine? Hadn't I learned my lesson? People were assholes. Jameson had it right all along. Why couldn't I have been more like him—always on the lookout for trouble, never putting anything past anyone.

People fucking sucked! And I was going to learn the hard way what Jameson had tried to warn me about. You can't trust anyone, not even when you're walking across a fucking parking lot. I should've been paying attention.

31

JAMESON

Jameson pushed away the thick file Alec Hall had prepared for the team. Months of Coast Guard surveillance and intel wrapped up in one tidy brief. Their newest contract with the Department of Homeland Security wouldn't officially start until next month, but Alec had asked the team to be prepared at any time—drug smugglers didn't follow a precise schedule. Though the traffickers had stuck to the same route and Jameson had to admire their ingenuity.

The waterways—some small, some larger, from New York to Maryland's Chesapeake Bay, then straight to the Atlantic—offered the criminals a clear, mostly unpoliced avenue to move their drugs, with plenty of places to stop and make deliveries, pick up product, and swap vessels.

The flaw in their plan had been the Delaware River.

Jameson glanced at the clock on the wall in his office and frowned. It was well past the time Kennedy should've called him. He'd lost track of time, maybe so had she.

He glanced at the file thinking he'd work another couple of minutes while he waited for her, but something felt off. Kennedy always checked in, even though she'd warned him when she was working she had no sense of time, she'd never not called when she said she would.

Jameson grabbed his cell, and with a sense of urgency, he scrolled to her number and tapped the call icon. Seven rings later, Kennedy's voice came on the line and asked him to leave a message.

Voicemail.

He sat back in his chair and tossed his phone from hand to hand. Jameson weighed his options and didn't care what it said about him or that he was probably over-reacting. He made his way to Nixon and McKenna's office and knocked on the frame of the open door.

"Gotta second?"

Both McKenna and Nix glanced up from their laptops but it was Nix who answered, "What's up?"

"Kennedy's not answering her phone. Can you track it?" Jameson asked McKenna.

Her brow went up and she smirked. "She's not answering, so you want me to track her down for you?"

"Yep."

"When was the last time you talked to her?" Nix questioned.

"A few hours. She was headed to Nature's Choice. Then she was going to Southern States and she was supposed to call me when she was done running errands and at the grocery store."

Jameson knew he sounded crazy, but he could feel it, Kennedy was in trouble.

"She probably ran into twenty people she knows at Southern States." Nix shook his head. "You know how it is around here. Everyone's nosey as shit and will have a hundred questions for her."

Jameson had already thought about that.

"Know that," he acknowledged his friend, then went back to McKenna. "Can you track her?"

"You're serious?"

"Very." The longer he stood and argued with the couple, the tighter the knot in his stomach grew. "Something doesn't feel right. I can't tell you what it is, but my gut is screaming at me."

"Why the hell didn't you lead with that, instead of coming in here sounding like a jealous stalker boyfriend?" Nix snapped.

McKenna was already tapping away on her keyboard when her hand stopped mid-stroke.

"Wait. Remember when she told us she disabled her GPS?" McKenna asked.

"No."

Jameson had no recollection of any such conversation.

"It was the night we were talkin' about hacking Reggie's phone. She said something about not realizing it was so easy, and she thought she'd protected herself because she disabled her GPS."

"Okay? So?" Jameson still didn't remember and wasn't sure why that mattered.

"I can't simply track her, because her GPS is off. I have to fully access her phone."

"So? do it."

McKenna's face got tight and the corners of her mouth tipped down. "I'll do it, Jameson. But it's a total invasion of her privacy and really intrusive. I'll have access to everything. Not that I'll look at anything, but I could, and she's my friend—"

"Listen, I get you're concerned and I hope like fuck I'm mistaken and you all can bust my balls later about being an overprotective idiot, but I'm telling you something's wrong."

McKenna looked to Nix and he nodded.

Jameson mentally ran down Kennedy's plans for the day one more time then tried to recall anything that had been out of the ordinary in the last two weeks. Kennedy had gone to work with Jameson every day. They'd gone to the store together. Out to eat. They'd visited her mother. And none of those times had anyone followed them or had behaved strangely. They'd been stopped several times while they'd been out and Kennedy had been asked if she was okay, and they were happy to hear Reggie had been stopped. The questions had been nosey, but as Nix said, it was a small town, that's what people did. No one had been overly aggressive, and in the last few days, the inquiries had seemed to stop.

No one had driven up to the Swagger Farm or had been lurking around the office.

Gossip was only as good as the next story.

People had moved on.

Gary was dead. Peyton was dead. Reggie was in jail and no one was coming to his defense because he no longer had anything to hang over people's heads.

Or did he?

"Hey, Jonas? Nixon Swagger. Sorry to bother you but what time did Kennedy Lane leave your store?" Nixon asked into his phone, then paused. "Right. Was anyone in the store today giving her a hard time or taking a special interest in her?" Nix waited again. "Okay, thanks. Hey, one more thing, are there any cameras in your parking lot?" Nixon frowned and nodded. "No problem, and thanks for your help."

"Her phone's off or she doesn't have service. I'm going to keep trying," McKenna announced.

"What'd Jonas say?" Jameson asked, trying to keep his patience in check.

"She left around two. No one else was in the store, period—lunchtime is the slowest part of the day. No cameras in the parking lot."

A little over three hours ago.

Fuck.

Jameson pulled up her number to try her again, but stopped when Nix's phone rang.

"Swagger." His eyes shot to Jameson's and he clipped. "Don't touch anything. We'll be right there."

Jameson's body coiled tight and Nixon stood.

"McKenna, keep trying her phone and call Weston, ask him to meet us at Nature's Choice." Nixon hadn't broken eye contact with Jameson, even though he'd been talking to his woman. "Jonas checked the parking lot. He found Kennedy's truck still in the lot with the door open."

Jameson's whole body caught fire and anger like an old familiar friend settled in his gut and got comfortable. He didn't wait for his friend to say more, he took off down the hall, skipped two steps at a time, and was out the door like a shot.

Nixon made it to Jameson's truck and jumped in as he was pulling away from the curb.

"I'll call Jonny—"

"No. He'll slow us down," Jameson returned.

"We need information from him."

Jameson made a right turn, ignoring the traffic light, and cut off a car driving through the intersection. "If he tells me to stand down, I'm not listening. Missing adult cases are not a priority and you know it."

Missing. Fuck.

Nixon had his phone to his ear and Jameson could hear the bite of Nix's tone, but the words evaded him over the roaring in his ears.

Jameson pulled into the lot and skidded to a halt behind Kennedy's truck. He sucked in a breath seeing the door open. Three hours. Three fucking hours her truck was less than five miles from him with the door left wide open.

Nixon and Jameson jumped out and Nix shoved a pair of latex gloves at Jameson.

"Don't contaminate the crime scene."

Crime scene. What the fuck.

Jameson stood frozen, unable to calculate his next move. As a matter of fact, Jameson was at a total loss. He couldn't believe this was happening.

"Doesn't she carry a purse?" Nixon's question snapped him to attention.

"No. Not normally. She has one of the phone cases that holds her cards."

Nixon nodded and opened the back door to her truck and poked his head in.

Jameson went to the other side to help him search, and two minutes later after they'd checked under her seats, center console, and glove box, he announced, "No phone. She must've had it on her."

They circled the truck looking for something—anything. Nixon got to his stomach and crawled partially under her truck. He backed out holding a piece of orange plastic.

"Looks like an old-school hypodermic needle cap."

Jameson's body swayed and he had to force himself to stay upright.

"Nixon!" a man yelled, and jogged across the parking lot.

On instinct, Jameson's hand started to move toward his hip but Nix grabbed his bicep, halting the process.

"Jonas," Nix greeted. "This is Jameson, Kennedy's man."

Jonas looked to Jameson and locked eyes. "I'm sorry I didn't come out sooner. We got busy and Lavender was in the back doing payroll. Things like this don't happen here, I didn't think to walk her out."

As much as Jameson appreciated the man's concern, he didn't have the time nor the inclination to assuage the other man's guilt.

"I talked to Ray," Jonas continued. "Come on, you're gonna want to talk to his son. The boy was taking out the trash and saw two women getting into a car."

Two women?

Jameson didn't have time to question Jonas further, he was halfway across the parking lot. A door opened and a big, heavyset man stepped out with a scrawny teenager.

Jonas made a quick introduction and explained that Ray owned a roofing company whose office was in the space next to Nature's Choice. Jameson's gaze never left the boy's as he shifted uncomfortably from foot to foot.

"Go on, RJ, tell 'em what you saw," Ray prompted his son.

"I was taking out the trash. Right there." The boy pointed to a dumpster ten feet away and Jameson looked from the metal container back to Kennedy's truck. Roughly fifty yards away, the boy would've had a clear line of sight. "I didn't...I didn't think anything about it. A woman was helping another woman into the back seat."

"What do you mean, helping?" Nix cut in.

"I don't know, like, the woman had her arms around the other woman from behind. Under her armpits, you know, and sat her in the back seat, then picked her legs up and put them in."

Jameson's jaw clenched until his molars hurt.

"Did you see her face?" Nix continued.

"No. Both of their backs were to me and I went back in. The woman being put into the car had blonde hair, or really light brown. And the other one had old woman hair."

"What does that mean?"

"You know, it was like gray and cut short. Above her shoulders."

"*Like* gray? Or gray?" Jameson asked.

"It was...I think it's called salt and pepper." RJ turned to his father. "Like Grandma's."

"He means dark with gray streaks," Ray clarified.

"What about the car?" Jameson persisted.

"It was a black Buick."

"You sure?"

"Yes. My buddy Todd's mom has one. It was a Buick for sure."

"Was there anyone else? Maybe in the car or standing close?"

"No. Just the two women. That's why I didn't think anything about it. I just thought the woman was helping her into the car."

As much as Jameson wanted to shake the kid for not intervening, he couldn't blame him. Cliff City was a small town, kidnapping was not the first thing that would come to anyone's mind. Especially if the woman doing the taking looked like a grandmother.

"Thanks, RJ. You've been very helpful," Nixon offered.

"I'm really sorry. I would've helped. I just didn't think..."

"Put that out of your mind. You had no way of knowing. Please call us if you think of anything else." Nix pulled a business card out of his pocket and gave it to Ray.

Jameson was already walking away from the group with his phone to his ear.

"Still no luck, Jameson," McKenna answered her phone.

"A woman took her. Older, salt and pepper hair, drives a black Buick," Jameson cut straight to it.

"Reggie Coleman has a black Buick registered in his name. Hold on." He could hear McKenna furiously pounding on the keyboard. "Lois Coleman has blonde hair and she's short and stout. But she could've been wearing a wig."

"Yo!" Jameson bellowed across the parking lot. "How tall was the woman?"

RJ frowned for a moment then answered. "She was pretty tall for a woman." Again he turned to his father. "Like mom's height."

"Five-eight," Ray once again explained.

"Thin? Heavy set?" Jameson questioned.

"Average?" The teenager shrugged his shoulders. "She wasn't *big*, but she wasn't thin, either."

"Did you hear that?" Jameson went back to his conversation with McKenna.

"Yeah. Not Lois Coleman."

Jameson caught sight of Weston pulling into the lot.

The smell of burning rubber filled his nostrils as Weston came to a stop, not bothering to pull into a parking spot.

"What about Deloris Marshall or Gary Earle's wife?"

"Anything?" Weston asked, coming to Jameson's side.

"Weston's here. I'm putting you on speaker."

"Negative on Gary's wife, she's wheelchair bound. I'm checking on Deloris now. Holy shit. Wait a second."

"What?" Jameson growled. The shock of McKenna's voice almost sounded giddy.

"Kennedy's phone is back on. Shut up for a second."

Jameson's heart thumped in his chest and his breath caught.

Come on, McKenna, work your magic.

"Why are we in Pennsylvania?" Unprepared to hear Kennedy's voice, Jameson rocked back in shock.

"You ruined everything!" a woman shouted.

"That's Deloris Marshall," McKenna announced.

"But why are we in Pennsylvania? You passed Idaville ten miles ago. There's nothing but barns out here."

"Shut up. You talk too much," Deloris complained.

Good girl!

"She's telling us where she is," Jameson declared.

"Smart," Weston agreed.

"Idaville, Pennsylvania, is one hundred and forty-six miles north. There are two main routes," McKenna cut in. "PA-34 north and PA-94 both are rural roads."

"You kidnapped me." Kennedy sounded insolent. "I think I deserve to know where you're taking me. You just passed a sign that said welcome to Goodyear."

"They're headed north. Come on, Kennedy. Keep going," McKenna encouraged, even though Kennedy couldn't hear her. "She knows we're listening."

"I'm headed north." Jameson jogged to his truck and watched Weston toss his keys into the open window of his truck. "Tell me where I'm going."

"Someone park this for me." Weston gestured to his vehicle. "I'll be back later for the keys."

"Pulling up a map now," McKenna told Jameson as Nixon and Weston piled into his truck.

"Do a property search in Pennsylvania, anything—"

"Already did it," McKenna cut Nix off.

"I didn't kidnap you," Deloris sneered. "My Reggie's in jail because of you. It's all your fault."

"You sure went through a lot of trouble drugging me and tying my hands behind my back for a nice afternoon drive."

Jameson's grip on the wheel tensed until his knuckles turned white.

That's it, babe, keep her talking. Hold tight, I'm coming for you.

32

KENNEDY

My headache had turned into a dull throb and my throat felt like I'd swallowed sand.

There was nothing I could do but talk while we were driving and pray that McKenna had been able to hack my phone. Jameson had to know I was missing by now.

All I had was hope and a prayer. I'd been trying to untie the knot behind my back but all I'd done was chafe my wrists bloody and the sticky liquid did nothing to lubricate. It actually made it worse.

Even after all these hours, I was still in a state of shock that Deloris had been able to get me into her car. I didn't remember her doing it, but I was surprised she was as strong as she was—I had to have been dead weight. I wasn't afraid of Deloris so much as I was of the thought of her having an unknown accomplice.

What if someone else was following behind us? She'd said *she* didn't kidnap me. And I was afraid to ask her what she'd meant by that. Did she not put me in her car, or in her mind was it not kidnapping me because she was taking me somewhere to kill me?

Either way, I was screwed until we stopped. Now that the drug had worked its way out and I could think clearly, I realized I still had use of my legs. As long as she didn't shoot me or stab me I could easily outrun the woman—even with my hands tied behind my back.

I was formulating a plan of attack when I remembered I hadn't been giving McKenna directions.

Please be listening.

"Why are we going to Fuller Lake?"

"Enough!" Deloris shouted.

"Just tell me why? Why are you doing this? Why are we on Lake Shore Drive?"

"Because you ruined everything. It's your fault my son was murdered. If you would've just sold Reggie your land, none of this would've happened. My son would be alive and me and Reggie would be together."

No surprises there, I'd already put two and two together and figured out why she'd kidnapped me, but I was happy she admitted it. If McKenna was listening, she'd also be recording the conversation. At least when this was over, Deloris Marshall would be right next to Reggie in the detention center and they could be together like she wanted.

"I didn't kill your son."

"It's all your fault!" Deloris screamed.

In her fit of anger, she jerked the wheel and I careened sideways. My abdominal muscles protested as I tried to remain upright.

"Be careful or you're going to crash."

"What do I care? Everything's gone. All gone. You took everything."

Oh, hell. For the first time in hours, real fear wound its way through my body. If she crashed either by accident or on purpose, I was fucked. She hadn't buckled me in, I'd easily be seriously injured.

I had to keep her talking but I was afraid to make her any angrier. "The lake is beautiful."

"Reggie took his son up here to hunt."

Another clue. Please, McKenna, find me.

What else? Think, Kennedy.

Deloris made a turn, taking us up a treelined driveway.

"I love the tall evergreens. They give off so much shade. I was thinking of planting a row next to my house—"

"Shut up."

Shit. I shouldn't have mentioned my house. Now she was pissed again.

A nice cabin came into view and panic hit. This was it. She was stopping.

"The...um...cabin is pretty. It looks like it was made from real logs. Have you...um...it's real nice. And you still have a view of the lake."

Deloris didn't say anything. She turned off the car, got out, and I was getting my feet in position to kick out as soon as she opened the back door to get me out.

But she never opened the door. Instead, she beeped the alarm and walked to the house.

I couldn't stop my heart from pumping overtime and beads of sweat formed on my forehead and started to roll down my face. Even though the car was parked in the shade, the air temperature outside was still stifling. *Only I would get kidnapped and locked in a car on the hottest day of the month.*

Shit. I was wasting time. I had no idea when Deloris would be back.

"McKenna. If you're listening, Deloris Marshall took me to a cabin in Pennsylvania. I don't see a house number and the last street sign I saw was Lake Shore Drive. She left me in the car and went into the house..." Even though I felt like an idiot talking to myself I gave a detailed accounting of what happened and everything I remembered about the drive. I didn't know how much time had lapsed but I knew it'd been two hours since I woke up. Or since I was able to get myself into a sitting position and look at the clock on the radio.

I fell silent when I ran out of things to tell McKenna. I finally got myself angled far enough so my back was against the door. It was frustrating as hell not to be able to see as I felt around for the lock. Sweat was now dripping down my chest and back and I really needed a drink of water.

Finally, I found the lock and slid the lever. The door handle was just below that. Almost there. The excitement died when the door didn't open.

"Child safety locks," I muttered. "It's so damn hot in here. I'm going to try the other side."

It took me a long time to scoot myself to the other side and repeat the process. "Nope. This side's locked, too."

An idea hit and I tried to get my legs over the center console. If I could get into the front seat I could get out. I twisted and tried to maneuver through the space but I couldn't manage it with my hands behind me.

"Fuck," I huffed in frustration. "I really hope you're listening, McKenna, and my phone didn't die or lose service. I'm stuck in here and I can't get into the front seat, I tried."

That was a seriously depressing thought. As long as I was locked in the car, she was my only chance.

I sat back and rested my head against the seat back.

"You're probably wondering why I'm not trying to kick out the window," I said conversationally. "I thought about it. But with my hands tied I'd have to dive out the window. If I hurt myself, I won't be able to fight the bitch when she finally comes back. And I don't know if someone else is in the house. I think for now I'm safer in the car. But if it gets any hotter in this fucker, I may have to do that just so I don't sweat to death.

That was a terrifying thought.

"How long does it take for someone to die from heat exhaustion? I remember something on the news about a poor little baby who was left in the car on accident. But I can't remember how long it takes."

Surely it would take hours, right?

I tried to work the knots again but the raw skin had me crying out in pain.

"This fucking sucks, McKenna. My hands are useless

and I'm stuck in this goddamn car. I wish Jameson was here, he'd know what to do. God, I hope you're listening. If you're not, I'm screwed. My only chance is if she opens this goddamn door."

I pounded my head on the seatback in frustration and immediately regretted the sudden movement.

"And I have a damn headache. I'm going to kick her in the face when she comes back."

I looked at the house and imagined Deloris sitting on the couch reading a magazine, not a care in the world I was dying of thirst and hot as hell.

"God! What a bitch. She blames me for Peyton's death. Me! Can you believe that shit? He broke into my house. He tried to kill me. It's Reggie's fault, not mine. God, I hope he rots in jail forever."

I don't know how long I sat there feeling sorry for myself but it was long enough to be soaked in sweat and for fear to replace my anger. My head no longer ached—instead I was dizzy, so dizzy my eyes kept drifting closed.

This must've been Deloris's plan. She was going to bake me in the car until I was dead. I fucked up, I should've kicked out the window when I had time. I should've taken the chance and if there was someone else in the house, I could've figured something out. Instead I'd waited too long.

"McKenna, if you're still there, tell Jameson I'm sorry I messed up."

I took a shallow breath and thought about his smile and what he sounded like when he laughed. I didn't have it for long, but at least I had it.

"If I die in here, I need you to tell my mom I love her. And don't let the police tell her. I know it's a lot to ask, McKenna, but Jameson and Nixon should do it. They'll know to go easy. They'll know how to help her."

I was so damn tired and my throat was so raw it hurt to speak, but if this was all the time I had left I needed to say a few more things before I fell asleep.

33

JAMESON

Jameson had slipped past anger over two hours ago when Kennedy had started talking to McKenna after Deloris had locked her in the car. Then thirty minutes ago when she started talking about dying in the car, Jameson felt his heart shatter.

They'd made good time but they were still twenty minutes away, and by then, Kennedy could be out of time. On a day like it was, it would take thirty minutes for the temperature inside the car to reach over a hundred degrees. Kennedy had now been locked inside for almost two-and-a-half hours.

"I can't breathe in here, it's so hot," Kennedy said. "I'm going to try to kick out the window."

"Stay still, Kennedy," Nixon muttered as if she could hear him.

The less energy she used, the better off she'd be.

There was a soft bang and Kennedy slurred, "I can't

fucking do it. I'm so stupid. McKenna. Tell Jameson I'm so sorry for being so stupid. God, I wish he was here."

Jameson cursed a blue-streak and swerved around two cars in front of him.

"You're turning left up here," Nixon instructed.

"McKenna?" Kennedy called. "Thank you for keeping me company. I'm so happy Nixon found you. He's so good. Always was."

"Goddammit, Kennedy," McKenna cried. "Don't give up."

"I hope you guys have lots of babies. I wish I could've seen them." Kennedy sniffed, then started to cry. "I wish I'd had babies."

That sob from Kennedy had wetness brimming in Jameson's eyes.

"Hold on, Kennedy," he growled. "Hold the fuck on."

"I love him," Kennedy cried. "Tell him that I was thinking about him when I closed my eyes."

"Kennedy!" McKenna shouted even though there was no way for her to hear.

"Tell him I loved it when he laughed. That's what I'm thinking about. The last thing I'm gonna hear is him laughing." Kennedy choked back a sob and Jameson couldn't breathe. "Thank you for being here, McKenna. Tell Jameson...just tell him...I'm tired. Too tired. I'm gonna go to sleep."

Silence descended like a blow, the weight of it debilitating.

"Jameson," Nixon called.

But he wasn't paying attention—all Jameson could think about was Kennedy's final words.

It can't be over. No fucking way can it be over.

"Fuck!" Nix shouted and grabbed the wheel, jerking it hard right just in time to prevent the near head-on collision. "Pull the fuck over and let me drive."

"No time," Jameson grunted, eyes now focused on the road.

"We'll have *no time* if you kill us all."

A sign for Lake Shore Drive caught his attention, but he skidded to a stop as a black Buick turned in front of him.

"Do you think that's the car?" Weston asked.

"What are the chances—?"

"Let me out. I'll run the rest of the way to the house." Weston already had the back door open and was jumping out. He rounded the bed of the truck and in a full sprint took off down the street. Jameson hit the accelerator to catch up to the Buick as it turned onto a gravel access road.

Rocks were shooting out from under the car's rear tires as the Buick picked up speed.

"What the fuck is she doing?" Nixon snarled. "She needs to slow down."

Please, God, don't let Kennedy be in the car.

Deloris Marshall was driving straight for a boat ramp and not slowing down.

"Fuck!" Jameson roared as the car splashed into the water.

He slammed on his brakes, jammed the truck into

park, and anticipation surged as he ran toward the water. By the time he made it into the water, the front end was already sinking and the car was filling up at an alarming rate.

Don't be in there.

Jameson was waist-deep with only the ass-end of the Buick bobbing when he dove underwater, Nixon right behind him. His boots were so heavy it felt like he had bricks tied around his ankles and his clothing caused drag, slowing him down more than Kennedy had time for.

His hand hit the metal fender of the Buick and he popped up, took a huge gulp of air, and dove back down.

Uncaring that debris was burning his eyes, he peered into the car and pushed through the open window. Kennedy was floating face down in the back of the car, her beautiful blonde hair flowing around her. His gut churned and for a moment panic and fear paralyzed him.

Nixon bumped his leg getting his attention and pulling him from his stupor, and determination kicked in. He would not let his woman die in a watery tomb. He kicked his feet, propelling him farther into the car and he grabbed Kennedy's bicep.

Nixon wrapped his arm around Jameson's middle, and with a shove off the car, yanked both Jameson and Kennedy out the window.

Jameson adjusted his grip around the woman who had changed his life and kicked as hard as he could to the surface. This was not how their story would end. He'd never recover, never get over the loss of her. She had to live—there was no other option.

His head came up out of the water. He turned Kennedy to her back and Nixon was there at his side checking for a pulse.

"No pulse," Nix announced.

Three minutes. They had three minutes before brain death occurred.

"Do it," Jameson demanded, and Nixon lowered his mouth to hers.

Jameson watched in horror as Kennedy's cheeks puffed out as Nixon attempted to breathe life into her. They'd been too fucking late. He should've known she was in trouble earlier. He shouldn't have been so wrapped up in work and lost track of time. Thirty minutes sooner and this wouldn't be happening.

If he'd just taken the goddamn day off and helped her work her field, none of this would've happened.

"Stop," Nixon barked as he lifted his head. *Had he said something out loud?* "Relax and turn her back toward me."

Shit, he hadn't realized he had been fighting Nixon's efforts.

This wasn't the first time they'd performed a water resuscitation while towing a person to shore. They had the rhythm down to a science. Nixon provided four respirations between each of Jameson's strokes. It was a precarious dance and slowed them down considerably. As much as they needed to get her to land as quickly as possible to start CPR properly, she'd been deprived oxygen for too long. They had no choice.

Jameson finally felt his foot hit dirt and he stood. Scooping her lifeless body out of the water, he ran the last ten feet. Nixon already had his knife out of his pocket and open, and with a slice of the blade, the rope fell away. Jameson dropped to his knees, gently laid her down and started chest compressions.

"Come on, Kennedy. Breathe, baby."

After a full count of thirty, he tilted her head back and gave her two fast respirations, watched her chest rise instead of her cheeks inflating—a good sign—and checked her pulse.

Nothing.

Fear nipped at his soul as he leaned over and restarted compressions.

"Breathe, goddammit. Breathe."

Sirens wailed in the background and he prayed they weren't too late.

"Brother," Nix said with caution.

"Don't. Don't fucking say it."

Dread crowded Jameson's chest and threatened to choke him as pain seared through his soul.

"Kennedy!" he roared. "Fucking breathe."

34

KENNEDY

I couldn't breathe through the retching. I vaguely felt my head being pushed to the side and agonizing pain burned my chest and throat.

Was I throwing up?

Dying?

"That's it." I heard Jameson coax.

Definitely dying. I was hallucinating. I'd finally conjured up his voice in my head. I spent much of my time in the hot car thinking about Jameson. Wishing I could hear him one more time before I died. I'd finally done it.

"Come on, Kennedy."

My chest seized again and fire shot up my throat and scorched my nose and mouth.

What a painful way to die.

"Get her on her side."

Nixon?

My body was not my own, I couldn't stop the force of

the movement, even though I wanted to. Something sharp was piercing my shoulder and it hurt like a son of a bitch.

"That's it. Breathe, baby."

Breathe?

"James—"

"Shh, baby. Don't talk. Just breathe."

Suddenly there was a flurry of commotion and more voices invaded my sleep. Commands were given, my body was moved, hands touched me, but I comprehended nothing.

I was so tired. Blackness pulled me under and I welcomed the peace.

"Turn off the alarm," I mumbled, then winced. I felt like I'd swallowed rocks.

The annoying beeping continued and I reached over to shove Jameson. He insisted on sleeping on the side of the bed with the alarm clock, the least he could do was hit snooze.

"Jameson," I grunted but my hand hit the mattress, not his chest.

Unusual, we never moved apart when we slept. He always held me close.

"Right here, baby." His hand took mine and he squeezed.

"Why are you out of bed?"

"Kennedy, open your eyes, babe."

"Sleep," I grunted.

"Time to wake up."

"I quit. No work today."

I begrudgingly opened my eyes, but only so I could drink some water to soothe the desert in my throat. Then I was going back to bed. Screw work.

Jameson's handsome face filled my blurry vision. But he wasn't smiling.

"What's wrong?"

Deep lines formed around his eyes and he stared at me with concern.

The beeping had faded into the background and awareness started to creep in. Something was wrong. My gaze flitted over his shoulder to the stark white walls and the smell of bleach filled my nostrils.

Where was I?

"Jameson?"

"Everything's okay. You're in the hospital."

"Hospital?"

I tried to jerk to a sitting position but Jameson gently stopped my attempt.

Something foreign was in my nose. My hands went to my face and I tugged at plastic tubing.

"Oh, no. That stays in."

So many scenarios assaulted my brain. Was I in a car accident? Nothing hurt but my chest and throat. So many questions, but I couldn't begin to formulate a coherent thought. What was going on?

"Good, she's awake." That sounded eerily familiar.

It was like I was having a bad case of déjà vu.

Jameson moved to my side, revealing a tall, smiling nurse.

"Hi, Kennedy. I'm Shar. Let me turn the volume down on some of these machines." The nurse walked around the bed and the beeping finally stopped. "Jameson here, insisted on the volume being up."

I glanced back at Jameson and he shrugged his shoulders. Now that some of the fog had lifted and I could see him clearly, he looked terrible. Black circles marred his face. Worry lines etched deep. I tugged on his hand and he gave me a small, sad smile.

"I already called the doctor. She'll be in soon." Shar's upbeat, chipper voice was the absolute opposite of Jameson's somber mood.

"Why am I here?"

Shar's body rocked back and her eyes went to Jameson before they gentled on me. She took a few steps closer to my bed and seemed to be contemplating something.

How bad was it?

"You almost drowned," she told me.

"Drowned? I know how to swim. Why can't I remember?"

Panic hammered in my chest. Drowned? That wasn't possible.

"Memory loss is normal when the brain is deprived of oxygen."

Deprived of oxygen?

No. I shook my head in denial. That wasn't possible. The last thing I remembered was delivering honey to

Jonas. I'd been nowhere near the water. Did I cross the Chester River Bridge and crash?

"Kennedy, baby, slow down. Everything's okay now," Jameson cooed.

"Okay? Nothing's okay. I can't remember. How? Where am I?"

My chest started to burn and my stomach was rebelling. Why couldn't I remember?

"I can't breathe," I wheezed.

A blood pressure cuff started to inflate and I wanted it off. I wanted everything off.

"You'll feel better when you wake up," Shar said with a sad grin, and warmth spread through my arm and finally through my body.

Peace.

"*IT'S ALL YOUR FAULT!*" *Deloris Marshall yelled.*

"No!" My body jerked upright and strong arms wrapped around me. "No. Get off me."

"Kennedy, wake up. You're safe. I've got you. Open your eyes, baby."

Jameson.

My eyes cracked open and Jameson was there.

He saved me.

"I'm sorry," I muttered. "I had another one."

Jameson gently lowered me back to bed, just like he'd done the previous three times I woken up in a fit.

You know, I'd heard the saying, be careful what you

wished for, but I'd never understood the true meaning until then. When the nurse had sedated me, I'd wished I could remember what had happened. Then I'd fallen into a restless sleep and the day's events unfolded in my dreams.

As the holes in my memory filled, I'd woken up terrified to a haggard Jameson who'd coax me back to sleep only for the merry-go-round to continue.

I'd remembered everything up to falling asleep in the car. I'd gone from blazing hot to freezing cold and shivering.

"Close your eyes, I'm here."

Oh, no. I was done trying to sleep.

"How'd you find me?"

"Let's—"

"Please, Jameson. I don't want to sleep. All I hear is Deloris and I re-live the drive. I want to know the rest."

He was quiet for a long time, and in the silence, I watched a thousand emotions cross his face. Some were angry, some were sad, but all of them looked tortured.

Then he spoke, his voice rough and raw as he explained what had happened. But what he didn't tell me was how he'd felt. His accounting was akin to a military brief. All facts, no emotion. He took me through step-by-step of how the team had gathered information from Jonas, Ray, and RJ, how McKenna had finally gotten into my phone when I had service, all the way to the end. He'd provided details about Nixon starting water resuscitation and about him giving me CPR.

Nowhere had he told me about himself. It was on-point and all about me.

It was also shocking. All of it.

"What happened to Deloris?"

"She's dead."

Matter of fact and emotionless.

"How?"

"She handcuffed herself to the steering wheel, rolled down all the windows and drove into the lake. She drowned. Not that it was a thought, but Nixon would never have been able to pull her from the car."

"It wasn't a thought?"

"Fuck no." *Resolute.* "The bitch tried to kill you. I hope she's rotting in hell right alongside her piece-of-shit son. I do *not* feel sorry either of them are dead."

I searched my feelings and found I couldn't summon up any remorse either. I'd thought Deloris had left me in the car to die while she was sitting in her nice comfortable house watching TV. But, apparently she'd been in there trying to find the gumption to commit suicide. I could've felt sorry for her, she was a woman who'd lost her child. Even if Peyton was an asshole and he'd hurt me, he was still her son. But the fact her suicide plan had included murdering me as well negated any sympathy.

"I'm sorry," I whispered. "It had to be hard on you."

"Don't apologize. You did nothing wrong. You were—"

"I was the one who had to sit in a car and wait to be rescued. Sure, I was terrified and I'd made several mistakes. But you were the one who was racing to get me.

You're the one who had to listen to me rambling. That had to have been hard."

I couldn't remember half of what I'd said. I just needed to talk. It made me feel like I had some connection while I was petrified I was going to die.

"Hard? It was fucking torture." Jameson blew out a breath and locked eyes with mine. "I was listening to you as you were dying and I couldn't get to you. I couldn't help you. I couldn't protect you. All I had was your voice. And as much as your commentary pushed me forward, it also paralyzed me. I knew I wouldn't survive if I lost you. I knew it down to my soul, my life would be over. Even if I was left breathing on this earth, I'd be dead." Jameson's jaw clenched and his eyes dulled. "And when I couldn't resuscitate you and I thought you were gone, I wanted to die right alongside of you."

"But you saved me." Jameson shook his head but I spoke over him. "I knew you would. Maybe that's why I wasn't as scared as I could've been. I was able to stay calm."

He picked up my hand and kissed the inside of my scarred wrist. "I was so fucking scared. I thought the day I found you lying in the grass with blood caked in your hair was the worst day of my life. But that was nothing compared to holding your lifeless body. I will never forget what it felt like to touch your neck and *not* feel your heart beating. I will never take for granted a beat of your heart or a breath filling your lungs. Not a single day will pass when I'm not acutely aware of how close I was to losing you."

"And, Jameson, not a day will pass where I forget that it is because of you I'm alive."

The chair he was sitting in scraped on the linoleum floor as he folded his big body forward and planted his head on the bed next to my hip.

"So fucking close." My hand went to his head and my fingers tangled with his hair.

I said nothing as his body shook. There was nothing *to* say. I'd almost died but he saved me.

I was wrong—there was something to say.

"I love you, Jameson, until my dying breath." His body went solid but I forged ahead. "And I can say that with one hundred percent certainty. When I thought I was drawing my last breath, all I could think about was you. All of the things we hadn't done. All of the time that was being stolen from us. But you were my last thought and you always will be."

"I will never let you go," he groaned. "Never."

"I know."

Silence fell, my lids were getting heavy, and my heart was full.

I was alive and Jameson was there.

35

JAMESON

"Last day." Kennedy held up an empty pill bottle before she tossed it in the trash.

Jameson stared at her over the rim of his coffee mug and smiled.

He had a lot to smile about. After Kennedy had spent five days in the hospital treating aspiration pneumonia, a complication she'd developed, and two weeks more of oral antibiotics, she was finally on the mend. Yesterday's chest x-ray showed her lungs were clear and no further treatment was necessary.

They'd gotten lucky. And Jameson knew it.

He'd refused to waste a second of their precious time on anger. Finally, he was taking a page out of Kennedy's playbook and was concentrating on the here and now. The past had no place in his life. He wouldn't dwell on the fear and terror he'd felt that day.

Kennedy was breathing, her heart was beating, and she was smiling.

Reggie was sitting his ass in a jail cell awaiting trial. Jonny had tracked down the woman in the pictures, who thankfully was not a minor, though she'd refused to press charges. Jonny had explained there were hundreds of pictures of her in compromising positions but she'd shrugged it off and said she didn't care. The woman would never admit she'd been paid for her services, Reggie wasn't talking, and the woman had no interest in involving herself in the case so Jonny's hands were tied.

Not that the State's Attorney needed more evidence or testimony against Reggie but due diligence necessitated Jonny tracking her down. That done the case was closed as far as Gemini Group was concerned.

Life was good.

"You ready to go pick up Killer?" Jameson asked and rinsed out his cup before putting it in the dishwasher.

"You mean Petal?"

"No. I mean Hercules."

Kennedy pursed her lips, trying to hide her smile. She was enjoying their banter just as much as Jameson was.

"Just take me to get my puppy, would ya?"

Jameson waited for her to get close before he hooked her around the middle and pulled her into him.

"After you kiss me."

With an exaggerated roll of her eyes she went to her toes and kissed him. Jameson, never being one to miss a golden opportunity, deepened the kiss and didn't let up until she moaned into his mouth and his cock was throbbing.

Sweet torture.

"THAT'S A GOOD BOY," Kennedy cooed at the puppy as he pissed in the grass across from the Gemini Group office. Jameson suspiciously eyed the green metal stand with a trash can attached that clearly ordered dog owners to pick up their animal's shit.

Then he looked back at Kennedy and the twelve-week-old German Shepherd and hoped urinating was the extent of the puppy's needs. Then he resigned himself to the fact he wouldn't allow his woman to pick up dog shit, ever.

How had his life come to this?

"Ready?" Kennedy scooped up Tank and smiled at him with so much love and happiness, he'd remembered how.

And he'd never been more grateful.

The three of them made their way across the street and up the stairs. Kennedy hadn't even gotten fully into the office before McKenna was rushing down the hallway.

"Let me see that cute little furball." McKenna held out her hands for the puppy but she was staring at Kennedy.

McKenna did that a lot. They all did. Jameson hadn't been the only one who'd gone through hell the day Kennedy almost died.

McKenna had been the one Kennedy had directed

her conversation to. The two women had been friendly before, but now they were damn near inseparable. Kennedy had been folded firmly into the family of brothers. She'd forged her own relationship with each of Jameson's friends and to say they were over-protective would be an understatement.

Much like after McKenna had nearly been beaten to death, Nixon, Weston, Chasin, and Holden had circled around Kennedy, vowing to never let anyone hurt her again.

"What'd you name him?" McKenna asked.

"Cutie Pie," Kennedy lied.

"For the love of all things holy." Nix came into the room. "Please tell me she's full of shit."

"Tank," Jameson corrected.

"Killer would've been better," Nix announced, and Jameson raised an *I told you so* brow to Kennedy.

"I'm not namin' my dog Killer," she protested..

"Does he have a brother?" McKenna cuddled Tank. "I want one."

Nixon's face lit with excitement.

"He does. You should get him," Kennedy answered.

McKenna looked at Nix and he shrugged. "Call the breeder, we'll go today."

Before McKenna could say anything, the buzzer chimed, announcing someone was downstairs trying to gain access to the office.

Nix pulled his phone out of his pocket, opened the security camera app, and frowned, though he said, "Come on up."

"Who is it?" Jameson asked.

"No clue," Nix answered as he walked to the door and opened it.

A pissed-off looking woman stood with her hand up ready to bang on the door.

"Is Weston Beil here?" the woman asked. Fire shooting from her hazel eyes.

"And you are?" Nix inquired.

"Silver? What are you doing here?" Weston asked, coming into the room.

"Are you always such an asshole or do you have something personal against me?"

Jameson shot his friend a *what the fuck* look and waited for his answer.

"I got nothing against you. I told Alec and the Lieutenant Commander with you in attendance, I think you lack experience. *Not* that you weren't good at your job or incompetent, but the operation needs something you don't have and that's experience and finesse."

"Well, thanks to you, I've been pulled. Which is utter bullshit, Weston. I brought this to the Coast Guard. I sat through months of meetings with Alec Hall. And all of a sudden, hotshot know-it-all Weston Beil barges in and takes over. Screw you."

Everyone's head in the room bounced back to Weston and waited for his reply.

"If you think that, you lack more than experience, you also lack common sense and self-control. Two more things needed to run the op."

"I know these waterways better than anyone. I grew

up on them. I have more hours on the water and piloting vessels down river than anyone else on the team. And most certainly more than you."

A few pieces of the puzzle clicked into place. Silver was the maritime pilot Weston had recommended being removed from the next month's contract. Her name hadn't been in the file Jameson had.

"Oh boy," Kennedy mumbled next to him.

"Oh shit's more like it." Jameson put his arm around his woman and pulled her close. "Buckle up, babe, I see explosion in our future."

"I like that." Kennedy smiled up at him.

"Which part? That there's never a dull moment?"

"No. The part about our future."

Jameson closed his eyes on a slow blink and when Kennedy's smile came back into view his chest ached with all the happiness in it threatening to detonate.

"It's bright and sunny with calm seas from here on out," Jameson told her.

"Maybe for us. But I think Weston's seas just got stormy."

Kennedy wasn't wrong. Weston's eyes were cloudy and alert at the same time and Jameson had a feeling it had less to do with their next contract and everything to do with the very pretty woman, Silver.

Jameson held his woman close, thinking he almost had it all. The only two things that were left were slipping his ring on her finger and putting babies in her belly.

And that would happen soon enough.

36

SILVER

Weston Beil was infuriating.

And what made everything worse was he'd been semi-right. Not that I lacked experience, because I didn't. I had more time on the water than every man on the team Weston had put together, including the members of the Coast Guard.

I'd grown up on the water. Literally. I'd lived on a boat since the day I was born. My dad was an adventure diver and instructor and part-time treasure hunter. Whatever money-making scheme he'd had always revolved around the water. Since birth, my father had been grooming me to take over his business.

Not that I had taken over my dad's diving company or decided to be a treasure hunter—instead I'd opted for a career as a professional mariner. A career path that at the moment was debatably the wrong choice.

I was sure my father was probably out cruising the beautiful cerulean waters of the Caribbean enjoying the view from his wheelhouse while I was currently hand-cuffed to a water pipe in the hull of a motor yacht.

Good times.

That was the part Weston had been correct about.

He'd warned me, the operation to stop the drug traf-ficking was dangerous. He'd repeated *ad nauseam* that criminals, and most certainly drug dealers, did not take kindly to their racket being stopped.

So, Mr. Know-It-All Weston Beil had been right. And the taste of crow made my stomach roil. Which sucked, because if I got out of this alive, I'd be eating a huge plateful.

The yacht rocked back and forth, a motion I'd always been accustomed to but that now was making me queasy, as I tried to figure out a way out of this mess.

I had no idea what the captain and the first mate had planned for me, but considering I was surrounded by bricks of cocaine; I didn't figure it'd be pleasant.

No one was coming to my rescue. If I wanted to live, it would be up to me.

Damn, I wished Weston were there, and that thought churned my belly for a variety of reasons. I was not and had never been a helpless female and I wouldn't turn into one now. But I couldn't deny the big man was strong and the air of danger that surrounded him was intoxicating. Had he not been such a dick, I would've said he was probably the hottest man I'd ever laid eyes on.

Weston would know what to do. The captain wouldn't have been able to overpower him and handcuff him to a fucking pipe.

Shouting upstairs had me shrinking back against the steel.

I needed to hurry up and figure something out before I turned into fish food.

Weston and Silver in Weston's Treasure

RILEY'S REBELS

If you are interested in joining Riley's Rebels newsletter
sign up here:
https://www.subscribepage.com/RRsignup
We love stalkers! Here are the links you'll need.

ALSO BY RILEY EDWARDS

Riley Edwards

www.RileyEdwardsRomance.com

Romantic Suspense

Gemini Group

Nixon's Promise

Jameson's Salvation

Red Team

Nightstalker

Protecting Olivia - Susan Stoker Universe

Redeeming Violet - Susan Stoker Universe

Recovering Ivy - Susan Stoker Universe

Rescuing Erin - Susan Stoker Universe

Romancing Rayne - Susan Stoker Universe

The Gold Team

Brooks - Susan Stoker Universe

Thaddeus - Susan Stoker Universe

The 707 Freedom Series

Free

Freeing Jasper

Finally Free

Freedom

The Next Generation (707 spinoff)

Saving Meadow

Chasing Honor

Finding Mercy

Claiming Tuesday

Adoring Delaney

The Collective

Unbroken

Trust

ABOUT THE AUTHOR

Riley Edwards is a bestselling multi-genre author, wife, and military mom. Riley was born and raised in Los Angeles but now resides on the east coast with her fantastic husband and children.

Riley writes heart-stopping romance with sexy alpha heroes and even stronger heroines. Riley's favorite genres to write are romantic suspense and military romance.

Don't forget to sign up for Riley's newsletter and never miss another release, sale, or exclusive bonus material. https://www.subscribepage.com/RRsignup

Facebook Fan Group

www.rileyedwardsromance.com

facebook.com/Novelist.Riley.Edwards

twitter.com/rileyedwardsrom

instagram.com/rileyedwardsromance

bookbub.com/authors/riley-edwards

amazon.com/author/rileyedwards

ACKNOWLEDGMENTS

To all of you – the readers: Thank you for picking up this book and giving me a few hours of your time. Whether this is the first book of mine you've read or you've been with me from the beginning, thank you for your support. It is because of you I have the coolest job in the world.

Made in the USA
Monee, IL
15 May 2023